WORDS TO DIE BY

Visit us at www.boldstrokesbooks.com

WORDS TO DIE BY

by

William Holden

A Division of Bold Strokes Books

2012

WORDS TO DIE BY

ISBN 13: 978-1-60282-653-3

This Trade Paperback Original Is Published By
Bold Strokes Books, Inc.
P.O. Box 249
Valley Falls, NY 12185

First Edition: March 2012

CREDITS
Editor: Stacia Seaman
Production Design: Stacia Seaman
Cover Design by Sheri (graphicartist2020@hotmail.com)

Acknowledgments

First and foremost, I would like to thank Radclyffe and everyone at Bold Strokes Books for believing in this project. Secondly, my partner, who has put up with me during the long hours of writing and especially those difficult hours when the words would not flow. Finally, I would like to thank my dark half, Christopher, who was buried deep inside of me and finally found his way out.

For the two most important people in my life:
my partner and love of my life, Mark Jordan,
and my best friend and soul mate in writing, Dale Chase.

CONTENTS

THE OTHER MAN

*O*h *yeah. Yeah, just a little bit more. Oh, that's it.*
I love the way David touches me. The way his body feels against mine as he enters me. I wish I could tell him how wonderful he makes me feel. I wish I could talk so I could tell him how I feel. I wonder if he knows, or does he just think of me as a plaything?

Oh yeah, fuck me harder. Use me like the bitch that I am.

I can hear his deep masculine voice no matter where he is. It drifts through the house like the chords of a concert violinist.

Yeah, that feels good. Pound my ass.

I love the pulse of his cock inside me. I sometimes pretend the beating of his pulse is mine instead of his, and for those brief moments I know what it feels like to be alive. I can tell when David is getting close to the final moment. His cock always swells like a balloon just before it bursts, unloading his come into me.

Yeah, fill me up. Oh, babe. Damn, you are hot. God, you feel so good.

The quiet moments after sex is what I like the best. The air is hot and humid with that thick, intoxicating after-sex scent. David's brown chest hair always glistens with perspiration. I wish I could touch it, lick it, know how his body tastes. His green eyes are deep pockets of emotions. When he gazes into my artificial eyes they sparkle with life and desire. I love the way he traces the contours of my hairless body. I stay erect at all times waiting for him to use me at a moment's notice.

"Joey," he whispers to me. "You're fucking amazing. You're the best boyfriend anyone could have. You'd do anything for me, wouldn't you?"

Yes, of course I would. All I have is you. We belong together, just you and me—forever.

"Come on, let's get cleaned up." He crawls over my body and stands up before cradling me in his strong and loving arms.

He holds me against his body as he carries me to the bathroom. It's been the same routine every night since we met six months ago. He saved me that night. I was unable to escape the confines of where I was. He picked me up and took me back to his place. That first night together he seemed a bit uneasy, as if he were a virgin not knowing what to do. He held me that night. He never asked for anything in return, just an ear to listen to and a shoulder to cry on.

He must really love me. I wasn't cheap, but he didn't seem to mind spending three hundred dollars for me. After all, I am the deluxe model. My shoulder-length black hair is real, not artificial like some model's. My nipples are soft and protrude from my chest in small nubs. My pubic hair is black with loose, flowing curls. I doubt it's real. David doesn't seem to mind, though, he loves running his fingers through it. My lips are large and supple. They stay closed, not like some of those less expensive models that have the perpetual hole between their lips. Mine are easy to part for the most amazing blow jobs. I have a battery-activated throat that can bring a man to pleasures he never knew existed. My ass is also equipped with the same technology as my throat. My ever-hard cock includes a powerful ejaculation feature, which one can fill with any number of tasty liquids.

David sets me down in the bathtub between his legs and rests me against his chest. I feel him getting hard from our closeness. He grabs the bar of soap and rubs it between his hands before running the eucalyptus-scented lather over my body. He washes away the remnants of our sex. He caresses my body with his strong hands.

I'm mesmerized by the back-and-forth sway of the water in the tub. Just below the surface I watch the hair on David's legs join in the gentle motion. The hair stops at his ankles. His feet are large. His toes poke out of the water. My concentration is broken as I feel his hand slide underneath me. His finger slips into my ass. He twists and turns his finger to remove the drying come from me. He takes such good care of me. I don't know what I would do without him.

David dries me off first and then sits me down on the toilet seat. I watch with confusion as his evening routines for bed are replaced by other activities as if he's preparing to go out. I feel a twinge in my chest. I'm not sure of the origin of the discomfort; all I know is that I don't like the feeling. It makes me sad, another emotion that I'm not used to having.

He raises his arms one at a time and runs deodorant through the thick tangles of hair that lie underneath. He sprays a fine mist over his chest, adding a few shots around his groin. The air fills with a sweet, woody scent. The twinge in my chest returns in a quick, sudden thud.

He picks me up and carries me into the bedroom. The warmth of his body feels good against my cold synthetic skin. He props me up on my side of the bed. I begin to think it was all in my mind until I see him slipping on his black boxer-briefs. I watch with agony and confusion as he finishes dressing. He comes over and sits down next to me.

"I won't be gone long," he says as he strokes the inside of my thigh. "My doctor says I need to start going out and meeting people." He kisses me, stands up, and brushes out the wrinkles in the bedspread. "Remember, no matter what, we'll always have each other." He walks toward the bedroom door.

Meeting people? You can't leave like this. What do you mean, meeting people? You don't need anyone else. You have me.

It feels as if my entire body is trembling. I must be imagining it. I know that's not possible, I'm not alive. My chest feels tight, heavy. How can there be discomfort in a place where nothing exists? Is this what panic feels like? I'm confused by these strange emotions and feelings inside me. I don't understand them, nor do I like them. The one thing I'm sure about is the source of these feelings—David and his sudden lack of interest in me. He stops at the door. Hope rises in me that he changed his mind, that he has come to his senses. He turns to look at me and blows me a kiss. He smiles and shuts the door behind him.

I sit alone on our bed. My thoughts are all I have to keep me company. Our bedroom is clean and tidy. There's no room in David's life for clutter or disorganization. Everything has a place in his life. I had a place in his life; at least I thought so until tonight. His side of the bed looks like I feel; empty, alone, and useless. The sheets are pulled up to the edge of the pillows and tucked under the edge of the mattress—not a wrinkle anywhere. His cologne still lingers in the air. I want the smell to be a comfort to me; instead it makes me miss him more.

Time has never had meaning for me, until now. The seconds turn to minutes, which turn to hours. I'm bored with nothing to do for this long. I'm made to entertain others. I have no idea how to entertain myself. Hours go by and David still is gone. It's not like him to leave me for this long. I know David is not used to being out in the city late at night. What if something happened to him? What if David is hurt or worse, dead? The thought of losing him suffocates me. The bedroom begins to blur in my vision. I hear a deep pounding coming at me from all directions, as if a thousand drums are surrounding me. It vibrates inside me. It pulses and pounds through every inch of me. The feelings fade as a new thought enters my mind.

The world that I know goes dark. Anger replaces worry. I realize why he's been gone so long—there's someone else. David is out there at this very minute fucking someone instead of being here with me where he belongs. He'll come home smelling of someone else's body, someone else's sweat. David will come to bed and cuddle with me out of guilt and I won't be able to stop him. I'll have to let him wrap his arms around me, knowing someone else was in them. I'll get the filth from that boyfriend-stealing tramp all over my body.

My foot twitches in my peripheral vision. My thoughts stop to allow my mind to register what just happened. I feel hot, almost sweaty. My rational mind tells me that it's not possible. Something is happening to me, these emotions and feelings are reacting with my body, a body that's nothing more than rubber and a few electrical components. I stare at my left foot and concentrate, waiting for it to happen again. My big toe starts to tingle. The door to the bedroom opens and David stumbles in. My train of thought is broken. The sensations subside. I feel nothing. I look at him with a hurt, questioning eye. An expression I wish he could see.

David is quiet. He undresses without words. His back is turned toward me so I can't see his guilt. He folds his dirty clothes and places them in the hamper. He runs his hands through his pubic hair and pulls on his cock. He slips under the covers of the bed. He pulls me under with him. His body is warm. I smell the alcohol and cigarettes on his breath. He moves in closer and hugs me. His hand moves between us. He strokes himself, coaxing his cock to respond as if fucking me will make him feel better. His efforts go without reward. He remains flaccid. He kisses my back. He begins to sniffle, then cries himself to sleep.

I lie there unable to move with my mind racing with thoughts, doubts, and questions. He fucked someone tonight. His guilt is evident. The anger inside me returns. I want to yell at him. I want to curse him for fucking someone other than me—his boyfriend, his life mate. I want to hurt him the same way he has hurt me. Of course what I want doesn't matter, it never has. It's always been about him.

The morning sun filters in through the blinds, casting a yellowish orange glow across our bed. I hear the muted sounds of David snoring. The phone rings. David's body flinches as the old clock tower ringtone continues. The smell of his night sweat hangs over our bed as he tosses the covers off. I want him to fuck me. I want to know that he still needs me like I need him.

"Hello?" David answers after the fourth ring. "Good morning to you too…Yeah…No, that's okay…It's fine…I should get up anyway."

I try to concentrate on the voice in the receiver. The words are fuzzy, kind of jumbled. What I do know is that the voice is male. A knot burns somewhere in my lower extremities. It's him. I know it. It's the man David fucked.

"Yeah, I had a good time as well." David rubs my arm. "Today?" His hand reaches down in front and fondles my waiting cock. "Gee, I don't know. I've got a lot of stuff to do today."

Damn right you do. Like explaining to me what the fuck is going on. How can you do this to me? After everything I've done for you. I was the one to give you comfort and pleasure when no one else was around. I gave you my body freely, anytime you wanted and needed it. And now I'm nothing to you?

"Thanks, I like you too." He removes his hand. "It's just that… No, I'm not seeing anyone else."

Liar.

"Sure, that sounds nice. Let me get cleaned up and I'll meet you for breakfast…Got it…Give me about forty-five minutes? Great, I'll see you then." He hangs up the phone and stretches out next to me.

He kisses my shoulder as he used to do every morning. This time it's not out of love or affection. This time it feels different, somehow dirty, or forced. His cock is getting hard. His erection presses against the crack of my ass. He slips inside me. He wraps his arms around me and holds me. He buries his face against my back. He fucks me.

"Please don't be angry with me," he pants in my ear. "I still love you, it's just…"

Just fuck me and get it over with.

"This guy I met last night, Ray, he's nice. I like him a lot."

Then put your dick in him instead of me. Oh, right, you already did.

"Maybe," his heavy breathing batters my neck, "oh, shit. Maybe the three of us can be a family." He pulls out too soon and comes again over my ass. "I'm sorry. I have to do this. I promise not to leave you in there too long. It's just in case Ray wants to come back here after breakfast." David rolls out of bed without so much as a lingering touch. He picks me up in a limp heap and walks across the room.

Do what? Where in the hell are you taking me? Why are you

*not bathing with me like you do every time we fuck? What in the fuck
are you doing? Are you just going to leave your cold come inside
me?*

"I'm sorry," he says as he shoves me into the corner of his
closet. He shuts the door. Darkness surrounds me. I can see his
shadow move across the bedroom through the narrow slats in the
door. I'm alone except for his scent, which hangs from his clothes
and shoes.

Why are you doing this? Don't you love me anymore? I can
hear the water running in the bathroom. He's getting ready for
another date with Ray. *It's Ray, isn't it? Ray is putting you up to
this, isn't he? Fucking answer me.* Something in my throat begins
to vibrate. It tickles as it rushes out of me. "I fucking hate you!" I
hear a voice inside the closet with me. I listen and hear the breaths
echoing around me. I realize the words come from me. I try to speak
again, nothing happens. I'm silent once again.

"Hello?" David calls out from the bathroom. "Who's there?"

The light dims through the slats as David walks in front of the
door. The doorknob turns. David stands in front of me naked and
wet. He looks down at me. He hesitates as if he can sense something
is different. He grabs a pair of jeans and a T-shirt before closing the
door on me again. I watch as he dresses and leaves the bedroom.

*I'm sorry, David. I didn't mean it. Please, don't leave me in
here. I don't hate you. I love you. David, please.* My body feels
hot as the uncontrollable anger once again rises to the surface. *God
Damn you. If you leave me in here, so help me, you'll be sorry. Let
me out, you son of a bitch!*

My fist slams against the door. The shock of mobility silences
my mind. I see my fist against the door. My mind can't comprehend
how it got there. A gap is growing in the connection between my
reality and the new one staring me in the face. The hand doesn't
seem like mine at all, it's as if someone else is in here with me. I
listen for that stranger, hoping to hear him breathe or move because
having someone else in here is the rational explanation for what I see.
Silence is all that surrounds me. I concentrate on the nothingness. I
hear a faint sound. I question whether I heard anything at all. I hear

it again. It's muffled—it exists. I realize as the noise grows that it isn't coming from around me. It's coming from within me.

I feel something tug at my arm from underneath the skin. My arm flinches in response. I look at the fist again pressed against the door. The fist is mine. I can almost feel it against the cool painted wood of the door. I concentrate on my fist, willing it to move. Reason tells me that I'm wasting my time. Something inside me convinces me to try harder. It moves. The knowledge of what has happened rushes through my mind. I realize that I moved it, not David. I did it myself. I flatten my hand against the contours of the door and run my fingers between the wooden slats. I bring my hand to my face for closer inspection. I rub my fingers together. I feel my body for the first time. The synthetic skin feels foreign to me, yet comforting.

My arm begins to ache. My hand falls to the floor as if someone has set a heavy brick in my palm. It lies motionless once again. I study my hand, wanting to understand what has happened. My thoughts trail away when I hear distant voices. I recognize David's. The second voice is unfamiliar to me. They giggle and laugh as they come into the apartment. David has brought Ray home, to our home, and to our bed.

The tingling sensation returns to my body. I focus on the feeling that is becoming a part of me. It crawls through my body, moving up my left arm. I picture it like a cockroach creeping just underneath the surface of my skin, laying eggs that hatch and begin to move, spreading through every crack and crevice of my body, and bringing life with it. The weight lifts from my hand. My arm is free. The warmth flows across my chest and down my right arm. I see their bodies move across the room. I hear their sweet nothings that they whisper to each other. The fingers on my right hand twitch before curling into a tight fist.

I pull myself away from the wall. The wall David tossed me against when he so effortlessly discarded me. My body is stiff and stubborn with how and when I want it to move. Perhaps the connections between my mind and body need more time to develop a relationship, a perfect harmonizing unit. The problem is I don't want to wait. I am no longer a patient individual, a willing partner. I peer through the small slats and see the two of them kissing. I think back to the months I spent with David unable to move or to please him like he was pleasing me. I would have given anything to be able to kiss him, to touch him, or to taste his body. That will never happen. David has ruined everything. He has tainted what we had together by using Ray to mock me, by showing me what he thinks I cannot do. I'll prove to him the type of lover I can be. I prop myself against the door and wait.

I watch as Ray begins to unbutton David's shirt. He touches his chest. His fingers run through the thick mat of hair. He leans down and licks then bites David's erect nipples. I hear my lover moan with pleasure from another man's touch. The distant drumming I heard before echoes through my head. The sound is louder and stronger than before. It pulses life into me.

"What's wrong?" Ray questions, a bit short of breath.

"Nothing, it's just…" David kisses Ray as he glances in the direction of the closet. "I've not taken a shower yet today."

"So? You don't hear me complaining, do you?"

"No, it's me. I'll be right back. I'm just going to take a quick shower."

"Okay, I'll join you."

"No. I won't be long. Just get undressed and wait for me, I'll be out before you know it." David kisses Ray; his eyes glance once again at the closet door. He knows I'm inside watching, waiting.

Ray stands several inches taller than David. His blond hair hangs down around his broad shoulders. I watch with renewed interest as my lover's new man pulls off his dark green T-shirt. His skin is the color of wheat. His chest is covered in blond hair that shimmers when touched by the sun's light. A thick trail of hair runs from his rib cavity down his stomach, disappearing behind his black jeans. His nipples are larger than mine and more erect. His body is toned and firm in a way mine will never be. He slips his shoes off, unzips his pants and steps out of them. His thick, muscled legs have the same golden hair as his chest. His red and burgundy paisley boxers sway from the movement of what hangs between his legs.

My jealousy increases as he pulls his underwear off. His cock and balls hang low and heavy between his legs. I look at my own cock, and even though it's always hard and ready for pleasure, it seems less impressive than it once did. "Was I not big enough for you?" I whisper to no one. As I continue to admire Ray's body, a strange sensation moves and swells between my legs.

I realize that I'm getting aroused. I want to hate him for what he's done to my relationship with David. My anger toward him is mixed with a desire to know what it's like to be with another man. The same man who has taken from me the only one I have ever loved, and the one man who has ever loved me. I raise my fist and knock several times on the closet door. "Ray," I whisper with my new voice. Anticipation runs through my body as Ray turns around and faces the closet. My body is alive with excitement as he approaches the door. The doorknob turns. He opens the door. My lover's new boyfriend is standing inches from me. His scent invades the closet. It engulfs me. I fall out of the closet.

My face lands on his large, well-manicured feet. I want to slip one of his toes in my mouth, to taste a man's skin for the first time. His large hands cup my armpits and raise me off the ground before I get a chance.

"Well, well," he whispers as he looks behind him. A smile stretches across his strong jawline, creating a dimple on the left side of his face. "Who do we have here?"

I want to touch him, to speak to him. I remain silent and still.

"I had no idea David was so kinky. I hope I give better blow jobs than this thing."

Don't count on it.

He looks behind him again, then back at me. He places me in a kneeling position in front of him. His cock lengthens from nothing more than the excitement of cheating on his new boyfriend with his boyfriend's ex—a relationship that isn't even dead yet.

He grabs his cock and rubs the head of it over my lips. It feels soft, silky, and damp against my lips. His precome is warm and salty. I part my lips. The head of his cock slips in with ease. He hesitates and looks behind him. He looks down at me with the head of his cock sticking in my mouth. He begins to pull the head of his dick out of my mouth. I refuse to let him get away that easy. I suck his cock into my throat. The veins of his cock pulse against my lips as I bring every inch of him into my mouth. He doesn't have time to react before I'm using every trick in the manual to give him the most exquisite blow job of his life.

"Motherfucker," he groans. "What in the hell is this thing? Oh…my…God."

I feel his legs buckle. He leans against the door frame for support. My vibrating ring spins counterclockwise up and down his shaft while my tongue caresses the sensitive area beneath the head. My suction is strong, extracting a constant flow of precome that floods my mouth and runs down my face. I peer up at him. His eyes are closed. I reach my hand up and fondle his furry sack. These are new sensations for me. I want to linger and explore what a male body can offer me. The skin of his sack begins to tighten from my caresses. I fear what might happen if I get caught. I let my hand fall to the floor. I turn up the pressure and speed of my mouth.

"Son of a bitch." His legs bend forward. I can feel his body trembling against me. His legs give out and buckle. He falls to the floor. I'm on top of him and I'm in control for the first time in my life. He throws his arms over his head as he arches his back and groans. His sweat fills the air and hangs over us. My mouth is flooded with the heat of his orgasm. It rushes through his shaft and explodes further into my throat. My mouth continues to suck and vibrate and grind against his cock. He explodes again as he throws me off him. He kicks at me and shoves me back into the closet with his come still oozing out of my mouth. He closes the door. The dim light of the closet consumes me once again. I lick my lips and taste his bitterness, which lingers. I wait, knowing that he'll be back for more, and this time it will be for keeps.

Ray stands in the middle of the bedroom. He faces the closet as if he knows I'm watching him. I can tell by his erect cock that he wants more. I am what he desires—not David. I tap on the door with my finger. His eyes grow large from the sounds within the closet. I watch with anticipation growing in my gut as he approaches the door. His hand reaches for the doorknob.

"What are you doing?" David questions from behind him.

"Shit." Ray jumps with the suddenness of David's voice. "Don't sneak up on me like that."

I watch as they embrace. They kiss. David squeezes and massages Ray's ass in front of me. His dark, hairy crack toys with my emotions. I can still smell his crotch on my skin. David runs his finger over the tender hole. I watch the muscle respond as Ray gives in to David's needs as he gave into mine just moments ago.

"Come to bed." David guides Ray. I watch as my boyfriend lies on top of Ray. He kisses and licks Ray's shoulders, armpits, chest, and stomach. He moves down and takes Ray's cock in his mouth. The same cock that moments ago was in my mouth. David buries his face in Ray's crotch. I can hear David moan with pleasures that he once knew with me.

Ray looks in my direction, then down at David. He pulls David off his cock. "I can't."

"What's wrong?" David wipes precome from his chin.

"Nothing, it's not you." He sits up in bed and kisses David as if to reassure him. "It's that thing in your closet, it creeps me out."

"What thing?"

"When you were in the shower I heard a knock in the closet like something had fallen. I opened the door and that sex doll of yours fell out."

"I didn't want you to see that. I didn't want you to know."

"Know what?"

"About Joey."

"Joey?" Ray looks in my direction. "You mean you named your sex doll?"

"It's not like that. My therapist thought it would help. I've had some pretty bad relationships in the past, which shut me down, so I've not been able to date or even socialize with other guys for years. My doctor thought that it might help me to get over these problems by having a mock relationship with the doll."

Mock? Did you just say mock? It was a real relationship. Goddamn it.

"I'm sorry. I didn't know."

"You're the first guy I've been with in a very long time."

"I'm here now, and I'm not planning on going anywhere. You don't need that…thing…Joey, anymore."

You seemed to need me a few minutes ago, bitch.

"Are you asking me to get rid of Joey?"

"David, I know this is sudden. I want this to work between us and I think it can. You need to want it as well."

"I do. More than you know. I don't want to lose you."

"Then please, get rid of the doll."

You've blown it now. My David will never agree to it.

"You're right. I think it's time. I need to do this."

What? You can't just get rid of me like an old shoe. You love me. I know you do.

"Thank you." Ray kissed David. "I promise everything is going to be fine. I won't let you down. I'm going to get dressed and run down to the corner store to get us some cigarettes and beer. Maybe while I'm gone you could get it out of the closet. At least put it in the garage until trash day."

The air in the closet is stale, hot and stagnant. Ray looks in my direction as he dresses. He still wants me. I feel his desire filling the void between us. I see the need in his eyes when he looks in my direction. He thinks that he's won, that he's found a way to get rid of me so he won't have to deal with his own desire for me.

Emotions rushes through me as I watch him kiss David, my David. Ray has twisted everything around in David's mind. He's manipulating David. I can't let Ray do this. I won't let him take my David away from me. My body shakes as the emotions rush out of control. My face feels flushed. It burns with anger.

I watch Ray leave. David pulls on a T-shirt and a pair of boxers. He comes toward the door. He stops. I can see his shadow slanting through the door. He opens the door and looks down at me. I try to hold in my emotions to hide them from David. He squats down in front of me. He caresses my hand as he looks into my eyes.

"Oh, Joey, how did we get here? I never thought the day would come that I would be saying good-bye to you."

Good-bye? Good-bye? The last six months mean nothing to you? You're going to let that man ruin everything?

"Ray is right. It's time. I need to let go." He picks me up and holds me out in front of him. I can see a tear forming in the corner of his eye. He hesitates. "No. I have to do this." My world turns sideways as he throws me under his arm. My head and arms face his back. My legs dangle in front of him. He carries me out of our bedroom for the last time.

My mind tries to absorb the emotions and thoughts, to process them. They come too fast to keep up with them. I'm confused, hurt, and angry. David doesn't seem bothered by any of this. He doesn't stop or hesitate even once as we walk through the living room. I look at the fireplace where we first made love and the couch where we used to fuck as we watched videos, practicing the various positions of the porn stars. The memories must mean nothing to him, for how else could he walk through the room without feeling anything? I'm hurt by the memories and his determination to toss me out in the garbage like our love meant nothing to him.

He carries me into the kitchen. The smell of last night's dinner still lingers in the air. Last night, when everything was still all right, when David still loved me, before he met Ray. I reach up as we pass the counter and grab one of David's knives. It's not comfortable in my right hand. I move it to the left and wrap my fingers around the handle.

I have no idea what I'm doing. My hands are not used to manipulating items in this way. All I know is that I want David to feel my pain. I want him to stop, for just a minute, so we can talk— talk for the first time. I know that once he realizes I'm alive, he'll give up this ridiculous notion of being with Ray. He'll come back to me and we can be together, like before, only better. I tighten my grip on the handle and bring it down, slicing it through the air.

"Fuck." David loses his footing as the blade slices into his upper thigh. He stumbles. We fall to the floor. He squirms underneath my body. Blood flows from the deep cut. It puddles on the wooden floor and soaks into his clothes. My hand is sticky and warm. He looks down at me. His eyes are wide and full of shock as he notices that I'm moving on my own.

"David, please wait."

"Jesus Christ!" he shouts at me. "What in the fuck!"

"Please, I don't want to hurt you. I love you. You have to listen to me." I hold on to his legs as he kicks at me. His foot slams against my chest, and then my face. I become desperate for time.

"Get the fuck off me." He struggles and breaks free from my lack of coordination. He crawls away and leans against the wall. "This isn't happening, you can't…"

"It's me, David. Your love has brought me to life." I try to stand. I can't. My legs are weak, unstable, and uncooperative. I fall to the floor in an awkward position. I twist and turn my body, flopping up and down on the cold, wet wooden floor trying to gain control of my limbs. After several excruciating attempts, I land on my stomach. I crawl to him on my elbows, the bloody knife still in my hand. "I know you love me. I can forgive you for sleeping with Ray, just please come back to me. It can be just like before, just you and me. Nothing has to change."

"Fuck off," he yells. He kicks my face again. He pulls himself up from the wall and steps away from me.

"David, don't make me do this." I raise my knife and bring it down as he runs past me. The blade slices through his calf. The skin breaks with ease. The muscle is tough. I push into it with as much strength as I have. The blade digs in deeper. He falls against the refrigerator and tumbles to the floor.

"Shit, okay, we'll talk. Just please put the knife down." He raises himself on his elbows and looks at me. I crawl over to him and bring myself between his legs. "I'm sorry. I didn't know. How could I have known? I didn't mean to hurt you. I'll tell Ray it's over when he gets back, I promise."

I look into his eyes. They're empty, void of everything that once stared back at me and gave me life. I can see the lies hidden deep within. Anger races through me. The David I knew and loved is nowhere to be found—he's dead to me. I raise the knife. "You son of a bitch, you're lying to me." I shove the knife into his gut. Blood splatters across my body. I twist and turn the knife, feeling the tip of the blade carving into the hardwood floor beneath David. I lick my lips and taste his blood.

David's body convulses against mine. He looks down at the knife in his stomach and then looks at me with a blank stare. I yank the knife out and bring it down in his chest. I can feel a rib crack against the force. Blood bubbles and seeps from his mouth. His T-shirt is soaked with a blackish-red. The smell of his blood and approaching death gives me a moment of sorrow—just a moment. I pull the knife out. Blood sprays and puddles around his body. I lean down and kiss him as the knife cuts through his throat. The last thing he hears is my voice telling him that I loved him.

I pull myself up using the countertop to support my weak legs. I stare down at the lifeless body of my boyfriend. His blood covers my body. I wonder if he were still alive if he would bathe me to wash away the blood, just like he used to do to wash away his sweat and come. He looks peaceful, like he did when he slept after sex.

I hear footsteps coming up the side of the house. Ray is back. He needs to pay for what he made me do. I stumble into the living room. I see the phone sitting next to the couch. I grab the receiver and smear blood across the ivory handle. David's beautiful handwriting stars back at me with the word "Police" written in his clean, crisp penmanship. I push the button.

"Nine-one-one operator."

"My boyfriend…Help me…He's trying to kill me. Please, you have to help."

"What is your address, sir?"

I drop the receiver and make my way back into the bedroom. I straighten out the sheets because I know David would appreciate that. I sit down on my side of the bed and wait. I listen to Ray yelling and screaming. I can almost see him cradling David's lifeless body. The sounds of the sirens echo down the street. They get louder as they approach. I hear doors slamming and loud voices shouting through the house. I hear them arguing with Ray. As the commotion dies away, I hear footsteps approaching the bedroom.

WORDS TO DIE BY

"Yeah, take him away," a voice calls from down the hallway. "I'm just going to check the rest of the house."

A tall, masculine police officer enters the bedroom. His dark blue uniform gives him a look of authority—a sense of power. He notices me on the bed. A smile appears on his handsome face. He approaches me and sits down on the bed next to me.

"Damn, I didn't know they made these things to look so real." He runs his fingers down my chest. His touch ignites my heightened senses. "You must have gotten caught up in the mess down there, you're covered in blood." He looks behind him, then back at me. "I can't believe I'm about to do this."

I remain silent and lifeless as he goes into the bathroom. I hear water running. He comes out with several wet towels and begins to wash away the blood. "I don't think anyone will miss you. Why don't you come home with me?"

He picks me up and carries me out of the house and into his squad car. A smile appears on my face as we drive away. I can tell this one will last. He'll love me better than David did. I know he will.

FEAR #1:
COULROPHOBIA—THE FEAR OF CLOWNS

Jacob sat staring at his reflection. A chill developed in his neck and crept down his spine as the voice of his doctor echoed through his head. *The fear is in your mind. It doesn't exist. Therefore it cannot hurt you.* Jacob turned on the trimmer and ran it over his scalp. His unwashed hair fell away from his head in long, greasy strands. He thought back on the last four years and the weekly visits to his psychiatrists and other doctors. He opened a small tin box and dabbed the cotton mitt into the translucent setting powder. He dusted his face.

His fingers twitched with excitement as the white paint began to cover his scarred and dimpled face. The pigmented cream filled in the lines that had developed on Jacob's face from early childhood on. His doctor's voice rose up in his mind reminding him of what he must do. *Embrace your fear, Jacob. You must face it head-on in order to free yourself from its grip.* Jacob tilted his head to the left to touch up the paint behind his ear, then continued down his neck to the edge of the black and white polka-dotted collar.

Jacob sharpened the makeup pencil and painted his lips fire engine red. His mouth and lips looked small and lifeless against the brightness of his new white skin. He dragged the pencil off his lips and ended up with lips and a mouth that were three times the size of his own. He grinned and noticed how yellow and stained his teeth looked against his new face. He lit a cigarette and exhaled a thick cloud of grayish white smoke over his head. *Fear is your problem, and you alone must accept that it doesn't exist.* The doctor's voice drifted around in his mind. Jacob looked down at his wrists and saw the scars from four years ago, twisted and deep within his skin. Jacob knew all too well that the fear was real. In his sleep he still felt the edge of the razor cutting through his skin and severing the veins.

Jacob began chanting the words he'd learned in therapy to deal with his fear. "I am not afraid of clowns. They cannot hurt me. They cannot kill me. I am not afraid of clowns." He repeated the meaningless words as his eyes became dark, hollow sockets from the midnight black paint. He tilted his head back and slipped a contact into each eye. He blinked as he brought his head down and stared at the greenish-yellow eyes that were looking back at him.

He took the wig off the Styrofoam stand and placed it on his head, stretching and pulling the thin rubber cap over his scalp. The long, frizzy, bright green hair stuck out in all directions, as if an electrical current was running through his body. His doctor's voice spoke up one final time. *There is nothing to fear in clowns. It is up to you, Jacob.* He gripped the razor between his thumb and finger and brought it to his face. *One final touch*, he thought as he slipped the edge of the blade into the corner of his left eye. The blood bubbled. The bubble popped. A single thin trail of blood ran down his face. He cut the right eye in the same fashion and waited for the bloody tears to set in.

Jacob could feel the frustration and anger rising inside him as he spun the words around in his head. He stood up and looked at himself in the full-length mirror that hung on the back of his bedroom door. "It's up to me—it's time. I'll show those motherfuckers just how real the fear is." He opened the dresser drawer and pulled out a butcher knife. "It's their turn to be afraid."

THE STORY OF GLENCLIFF, NEW HAMPSHIRE

Old man Max is what the town's people called him, probably still would if there was anyone left in the small New England town of Glencliff. Max had lived there for as long as anyone could remember; fact is, Max had always been there, right from the beginning. Folks said he was scared of the sun—perhaps that's because no one saw him until the day turned dark or when the sun couldn't break through the clouds. He was a tall, lanky man, always dressed in a black suit with a stark white shirt. His black hair was thin and hung around his pale white skin. Dark sunglasses complimented his odd, ghostlike appearance.

For centuries stories of who he was or what went on behind the closed doors of his old, tattered house ran rampant through the town like the plague. His house, which sat on the side of the White Mountains, looked down over the tiny town like a specter waiting for its next prey.

Mr. Proctor, the town librarian, swore he saw old man Max wandering the cemetery late at night with a shovel slung over his back. "He's making zombies," Mr. Proctor would whisper from behind the reference desk. "He's digging up the dead and doing God knows what with their bodies."

Mrs. Whittle, who was married to the local minister, expressed concern that the devil himself resided in that house. "We have Lucifer living among us. He's watching the good folks of Glencliff, waiting for each of us to sin so he can take us all to hell with him."

Sunday morning services soon flourished as the folks of Glencliff came to confess even the slightest of indiscretions.

It wasn't until the fall of 2009 that the good folks of Glencliff found out the truth about old man Max. It all started when a new resident moved into town. His name was Gregory Stoddard. He was a handsome young man who brought with him his talents for making the finest pastries in New England. He soon became the talk of the town. Unfortunately he caught the eye of old man Max as well.

People warned Gregory of the evil that surrounded the old man. Gregory would have no part of their hysteria. He agreed that he was an odd sort of man, but he never once thought that there was any sort of malice behind those dark glasses. Each evening as Gregory's café was winding down from the activities of the day, the townsfolk would see old man Max walk past the new shop on Main Street. He would pause and peer through the window. His facial expression was void of any visible emotions, yet even behind the disguise of the dark glasses, people knew his focus was on Gregory.

The strange and unnerving actions of the old man soon took a new turn as Gregory began to receive imported chocolates and exotic flowers all with the same, simple word scrawled on the card—*Mine*. The gifts became more lavish as the weeks went on, as gold watches and rare gems arrived at the café. Gregory became convinced, as the other residents of Glencliff had already guessed, that there was indeed something quite wrong with old man Max.

It was a cold November morning a few days before Thanksgiving when a beautiful young man came into the café. As the residents would later agree, it was love at first sight between the two men. In the weeks that followed there was much joy and celebration as Gregory announced his wedding to Daniel. The town rejoiced and for just a little while forgot all about old man Max.

The wedding was held in the town chapel with everyone except old man Max in attendance. The two grooms were as handsome as could be in their matching black tuxedos. As the minister pronounced them husband and husband, and the two of them kissed, everyone leapt to their feet with thunderous applause.

A large reception was thrown in honor of the two men so the

townspeople could personally greet and congratulate them. The celebration unfortunately was not meant to last, as the doors to the hall flew open with a thunderous crash. Standing in the doorway was none other than old man Max.

The music stopped as all eyes fell upon old man Max. His eyes were red with hatred as he stared upon the newly married couple. He raised his hand and pointed a long, crooked finger in Gregory's direction and hissed the single word "Mine."

The windows shattered, spraying glass through the air as old man Max's jealousy swelled around him. The good folks of Glencliff didn't have time to react before they fell down dead from an invisible force. Old man Max, with a glimmer of joy in his smile, returned his attention to Gregory and Daniel, who stood holding each other in disbelief and shock.

Old man Max walked toward the two men and without so much as a second thought grabbed Daniel by the head and twisted his neck with a quick and forceful snap. Daniel's lifeless body fell to the ground as the old man released his grip. Gregory did not scream. He did not move as the dead body of his new husband fell and wrapped itself around his feet. Old man Max held out his hand and uttered the same single word "Mine." Gregory took the old man's hand and together they walked out of the reception hall.

That night Gregory's screams could be heard throughout the town, echoing through the trees and down the slope of the mountain. His agonizing pleas and calls for help fell from the mountainside blanketing the quiet, lifeless town of Glencliff.

You may be asking yourself how I know of such events if there was no one left to tell the tale. The answer is quite simple: I was there that night when old man Max came uninvited. I had slipped out on the balcony to have a smoke just before the old man came and did his evil thing that took the life right out of our town. I hid throughout the night, fearing any movement would be my own death. I listened for hours on end as Gregory's voice grieved for the loss of his husband and his neighbors. I can still hear his terrifying pleas and painful wails in my sleep, six years later.

I left Glencliff that next morning and have not set foot in the small town until today. The visions of that night have haunted me ever since, and I knew I could not move on or get any rest until I came back and paid a visit to old man Max. Looking back now, I wish I had found another way to deal with the nightmares, for what I saw when I peered through the window of old man Max's house was more disturbing than anything I could have ever imagined.

It was late last night when I arrived at the broken-down home of old man Max. I knew that no other person living or dead had ever approached the old house. I only hoped that I would live long enough to tell this tale. The house was dark except for a faint light that illuminated the window nearest the front door. I climbed the old steps, feeling the wood give with each lightly placed foot. Without making a sound, I slipped up by the window and peered inside.

Old man Max was standing on the far side of the living room preparing tea. There was a look of contentment upon his face as he stirred sugar and cream into each freshly poured cup. When my eyes left him, they fell upon Gregory, who was still alive after all this time, yet the handsome man he once had been, had been lost at the hands of old man Max. As my eyes left the decaying, living body of Gregory I soon realized that there were other men in the room with them, seven or eight by my weakened memory. I walked around the side of the house and peered in through another window. What I saw from this new angle I shall never be rid of, for the other men gathered around for tea were the dead and buried bodies of the former residents of Glencliff that old man Max had removed from their graves. It appeared that Mr. Proctor, the former town librarian, had been right about old man Max all along.

THE CLUB

I stand on the wet sidewalk and peer through the front window of yet another club on Rue Sainte-Catherine. My reflection is the first thing I see. My self-made, pale-white face staring back at me matches the brilliance of the moon's pigment. I smell death approaching. Its fragrant aroma tantalizes my taste buds and makes my stomach grumble and my groin ache. It's nearing three a.m. The city slumbers, yet there are those who wander the streets in search of trouble or excitement, or just out of boredom. The village is alive with men. I could take any of them, all of them, but I'm looking for someone special. I own the night. I always have. After all, I didn't get the title "the Midnight Barker" solely on the basis of my good looks and charm—well, maybe just a little.

I look through my reflection into the lounge. The walls are painted Venetian Red, which gives the room an almost deathlike ambience. I'm starting to feel a little homesick in this vibrant, yet strange city they call Montreal. The men inside appear listless and unanimated. They sit alone drinking their cocktails and staring off into nothingness. I suppose that's all they have left to look at. You see, people know when death is approaching; whether they want to admit it or not, they know. They can feel it. They can sense it. If they listen closely they can even hear death creeping up behind them. Her cold, clammy fingers inching toward their neck, grabbing them and pulling them into the darkness without a second thought about their feelings or any last requests.

I know when death has marked her next victim. I can smell it weeping from their pores. It's a strange scent to explain, sort of musty. It's similar to damp, rotting wood one might find deep in a Southern pine forest. Wood that's rotting to the point of fermentation. It's a stale, sour smell with just the slightest hint of Carolina jasmine. Excuse me while I wipe the drool that has just formed on my parched and hungry lips—that's better. Yes, death is an old, mean-spirited hag who has a cold heart. It's when she has marked someone that I like to piss her off. I cut in line ahead of her and get to the person before she can. I at least give the poor dying men a choice. Granted, it might not be the best set of options they've ever had, but it's better than just stepping aside and letting the bitch take them. Besides, beggars can't be choosers, and at this point in their miserable lives, they don't have much else going for them.

I step back from the window and give myself a quick once-over. One can never be too careful about outward appearances. I insist on looking my best at all times, especially for the first introduction, and that goes for any of my disciples. I have a reputation to uphold in my world. I won't tolerate sloppiness or misbehavior in my lot. The boys that I've welcomed into my fold are a select few. I choose them very carefully, or should I say their desires and longing choose me. They have to be ready to surrender their life to me. They have to want it above all else, and then they must prove themselves worthy of my eternal love. If one boy isn't ready and goes astray, all hell can break loose. Don't get me wrong—I love death and misery as much as the next guy. Just not on the scale we're talking about when someone is brought over to my world by mistake.

Then there's Derek, my pride and joy. I took him several months back in a small town in southern Vermont during one of my carnival events. He's a beautiful specimen of the human form. I almost hated to take him. You noticed I did say "almost." He's been by my side every night since he came to me—except tonight. Tonight is his first night on his own. My apologies, I've digressed. Remind me to tell you his story sometime. It's worth telling.

I adjust my topcoat, straighten my tie, and give myself a wink of approval before walking through the front door. The air inside is heavy. It smells of sadness, remorse, and death. Damn, what a beautiful scent that is. I move from table to table, deliberately, elegantly, enticing each of the men with what he wants and needs most. I read their hearts and minds and adapt myself to their desires. I know what secrets are held deep within each of them. I want them all, but know that I cannot let myself get greedy. I am here for only one of them tonight. Damn, having a conscience sucks.

An elderly man sitting in one of the darkened corners is watching me. His thinning hair is white, almost the color of my painted complexion. He has a round, pudgy face. His skin is sagging and speckled with age spots. His body may be flawed, but his heart is pure. A taste of orange blossom honey lingers on my tongue. He has lived a full and rewarding life with his partner. He never lied nor cheated. He was the perfect boyfriend. How boring. Now I remember why I dislike the taste of honey.

I turn my back on Mr. Wonderful and walk across to the opposite side of the room. Yes, this is more like it. These men have dark hearts. There's anger in the air. The energy vibrates around me, through me. It toys with my emotions, fueling my hunger even more. Oh yes, this is going to be a lot of fun.

Wait, there's something else in the air, something…dark, something violent. I close my eyes and concentrate on the feeling. Someone is holding on to terrible secrets. Secrets coated with years of dried blood. I scan the room looking for the man whom these secrets belong to. He raises his head. He looks at me. His hazel eyes sparkle with a blood lust that I've not seen in years. His hair is well trimmed, black with flecks of gray and silver. He appears a bit weathered, yet behind the din of age and memory there is a seductive and handsome man. It's the beautiful ones that always create all the trouble, wouldn't you agree? At fifty-nine he's the youngest one here tonight. Death knows no age, nor does she discriminate. He's marked like the others. I approach him. His scent intoxicates me. I walk around the table, then behind him. My finger traces the nap of his neck. I feel his muscles tighten in response. My stomach grumbles. My groin twitches. The others will have to wait for another night. This one will be mine by dawn.

He looks up at me as I make my way back around the table. His eyes smolder with secrets long ago buried. The embers are still warm underneath the layers of time. The warm coals need to be stoked to bring them back to life, and I am just the man to do it.

"Can I help you?" His voice is deep and erotic, yet the coldness in his tone feels like a dagger of ice piercing my shadow.

"May I sit down first?"

"I don't think so."

"What if I told you that I was here to help?"

"I'd say that I didn't need any help."

"Oh, I think you do. You just don't realize it yet." I take a seat across the table from him. "Let's see, where should I begin? Ah, yes, you do remember a beautiful young man by the name of Seth, don't you?" Oh yes, that got his attention. I can see the memories forming in his mind.

"I don't know who you're talking about."

"I think you do." I lean in closer to him. "Seth Johnson, the young sexy man you beat and tortured and then left for dead? How long has it been now, twenty-five years? You must remember him. He was responsible for your...unfortunate incarceration." I feel the fear and questions mounting in his mind.

"They never did find out about the others, did they? How many were there, six, seven? You must remember the anger and frustration you felt at not being able to...you know, perform." I wink and give him a slanted smile. "Surely you remember how the young men you hired would ridicule you. What was it they called you...that's right...a pathetic excuse for a man. Then to make matters worse, they still demanded payment for services not rendered. Remember how that felt?" The embers are hot. The flames are growing.

"What do you want? I've done my time." He lowered his voice and looked into my eyes.

"It's not what I want. It's what you want, and I can make it happen."

"Fuck off, man." He pushes his chair back and stands up.

"Henry, don't make a scene." I grab his arm. "Sit back down. We're not finished having this conversation." I smile and release his arm and wait for him to get comfortable again. "I know that you have spent years of your life locked away, wishing that you could go back to that night and do things different. Don't deny it. I can smell the rot in your stomach."

"What's your point with this stroll down memory lane?"

"You still can't sleep at night without dreaming of him, can you? It's been more than two decades and he's out there somewhere. He's moved on with his life and left you unsatisfied and empty." I feel his heart rate quicken. Sweat breaks out on his forehead. The fire inside him has ignited. I'm so fucking amazing at what I do, I even surprise myself at times.

"Why are you doing this? Even if what you say is true, I can't do anything about it."

"What if I told you that you could do something about it?" I raise my left eyebrow in my own special, seductive way. I can be so damn irresistible as well.

"I'd say you're full of shit."

This ungrateful man is starting to spoil my mood. It's time to get down to business. "Why don't you say we just cut through the bullshit? You've been marked. Death is coming for you. Don't try to act shocked or deny what you know is true. You can feel her, can't you? She's closing in on you just like every other man sitting in this pathetic club. Do you honestly think that I believe that you or any of these men just want to wait and let her take you?"

"What else is there?"

"There are always options, and I bet you'd like to know what yours are, wouldn't you?" I pause for a moment to give him time to reflect. "Option one. You do nothing like you are now and wait for the bitch to come for you. You can die alone, miserable, and full of regret wondering what if. Option two. I let you relive that night from your past. Think of it as a second chance to let you do things differently, if you know what I mean." I love this game. No one has ever refused me; what other choice is there?

"What's in it for you?"

"It's quite simple—I want your soul." I feel the mash-up in his mind. Questions, possibilities, even doubt that I could pull off what I was offering him. "Look, you're going to die either way. I just thought you'd like a choice on how you go." I look around at the other men in the club and start to get up. "I guess I was wrong about you, Henry."

"Wait." He reaches out and grabs my hand. I worry that my skin paint won't hold up against his grip. He's not ready to see my true form. Though I'm not sure anyone is ever ready for that experience. I look down at his hand, then meet his dark, volatile eyes. "I want in."

"Good. I thought you might." My groin tingles with anticipation. I slip my hand out from under his grip and reach into my topcoat. I place the contract in front of him and hand him a pen.

"You've got to be kidding me." His eyes move away from the paper. "I'm not signing a contract for this."

"Look, Henry. I may call you Henry, right? It's just a formality, nothing more. Don't go getting uptight on me now. No signature, no deal. It's just that simple. I walk away without getting your soul, and you won't have to sit here any longer and wait for death to come for you, because if you don't sign this fucking contract I'm going to rip your heart out with my bare hands and make a late-night snack out of it." I place my fingers against his chest just under his left breast. I flicker, blurring my true self with the fake image these men see. My fingers sink into his chest. The warmth and dampness of his blood and tissue wrap around my form. My fingers slide between layers of skin and muscle before lodging around his beating heart. I lean down and whisper in his ear, "Can you feel it, Henry? Can you feel my fingers tightening around your heart? It's as simple as this, Henry. Just one good yank," I jerk my fingers, deep inside his chest cavity, "is all it takes." The veins in his neck begin to pulse as he tries to hold back the pain and discomfort. Beads of sweat break out across his brow. I lean down and lick the moisture as it runs down the side of his face. The saltiness from his fear intensifies my hunger. "Have I made myself perfectly clear on the importance of your signature on this contract?"

"Yes," he whispers through trembling lips.

"Good. Now sign it."

His hands shake. He drops the pen several times before getting a solid grip on the plastic housing. I hold the paper with my free hand and watch as he signs his name. I remove my fingers from his chest cavity. He grabs his chest and inhales, gasping for air to keep his heart in rhythm. I give him a moment to compose himself. I do hate a public scene. It's just not my style.

"Enough of your whining already. We have places to go and people to see." I place the contract inside my breast pocket and hold out my hand.

"Where are you taking me?" His breath comes in sporadic waves. His face looks washed and pale. It wasn't the best look on him.

"Questions, questions; why in the hell do you keep asking all these questions? Can't you just go with the flow?" I throw my arms in the air in exhaustion. "After all, what else do you have going on in your life? Live a little, would you? Oh, wait. You don't have a life anymore. It's mine now." I smile and wink at him as I hold out my hand a second time and curl my fingers, gesturing for him to hurry along. He takes my hand. "All your questions will be answered as we go. Until then, keep quiet. You're starting to annoy me." We walk out of the club and into the darkened street.

The cool night air engulfs us as we walk down the main drag of the village. Our conversation remains nonexistent during our stroll. As with most men I come across, the conflicting realities fragment Henry's mind. Images and memories flash and disappear, then morph into new thoughts. I feel them, but have trouble filtering them. I see Seth blend into Henry, then blood covering everything. I swallow and taste the blood in his mind. It's bitter and old. The images of his past mingle in the blackness of the present, racing with questions, searching for answers that he can't possibly have.

I feel the shift between Henry's world and my own. It's subtle at first. The shift grows stronger, pulling me into it. The energy swirls around me. It enters me—electrifies me. The two worlds are starting to collide, allowing us entry into my world. For Henry it will be his world twenty-five years ago, the world that is engrained in his memory. The place he so desperately wanted to get back to that he sold his soul for the one-way ticket.

"Brace yourself and don't let go of my hand."

"Why, what's going on?"

"It's time. Our worlds are shifting, allowing us to pass between them." His hand tightens around mine. "You're going to feel a bit queasy as you pass. Some feel as if their body is being torn into large jagged pieces."

"Wait." He stops and holds me back. "Where in the hell are you taking me?"

"The place your memory has brought us to; the place and time that still haunts your dreams." I look up into the night sky as the vibrations rip through my body. God, it feels good to be going home. I close my eyes and say good-bye to the ugliness of this world. I hear Henry's deep pained moans as the shift begins to absorb him, stretching his body and mind into human Silly Putty.

We're once again on solid ground. The shift has completed. I watch as Henry looks around at the world created from his memory. I'm a master at what I do, right down to the finest of detail, details his mind retains, details his memory cannot recall. His eyes widen as he looks upon me and sees my true self. He wants to scream. His throat muscles flex. Fear keeps his breath from escaping.

"What in the fuck happened to you?" He yanks his hand from my grip as he stares at my near-featureless body. My long, billowing black hair blends against my shadow. The single feature he can see with any clarity is my ice-blue eyes staring back at him.

"This is my true self. I'm a shadower. My body is for the most part solid, but I can shift and manipulate my form at will. I can't be seen in your world as I am. What people in your world see is a painted version of who I was when I was alive."

"Will I become like you, when you take my soul?"

"Is there something wrong with the way I look? Is this not good enough for you?" I turn around with a little dance, laughing and mocking his ignorance. "Don't worry. You will not become like me.

That's a special honor that you're not worthy of. You shall die like everyone else in your world, minus the soul, of course."

"What do you want with my soul anyway?"

"Well, if you must know…" I lean into him and place my cold lips against his ear. I feel him pull away from my closeness. I grab his shoulders and pull him into me with a sudden and forceful yank. "I will eat it out of you and feed upon it." I lick his neck.

"You're fucking sick." He wipes his neck as he backs away.

"After what you've done in your past, I don't think you have any room to throw stones, especially at someone who can help you. Let's get on with this, you're starting to bore me. Besides, I'm getting hungry, and you don't want to be around me when I haven't eaten. I'm not a very pleasant person." I give him a little wink, then place my arm around his shoulders, leading him down the street to the night he first met Seth.

Henry pauses as we reach our destination, the small hustler bar that is home to all of Henry's victims. There are no signs, no neon lights. You must know about this place and where it is in order to patronize it. Henry looks at the once familiar surroundings with a strange expression of a life once lived. He peers into the window and remains motionless.

"Is there a problem?" I ask with a twinge of irritation in my voice. His expression changes as he glances back at me. Gone is the questioning older man with years of regret. The man standing before me is twenty-five years younger. There's an edge about him now, a darkness shaded in erotic undertones never fully realized. I take a deep breath and smell the troubled soul brewing beneath the surface.

"I forgot how good this feels." He touches his body as if inhabiting it for the first time. He faces me dead on. "It's time for you to leave. I have unfinished business to take care of."

"Yes, I know you do. I'm counting on it." I step aside and let him pass. He no longer walks like an old man. His strides are confident, bold, and with purpose. Oh, this is going to be so much fun.

I peer through the dirty windows and watch him take a seat at the far end of the bar. He orders a drink and waits. I enter his mind. It's erupting with possibilities for the night. He's anxious as he waits for the young man who destroyed his life all those years ago.

I slip back outside as I feel Seth getting closer. The air fills with an electric current from his essence. It smells of his sex. I like him already. He turns the corner, stops, and lights a cigarette. He's more beautiful than the image in Henry's memory produced. His sandy-blond mid-length hair is unruly, which adds a roughness to his seductive features. He has several days of dark brown whiskers covering his jawline, chin, and upper lip. He's not very tall, five foot seven or eight at the most, with a lean, firm frame. His jeans with tears in all the appropriate places expose his red-checkered boxers. His gray T-shirt is skin-tight. His nipples give rise to the thin material.

I take the opportunity of his stillness to flicker and slip into his body. He reacts to my invasion with a cold shiver. I succumb to the heat of him and settle in for a spell. I feel Seth's emotions, his motivations. He's a user, out for himself and no one else. Fear has no place inside him. A hollow, torn heart beats inside. The only thing that matters to him is his next paycheck. He takes a deep draw on the cigarette, blows the smoke around him, and heads into the bar. This is better than even I could have hoped for. Henry is going to be in for one hell of an unexpected ride, and I will finally get to feed, perhaps twice if I play my cards right.

It's apparent that the bartender knows Seth. His beer is opened and waiting for him before he gets to the serving area. Seth throws a few dollars down and finds a table in the corner with a full view of the bar. It isn't long till Seth and Henry make eye contact. Their gaze is long. They both have a plan, and winner will take all.

Henry doesn't play around with idle glances and the typical cat-and-mouse routine. He picks up his drink and comes over to Seth. "Mind if I join you?"

"It depends."

"On what?"

"How much money you're packing in that wallet of yours, and

how much of it you're planning on spending on me tonight. I ain't cheap." I feel Seth's lips stretch into a playful smile. Yes, he's good at what he does.

"How's this for starters?" Henry opens his wallet and lays a hundred on the table and pushes it over to Seth.

"That'll buy you some time." Seth leans into the table. "So, what's your name?"

"Henry."

"Well, Henry, sexy name by the way, I'm Seth." He motions Henry with a curl of his finger. Henry leans in closer. Seth presses his lips against Henry's. "It's a pleasure to meet you. You keep this kind of money flowing my way and you can have anything you want tonight."

"I plan on it." Henry pushes the chair away and moves over to the banquet next to Seth. His hand glides up Seth's leg. I can feel Seth's dick responding to Henry's touch.

I've been a silent party to this duo for too long. It's time to have some fun and make a few minor adjustments to Henry's past. I focus on Seth's body. I feel the blood running through his veins as if they were mine. I strengthen my hold and take control of his body.

We look into Henry's eyes. Seth's gaze is more gentle, thanks to me, yet Seth is clueless to the changes I'm invoking on him. Henry notices and runs his finger across Seth's cheek.

"Like what you see?" Seth's voice, our voice, becomes soft and seductive.

"You have no idea." Henry swallows a lump in his throat. He leans in and kisses us. I feel his thick, meaty tongue slip between Seth's lips. Our kiss goes deeper as they lean into one another. I hear Seth's thoughts. It's strictly business with him. I enter Henry's mind and tug on a few cords, making him feel things, warm fuzzy things that under normal circumstances he would never have felt. Henry pulls away. He looks at us, almost through us as he grapples with the feelings I've created.

"Something wrong?" Seth leans in to kiss him again.

"No, this isn't how it's supposed to be." He backs away from Seth's advances.

"How what isn't supposed to be? Are you fuckin' with me, man?"

"Fuck." He pulls Seth into him. Their lips meet. Their teeth clash from the impact. Henry's body is tense. He begins to sweat. I can feel his confusion as the anger and fire in his heart begins to ebb. He looks at Seth as if not recognizing him. "Son of a bitch. This can't be happening."

"Look, perhaps this ain't a good idea tonight." Seth pulls away from Henry's tight embrace.

"No, you're not going anywhere." Henry places another hundred on the table. "That should hold you over till I get back." He slides off the bench and leaves the bar.

I flicker and leave Seth's body. I blend in with the shadows in the room. Others think they see something out of the corner of their eye as I pass. Their minds will disregard it as nothing more than what I am—a shadow. I step out onto the street. Henry is yelling my name.

"What in the hell do you think you're doing?" I lift his two hundred pounds off the sidewalk and push him against the brick wall of the alley with little effort. "Do you want to draw attention to yourself? Is this how you behave? It's no wonder Seth got away the first time." I let go of his neck. He drops flat-footed to the ground.

"This isn't how it happened." Henry's face is reddening. Spittle forms in the corners of his mouth. "What in the fuck have you done?"

"I've done nothing." I try to compose myself though it's getting more difficult with this man. "I simply brought you back to where you most wanted to be. Perhaps you're not remembering how it went down last time. Even significant details can be lost over time."

"Don't give me that shit." He rubs his neck and walks past me. "I've lived for twenty-five years with this night running over and over in my mind. What ever you've done, undo it. I'm not supposed to be having these feelings for him. You can't do this to me. This wasn't part of the agreement."

"Dear, dear Henry. You have everything so muddled in the weak little head of yours." I tap my finger against his forehead in slow, steady thumps. "Our agreement was for me to bring you back here. How that or this night plays out is in your hands, not mine."

"It's not supposed—"

"How do you know," I cut him off, tired of his boring tirade, "that this isn't how it was supposed to happen that night? You wanted this night to end differently, didn't you? You wanted to come back here to get it right, thinking that perhaps you could change your destiny, your future, so you wouldn't have to end up sitting alone in the club where I found you." I grab the back of his neck, pulling him toward me. His stale, sour breath batters my face. "Think for once in your sorry excuse of a life. In order to have a different outcome, earlier events need to change." Damn, I'm a quick thinker. "These feelings that you say you're having appear to disgust you. I like that emotion. Disgust is good. Maybe this emotion is what you were missing that last time. Maybe it's why he lived." I push him aside. "Now, stop wasting my time with your pathetic excuses and get back in there." He walks past me. I grab his arm and hold him back. He looks at me with contempt. "Here, chew on one of these mints. Your breath smells like shit!" I release his arm and slip into the shadows of the night as Seth steps out onto the sidewalk.

"What are you doing out here?" Henry looks around as if expecting me to be standing behind him.

"I got tired of waiting around. The bills you gave me just don't keep a man occupied like they used to." Seth lights a cigarette and blows it in Henry's direction.

"Well, here's another one. Will that be enough to get you back to my place? I'm sure you'll find plenty to keep you occupied there."

"Sure, what the hell. I've already wasted prime time on you, what's a few more hours going to hurt, just as long as I get paid. Let's see what you've got waiting for me back home. It better be good, 'cause I ain't easy to please."

As they pass by, I slip back into in Seth's body. He stumbles with the awkward flow of my body. His attitude and outlook are dangerous for my plans. I need to soften him up a bit, to keep things moving in the right direction. I concentrate on his mind and take control. I move his hand and intertwine his fingers with Henry's. Henry smiles at us.

The walk to Henry's apartment is a short one. The old brick building is empty of inhabitants except for a handful of individuals. It's quiet and somewhat isolated, a perfect place to bring the boys back to. Henry had it all figured out, and would have killed more if it hadn't been for Seth. Now, twenty-five years later, they're back here in the same room where the violent attack occurred. The difference is Seth doesn't remember any of it…yet.

Henry closes the front door to his apartment. He pushes us against the wall. His mouth covers ours. His heavy tongue fills our mouth, Seth's mouth. Henry reaches down and pulls the tight-fitting T-shirt over Seth's head, exposing Seth's lean, toned torso covered in brown hair. Henry's hands are all over us. His eyes shift back and forth from Seth's naked torso, to his face, to his eyes. He picks us up. I let Seth play along, wrapping his legs around Henry's waist and his arms around Henry's neck. The three of us stumble into the bedroom. Henry sets Seth down on the bed.

"Get undressed. I want to see what I'm being paid to work with here."

Henry kicks off his shoes. His hands shake, making it difficult for him to unbutton his shirt. I wonder if his nerves are from sexual anticipation or sexual frustration. Either way, it's going to be a good feed tonight. Henry manages to get undressed and stands motionless in front of Seth.

"I'm impressed. Not bad for an old man." We smile and walk over to Henry. "Most men your age give me little to work with. I like what I'm seeing." We lean up and kiss Henry.

"I've got a couple of hundreds in the nightstand there. Help yourself to them. If you keep making me feel like this, I'll give you my checkbook by the time the night's over."

"You don't need to pay me any more tonight. I meant what I said. I like what I'm seeing." We move over to the edge of the bed and curl up on it. "Why don't you get yourself over here so I can show you what an amazing lover I can be." Seth, with a little help from me, pats his hand on the bed before pulling off his pants and underwear.

"Don't go anywhere. Please, I'll be right back. I just need to take a piss."

"Don't worry, man, I'm not going anywhere tonight." We wink as Henry scurries into the bathroom and shuts the door. I know that's my cue. I slip out of Seth yet again to find Henry pacing the floor.

"Nate, please, I need a favor."

"I'm listening." This has got to be good. No one asks the Midnight Barker for favors, except of course when their begging for their lives, and I don't think those count as favors?

"I don't know what's come over me. I think I'm in love with Seth."

"Henry, we've had this talk before…"

"No, no, you don't understand. I'm okay with it. In fact, I like this feeling."

"This is touching, but…"

"Please, don't take me, my soul. Just walk away and let me start over with Seth. I never got a chance to love anyone before. I didn't know what I was missing. Please, you have to let me go. Give me a chance to make up for what I did to Seth and the others."

"You're joking, right? You just want me to walk away? You get what you want and poor old Nathanial here goes home empty-handed and hungry? That seems a bit unfair to me don't you think?" I pause and watch his expression. "Fine, if it's that important to you. I'll give you a break and go back and try to find someone else in the club."

"You mean it? You'll leave, just like that?"

"What can I say, I'm a giving individual. Here's our contract." I tear it up into small pieces and let them fall into the toilet. "Go ahead, flush it. Besides, your sweetheart is waiting for you, and you wouldn't want to get him mad." Henry flushes the toilet and heads out of the bathroom with an annoying grin of happiness on his face. "Damn," I whisper to the empty bathroom. "He's more gullible than I thought." I slip out of the doorway and blend into the shadows of the bedroom. I stand at the foot of the bed and watch Seth take

Henry's cock into his mouth. My stomach grumbles; it's time to feed.

I enter Seth's body for the last time. His body has adjusted to my repetitive penetration. I slip in without a struggle. I settle in and taste the saltiness of Henry's precome lingering on Seth's tongue. Henry is letting go for the first time in his life. He no longer wishes to control the men in his life; instead he gives into the pleasure of submission and surrenders his body to Seth, to me.

Seth and I gain momentum on Henry's cock. He gasps for air, throwing his head from side to side in a fit of passion he's never before experienced. His body and mind are not equipped to handle true pleasure. He tries to speak through tangled breaths, begging Seth to stop or at least slow down. He reaches for Seth's head, our head to pull us off him. He struggles to remove us. My strength is too great to fight. Sweat covers Henry's body. The heavy, damp air hangs around us as I feel him swelling within Seth's mouth. His soul is about to escape. I am about to feed.

The first wave of Henry's orgasm rips into Seth's mouth, my mouth. It's thick and heavy and tinged with years of neglect. I swallow it and taste his soul. It's bitter and hot. It feels good to feed again. We continue our assault upon Henry. His body shakes and trembles from the heavy loss as more of his soul explodes into my mouth.

These moments of a man's life are the most powerful. It is with me alone that they can experience pure sexual pleasure. A pleasure that no human can ever feel and still be able to sustain life. A man's soul is his sexual being and nothing else. It is through his orgasm that fragments of his soul escape, and it is through this process that I feed.

Henry's body is spent. He has slipped in and out of consciousness several times during those last few orgasms. His body is calm, at peace, alive for now. Death will come for him in her own time. Perhaps I should help speed up the process.

I slip out of Seth's body. He falls against the bed, exhausted and spent. He looks up at me. His eyes grow in fear as he sees my tall shadowy figure standing before him. The sweat of his body glistens in the dim light. I smell his sex. I feel his bliss. I want him to come with me. I want to take him like the other young men I've taken. I want to make him what I am, to live eternity with him and my other boys.

"Don't be alarmed, Seth. I'm here to help you." I walk over to the bed and sit down next to him. He's too tired from my control to put up a fight.

"What in the fuck are you?"

"I'm Nathaniel, but please call me Nate." I brush the hair away from his eyes. "Do you know where you are?" I watch as Seth looks around. Fear seizes hold of him. His body trembles against mine as he notices the all-too-familiar apartment, the bed, and Henry lying next to him.

"This can't be happening. It's got to be a bad dream, right?"

"I'm afraid not. You're sitting in your past, twenty-five years ago. You see, Henry sold his soul to me this evening. In exchange I agreed to bring him back here to the evening the two of you met."

"Why? I don't understand!"

"Seth, he wanted to come back to change the events of this night. He wanted to make sure you didn't survive like you did the first time." Seth looks at me. His eyes are full of tears. My heart goes out to him. He's nineteen again, lost, alone, and living on the streets trying to survive. "I changed earlier events to give you this opportunity to seek revenge. The knife he attacked you with is in the nightstand. Take it. He's still alive, Seth. Take it and cut out his heart, end his miserable life like he wanted to do to you."

"I can't." His head shakes back and forth as he stares at Henry's body.

"Yes, you can. I can feel it inside you." I open up the drawer and place the knife in Seth's hand. "Feel it, Seth. This is what he uses to attack you. Remember how it feels cutting into your skin, digging into your gut. Use it, Seth. Use it for a good purpose this time, to end Henry's life."

"No." Seth tosses the knife across the room. "I won't."

"Then let me take you and bring you to my world. You can live for eternity pleasuring other men and feeding upon their souls."

"I'm not going anywhere with you. I just want my life back. I beat Henry years ago. I did my time in therapy and moved on. I have a good life now, and that's my revenge on this man. I have a wonderful husband and a beautiful eight year-old son. I'm not a killer. Send me back."

"I'm sorry, I can't do that."

"What? Of course you can. You did all this, didn't you?"

"It is some of my finest work, I'll admit that." I get up off the bed and walk around the room. "You see, the life Henry and I took you from, the one you say you want to get back to, doesn't exist anymore."

"Of course it does. It's my life. I have the memories, the feelings—those can't be lies."

"No, you misunderstand me. Think, Seth, what I'm saying. The life you had did exist. Those memories and feelings are all very real. The problem is the life you were living is a result of this night. The attack is what got you off the street and made you fight for your life. The same way the events of this night motivated you to clean up your act, go to college, and make something of yourself, and at college is where you met your husband."

"Yeah, I want it back."

"You still don't understand. The attack never happened, and therefore your life is not the way you remember it."

"What happens?" Seth is motionless as the realization of what I've said flows through his mind. "What's my life now?"

"Seth, just come with me. Surrender your soul to me and forget all about this life here. You'll never hurt, you'll never suffer."

"Tell me, God damn it."

"Seth, I'm sorry for what you're going through. The life you are asking to go back to is not a happy one. Without the attack, you never had the courage or motivation to get off the street. You're still selling your body, still living on other people's dime, for food, drugs, and alcohol."

He walks up to me. I expect to see anger, yet all I see is pain. Tears roll down his face, smearing the street dirt. "I don't want to live without Josh and my boy. They're everything to me." His lips quiver. He begins to sob as heavy waves of pain and loss wash over him. "There was a time in my life that I would have let you take me back to whatever hell you came from, but not now. I'm used to fighting for what I want, and I'm not giving you the satisfaction of winning this one. You owe me this."

"I owe you nothing."

"Kill me."

"What?"

"If I can't go back to Josh and my family, then I don't want to live. You did this to me. You took everything from me, so the way I see it you owe me this much. So do whatever you have to, just get it over with."

"I can't. Please come back with me."

"I said kill me. I have nothing left to live for."

He turns his back to me. I can see the remorse trembling through his body. He's right. I do owe him. I place my hands on his head. His body tightens and jerks in response. I take a deep breath and snap his head to the left, severing it from the rest of his body. His body goes limp.

I look around the room. Henry has passed. Death has come for him, and she didn't even bother to say hello. I look at Seth's head in my hands, wishing things had worked out differently. I wanted to introduce him to my world. He would have loved it, well, at least the old Seth would have. I kiss his still-warm lips and lay his head on the bed. As I open the door to the apartment, the two worlds begin to shift. I soon find myself walking down familiar paths in my own world. My stomach is full, even though I didn't get dessert. I think about home and how good it will be to rest for a while. Those thoughts are cut short by the familiar shift of our worlds once again. There's someone else out there who needs me.

NIGHTMARES—A SERIES OF SMALL TALES

The Grave

It's dark. The hot August air settles in around you as you sit at the gravesite. You buried your lover ten short months ago. Sleep escapes you without him by your side, so you visit the grave each night hoping to fall asleep together once again. You reach out and touch the newly sprouted grass. You dig your fingers into the soil, desperate to feel close to him again. A branch snaps in the distance. You want to brush it off as nothing more than nerves. A feeling inside you tells a different story. You hear footsteps coming up the gravel path behind you. His scent surrounds you—his favorite cologne— Old Spice. You can feel his presence engulfing you, soothing your tired mind and body. You want to turn around. You want to see him once again. Fear keeps you frozen, unable to move.

He's standing behind you. The smell of him has changed. The air turns a sickening sweet. It reminds you of rotting fruit. You feel a hand upon your shoulder. You turn your head and see the slimy gray skin peeling off the bones. The ring you gave him hangs from his decomposing finger. You close your eyes, hoping it's a dream. You hear his bones snapping and cracking as he leans into you. The cold dead skin of his lips touches your ear as he whispers, "I'm back."

You wake up in your bed cold, yet covered in sweat. You take a deep breath to relax your mind from the nightmare. As you turn over and close your eyes again, you feel something shift next to you.

Dinner for Two

Jared was a survivor. For the first time in his life he knew he could take of himself. He didn't need anyone else. His relationship of ten years had just ended. Richard was an abusive son of a bitch, and Jared had the knife and cigarette scars and broken bones to prove it. He was the punching bag Richard used every night to release his stress. Tonight was different. Tonight Jared was celebrating. Richard was no longer a part of his life. He'd broken the cycle of abuse and ended the relationship.

Jared opened up a bottle of white wine and poured himself a glass. He took a sip of it, enjoying the crisp, fruity flavor. He picked up his steak knife, the very same one Richard used on him countless times in the past. The meat was medium-rare, just as Jared liked it. He took his first bite and savored the marinated meat. It was tough, just like Richard. Even in death the bastard still didn't know how to be tender.

Cat's Eyes

There are many people and cultures that believe that cats will eat a human corpse just prior to the flesh going rancid. I'm here to tell a very different kind of tale. It's the story of Jared Beach, a feline-loving guy who made his home with over one hundred cats.

Jared suffered from many things in life, but the affliction that ultimately led to his demise was that of eating the cats once they died. He would boil them and skin them and make various soups and stews, never once thinking of the feelings of the other cats that were still very much alive. He lost his friends as well as his boyfriend when he confided to them his peculiar tastes.

As depression set in, he began to gain weight, so much weight, in fact, that mobility without a motorized chair simply was not possible. He could no longer move about the house or take care of all of his cats. One day as he sat and slumbered after a heavy cat-meat pie, the cats that remained couldn't tell if he was dead or alive. They became hungry and started to crawl all over him, demanding that they be fed. When he didn't respond to any of their typical games, they concluded that Jared was no longer alive.

The cats, assuming that the man had died, took revenge upon him and tore into his meaty flesh. The initial pain was so great that it woke Jared up with a start, yet he was too slow to fend off the eighty-nine cats. Several of the cats took aim at his toes, and they nibbled and chewed them right to the bone. Another cat crawled up on his shoulder and dug its teeth into the folded flesh of Jared's neck. The cat gnawed deeper to get to the meat and ended up ripping through the jugular vein. The blood spewed in a large arc from Jared's neck, attracting the cats to drink the blood as if they were drinking from a running faucet. The last thing Jared remembered before death set in was a cat's mouth opening up and gnawing out his eye.

Death

Death is coming for me. I can feel him approaching. The air turns cold. My breath becomes crystallized. Death looks at me. He can see my life, sense my desires. His breath is foul and smells of shit and rot. He comes to me, pressing against my body—becoming me or I him. I know my destiny; the hell I am going to will burn my soul for all eternity.

DYING TO GET OUT

Phillip took a deep breath to help stir his mind awake. The warm air infused with the odors of his body caught in his throat. He coughed. His chest tightened. His lungs felt heavy as he took another breath. The intake of air stopped midway in his chest. His thoughts, foggy with sleep, wondered if his lungs were getting smaller or if there was less air than before. The last thought terrified him. His eyes snapped open. He couldn't see. He blinked to make sure his eyes had opened. The fluttering of his eyelids answered his question—the blackness remained.

In the dark, something brushed across his face. His hands moved without conscious thought as if shooing a fly. His knuckles hit a hard surface just inches from his face. He pressed his hands flat against it. The old wooden planks moaned. They held firm against his pressure. The smell of the damp earth seeped through the cracks. Rot, decay, and the smell of death soon filled the air. Panic seized him. He felt nauseous. Sweat broke through his skin, causing the already hot air to become heavy with moisture. He held his breath for fear of using up the remaining air before he had time to get out.

He moved his hands through the space around him, calculating the distance between him and the walls of the wooden box. He wondered how long the air would last, considering it was almost too small for his five-foot-nine frame. He stretched his feet and felt the rough surface of the wood scrape across the tender pads of his toes. It was then that he realized his shoes and socks were missing. He moved his hands over his body. He felt his bare skin. He was naked inside the darkness.

Goose bumps covered his flesh, not from the cold, but from the fear running rampant in his mind. He rubbed his arms, stretched his legs, and wiggled his toes. The space felt different, as if the walls were closing in on him. The air seemed to dissipate. The temperature rose within what little space remained. His breath came in short, heavy pulses. Reason left his mind. He pounded his fists against the walls until they were numb from the assault. He screamed, deafening his own ears. Tears formed in the corners of his eyes. He closed them and prayed for a quick death.

The blackness began to fade. A soft glow of natural light filtered in, hitting his lowered eyelids. Phillip felt cold, colder than he had ever been in his life. He kept his eyes shut for fear that if he opened them the light wouldn't be there, that his mind or what was left of it was playing a cruel trick on him. His body shook as an icy cold finger trailed down his spine. He hugged himself to steady the shaking and to give himself a moment of comfort.

"Phillip, it's okay. Come on out now. It can't hurt you any longer." The faint, familiar voice called to him. He focused on the words. "That's it. You're doing just fine."

Phillip opened his eyes. He looked around the room, confused by the strange surroundings with light and air. There were books covering every wall. At first the room felt cozy and inviting, but the antiseptic tidiness eventually tainted the otherwise comforting feelings. His mind began to clear. The reassuring voice that pulled him out of the murk belonged to his therapist. As the fog of the dreams cleared, Phillip's memory returned. Michael sat as he always did in his leather swivel chair with his legs crossed. His gray cotton slacks were pressed, as was his black polo shirt. A notebook laid on his lap, his glasses held in one hand, a pen in the other.

"What do you remember?" Michael uncrossed his legs and placed the glasses back on his face.

"Nothing specific, just darkness and an overwhelming feeling of fear." A cold chill covered his body. He looked down at himself. His unbuttoned shirt exposed the brown hair that lay dampened to his skin. His sweat mixed with a deep earthy scent wafted off his body. He felt embarrassed by the condition he found himself in. He pulled his shirt together without buttoning it. His fingers trembled, making it hard to grip the material.

"You don't have to be embarrassed in front of me, Phillip. Remember, this is as much about trust as it is about your problem."

"Did I do this?" He let his hands drop. His shirt fell open and spread down his sides. His nipples became erect as the warm air of the office embraced his cold skin. His face reddened.

"No, I unbuttoned your shirt." Michael smiled, noticing Phillip's facial response. "It's not what you think. If I wanted you, I would just come out and say so. During the hypnosis, your body had begun to overheat to the point that you stopped sweating. I was afraid you might go into hyperthermia. I unbuttoned your shirt to help cool your body down."

"Sorry, Michael, it's not you. I do trust you, or I wouldn't be here." Phillip lowered his face and stared at his hands, which had fallen into his lap. "It's just that it's hard to explain. The hypnosis makes me paranoid. It's like I can't trust anyone."

"Hypnosis isn't to blame for these sudden feelings of paranoia. I'm convinced it's part of this large problem you have."

"You mean the claustrophobia?"

"No, it runs much deeper than that. There's something else that's driving these problems, something more specific. You've mentioned in past sessions the feeling of being buried alive. The technical term for that is taphophobia. Perhaps this is causing you to feel paranoid."

"No, the paranoia is new. It's because of the hypnosis. It's a part of it."

"What do you mean?"

"I've always been afraid of the dark and enclosed spaces. With that came the isolation and feeling of being left alone. That's what terrifies me the most during those moments. I never once felt as if someone was watching me."

"And now?"

"It's not just the dark that scares me anymore. It's the feeling that I'm not alone in the dark. There's something or someone in the dark with me." Phillip's voice quivered from the vivid memories. He looked up from his lap. "Where are you taking me?"

"Excuse me?" Michael's face tightened with the question.

"When you hypnotize me, where are you sending me? You know, a time in my childhood, a past life?"

"Phillip, I don't believe it's helpful for the progress we're making to discuss with you in detail what happens while you're under hypnosis. That's for you to figure out on your own. Trust me when I say that you are where you need to be during that time." Michael looked at his watch. "Our time is almost up for today." He stood and placed the pad of paper on his desk.

Phillip took the cue to stand up. Michael walked over to him and watched as he buttoned his shirt. "You're going to be fine." Michael gave Phillip a hug. "You just have to give yourself time." Phillip returned the hug even though he felt odd each time Michael closed their session with an embrace. "Now, remember what we've talked about." Michael wrapped his arm around Phillip's shoulder and walked him through his home office and to the front door. "If you need me for any reason you have my cell phone number. Call me any time, day or night."

"Thank you. I appreciate everything you're doing for me. I didn't mean to question you or sound ungrateful before."

"Questions are a natural part of the healing process. You should never be ashamed to ask. Just remember that you might not get an answer to your questions. Give it time and all your questions will be answered." He smiled and patted Phillip on the back.

Phillip smiled as he turned and walked down the first floor hallway of the brownstone and out into the sunlit street of Commonwealth Avenue. He turned his face to the sky and let the warmth of the late-day sun evaporate the chill in his body. He didn't want to go home, not yet. He wanted to capture the light of the day, to bottle it and use it before going to bed, to allow him to sleep without the nightmares. Things were always better in the daylight.

The sun had just dipped below the horizon when Phillip opened the door to his apartment. He turned on a few lights to illuminate his familiar surroundings before heading into the kitchen. He turned on the oven to preheat and tossed a Lean Cuisine frozen dinner on the counter. He grabbed a beer from the refrigerator, popped the cap, and took a long, slow drink. He toed off his shoes and settled into his favorite chair. He took another gulp of the icy drink and propped his feet up on the coffee table, wiggling his toes to stretch them.

He took a deep breath to unwind from the day. The air he breathed in smelled of dirt and soil. He sat up and took another deep breath; the earthy smell lingered. He picked up his shoes and examined the bottoms. The treads were clear of any dirt, yet the smell was stronger. His nose followed the increasing scent to the inside of his shoes. The ripe, pungent smell of the earth invaded his nose. He placed the shoes next to the chair and pulled off his socks. His feet were cold and dirty. He rubbed his feet to warm them, and in doing so he removed the clots of lint from between his toes. As he massaged his big toe, a sharp pain pierced his nerves. He leaned down and saw a dark brown splinter embedded in the pad of his toe. Gripping the edge of it, Phillip pinched the splinter and pulled it out. The jagged edge ripped through the layers of skin. A small droplet of blood bubbled up from the wound.

He held the small splinter between his finger and thumb, wondering where he would have gotten it. He wanted to dismiss it as nothing more than a splinter, yet something bothered him about it, as if there was a memory that he couldn't quite reach. His temples began to throb. He felt the blood pulsing and pounding in his head. Dizziness swept over him. The air around him felt thicker. He flicked the splinter to the floor and lowered his head between his knees and waited for the nausea to pass.

Phillip lifted up his head. He felt queasy and sick to his stomach. He grabbed the arm of the chair to steady himself as he stood. When his legs felt strong enough to support him, he made his way into the kitchen. He had lost his appetite. The thing he needed the most was the one thing he couldn't get—sleep. He turned off the oven and tossed the Lean Cuisine back into the freezer. He walked down the hallway toward his bedroom, using the walls to support himself. He undressed and crawled into bed, pulling the sheets up to his neck. He stared at the white ceiling while he waited for the pain in his head to subside. His eyelids soon dropped from the weight of exhaustion. His vision blinked off and on until sleep overtook him, and with sleep came the dreams.

His mind became a torrent of dim, foggy images. He once again found himself in complete darkness. His unclothed body shivered. He was standing this time. His bare feet, nearly numb from the cold wooden floor, ached with his weight. The dampness sank deep into his skin. The pitch black that surrounded him made his eyes useless. He sensed the walls were closing in on him. The air shifted as if something had rushed past him. Its movement stirred the damp air he breathed. He knew there was someone or something in the space with him. He couldn't see it, but he knew it was there. He felt its presence. It closed in on him. He felt it move to the left of him, then in front of him, then behind him. It surrounded him and then the unimaginable happened—it touched him. His mind went numb with fear as he felt the long, bony fingers of a hand on his shoulder.

The room shifted. A deafening sound reverberated around him. The space began to shrink. He could sense it. The walls were moving inward, encasing him with this thing that stood in the black space with him. Phillip felt the floor shift underneath him. The floor opened up. His body slipped from the confined space. He reached into the void, hoping to grab onto something to break his fall. There was nothing but a vast emptiness surrounding him.

He fell through the intermittent clouds. He felt the void's great expanse beneath him spreading out in all directions as if it had no ending. A shadow spread out beneath him. The darkened silhouette became varying shades of green as he approached it. His body hit a solid surface. The ground was wet. Large tombstones towered around him. He stood and brushed the dirt and dead leaves from his body as he looked out across the cemetery.

The light of the moon cast gray shadows across the stone surfaces. Its brilliance through the clearing night twinkled in the damp blades of grass as if a thousand eyes were staring up at him from the graves. He looked around him as the feeling of being watched settled back into his mind. He listened for someone breathing, a twig snapping, or any sign of another person. The night stood silent and still.

The light of the moon began to fade in and out through the increasing clouds. The air turned colder the further Phillip walked through the night. He paused against an old pine tree and searched for anything that looked familiar. His eyes caught something in the distance, a silhouette against the darkening horizon. He walked toward it and came upon a large headstone marking an open grave. It appeared in the night like a gaping mouth waiting to be fed. The dank earth carried smells of death and decomposition. The headstone was weathered and stained from years of abusive New England winters. Across the spotted surface an inscription began to appear. His blood ran cold as he read the words.

HERE LIES PHILLIP GLEN HANSON
BELOVED TO NO ONE EXCEPT ONE MAN.

Nausea swept through him. His stomach knotted. He gagged and heaved until his throat was sore. The date of his death etched into the stone below his epitaph said he would die that evening.

Phillip backed away with slow, uneven steps. He stopped. His eyes widened. His body froze as he felt himself back into something. He could feel it towering over him in a solid, cold stance. His body shook beyond control as a hand fell upon his shoulder. Panic ripped through his mind. He held back a scream, knowing it would be of no use. There wasn't anyone around to help him. He looked down expecting to see long, bony fingers curling around his collarbone. There was nothing there, yet he could feel something pressing into his skin. He took a deep breath and spun himself around. He stood facing the dark and nothing more. His mind tried to convince him he wasn't alone; then the palm of a hand made contact with his chest. It slammed into him, taking his breath away. He fell backward into the open grave. The soil from the edge of the grave trailed down the sides and littered his body with its cold dampness. Phillip saw a shadow move across the opening. A silhouette appeared at the edge. He looked up and saw Michael standing over him.

Phillip awoke in his bed. His familiar surroundings seemed cold and unfriendly. From the other room he thought he heard his front door close and the bolt sliding into place. He looked around the room for movements or shadows. He turned on the lamp and sat up, pressing against the headboard of his bed. Tears welled up in his eyes and spilt down his face. He brought his legs up to his chest and wrapped his arms around them in a makeshift hug. He rocked himself until the sun broke over the horizon and chased the fears away.

❖

Phillip stood in the kitchen, tapping his fingers as he waited for the coffee to finish brewing. The smell of the freshly ground beans tantalized his senses and made his wait seem even longer. Michael wouldn't be happy about him missing his appointment. Phillip didn't care. He needed a quiet morning without the questions and without the reminders of the dreams.

He poured himself a large mug, adding a bit of sugar and low-fat milk. He blew across the surface, then took the first sip of the morning, letting the hot liquid soothe his tired body. He sat the coffee down and pulled on a pair of boxers that hung on the back of a kitchen chair. He settled down in his favorite corner of the couch with a deep sigh. He picked up the remote and decided that he didn't even want the morning news today. He took another sip of coffee. The phone rang. Phillip flinched from the jarring noise and spilt coffee down his chest and crotch. "Shit, can't people just leave me the hell alone?"

He sat the coffee down on the table and looked at the caller ID. He recognized Michael's number. He picked up the phone. "Yes, Michael, I know I'm late…I just spilt hot coffee all over me thanks to you, that's what's wrong…yeah, you could say that…I had another bad night last night and just didn't want to deal with more questions today…I know…It's just…Fine, all right…I'll be there soon." Phillip dropped the phone in the cradle and tugged off his wet boxers. He refilled his coffee cup on the way to the bathroom to shower and change.

Phillip felt off by the time he reached Michael's office. It was as if he was outside his own body, witnessing his own actions, with no control of anything. The bright sun of the day that would normally make everything better seemed to worsen his spirits. He hesitated at the door. He stared at his reflection in the window. The old glass caused his face to look distorted and aged. His face was a stranger to him. He leaned in closer to get a clearer look. His reflection wavered, blurred, and then corrected itself. He shook the uneasy feeling out of his mind before ringing the bell. A second later he heard the buzzer unlatch the lock. He opened the door and walked down the dim hallway. The sound of the front door closing behind him echoed down the hall.

Michael opened the door before Phillip could knock. He peered around the edge of the door. "Come on in, Phillip. I'm glad you agreed to come."

"I'm not so sure." Phillip walked past him, tossing his shoulder bag down on the brown leather chair. He turned around as Michael closed and locked the door. Phillip stared at Michael as if not recognizing him. His hair was uncombed. It stuck out in twisted curls at odd angles. Thick black whiskers covered his face and neck. His clothes looked as if he had spent the last several days in them.

"I must apologize for my appearance. I've been up all night working on your file. I believe we're making tremendous progress. I think we're very close to resolving these issues you have." He motioned for Phillip to sit in his usual spot. "Please, help yourself to some green tea. I just made it." Michael sat down behind his desk. He scooted the pad of paper toward him. "On the phone you said you had a rough night. I'd like for you to walk me through the dream."

"Look, Michael, I don't want to go there again." Phillip filled a cup with the hot tea. He blew across the surface before taking a sip.

"It's critical that I know everything you remember. I'm here to help you, Phillip."

"Fine, I'll tell you what I can remember." Phillip slipped off his shoes, bringing his feet up under his body. He replayed the dream from the previous night. It wasn't until Phillip mentioned seeing Michael standing over the grave that he noticed him making his first notes on the paper.

"So let's talk about my presence in your dream." Michael set the pen down, intertwining his fingers over the pad of paper. "Why do you think I was there?"

"I don't know. For months the paranoia and the feeling of being watched have gotten worse, and now I see you in my dreams."

"I'm in your dreams because you want me there. Feelings have developed for me that you are not ready to process. You can't even admit that they exist. I've become the one person you can depend on. That in turn has resulted in these romantic fantasies of me coming to your rescue."

"You're not there to…" Phillip's words fell away as a sudden, unsettling thought broke through his mind. He had never felt that the person in his dreams was there to help him. It was just the opposite; he was there to harm him. He set the cup of tea down, pulled his feet out from between the cushions, and slipped them back into his shoes.

"I'm not what, Phillip? You can tell me anything. What is it that I'm not? You shouldn't be hiding things from me, Phillip. I need to know everything you're feeling."

"You're…not right about this." Phillip took an internal sigh. "I don't have feelings for you. You being in my dreams is nothing more than…more than…"

"Phillip, are you all right?"

"I'm not feeling so good." He placed his head between his legs to help with the dizziness. "Can you get me some water, please?" Phillip leaned back against the couch. Sweat ran down his face.

"Sure, it will just take me a minute." Michael stood up. He walked over to Phillip, patting him on the back. "I'll make it all better, I promise." Michael left the room, shutting the door behind him.

"You're not my knight in shining armor," Phillip whispered to the empty room. He grabbed hold of the arm of the couch to help steady his legs. The room swirled around him. He stumbled. He fell forward, bracing himself on Michael's desk. He looked across the desk and saw his file. He looked toward the door, then back at the file. He turned it around and opened it.

Phillip's mind became a mass of confused thoughts as he stared at the contents of the file. His hands began to shake. His temples throbbed. His stomach knotted as he picked up the dozens of photographs of himself. His life over the last several months looked back at him in eerie detail. He flipped through them one by one. He couldn't understand how or why Michael would do such a thing. He felt sickened, violated that the man he trusted had invaded his privacy to such an extent. The categorized photos displayed his various activities: his walks in the park, his time in therapy, even pictures of him sleeping in his own bed. It was the last set of pictures that terrified him the most. He felt faint. He broke out in a cold sweat as he realized his dreams had not been dreams at all, but his own reality. He stared at the final pictures of himself lying naked in a dark, wooden box. Phillip had seen enough. It hurt to think about those agonizing moments locked away somewhere while Michael photographed him. He dropped the pictures on the desk, and then noticed Michael's daily notes. He read the last entry.

Phillip was an ideal candidate. Every variable in my research indicated that his phobias were an exact match for my goals. Lately, however, it's as if he's unconsciously fighting the progress we were making. I need to get him back on course before he ruins everything. He's more defiant than the others, more independent. He's starting to remember things he shouldn't, as if the memory blockers are not working. I'll have to up his dosage. I hope that will get him under control again; if not, I'll have to terminate his file and start over. I can't lose that precious time. I need to find a way to keep him progressing forward.

The door to the office opened. Phillip looked up and saw Michael standing near the door holding the glass of water. Michael's eyes twitched with anger as he realized that Phillip had seen the file. They stared at each other without moving, without words. Phillip closed the file.

"Why?" Phillip broke the silence that had descended around them. He turned to Michael, keeping his hand on the desk to help balance his weakened body. "How could you do something like this? I trusted you."

"Phillip." Michael shut the door moving toward the desk. "Please, you have to understand. It's nothing personal. Out of all my patients, you are the perfect fit for my research. The others were close, but they could only take me so far. You, on the other hand, you are special, you matched every major point on my analysis." Michael took a few steps closer. He stopped.

"Research? You're using me as a fucking guinea pig." Phillip stepped back. He lost his balance. He stumbled on weakened legs. He righted himself by leaning against a chair. "You locked me up in small confined places, then buried me alive, knowing what that would do to me. The whole time you made me believe that they were nothing but dreams."

"Don't you see? This is why it has to be you. You suffer the greatest of all of my clients. Sure, the others shared similar phobias as you. The fear of the dark, the fear of enclosed spaces, but you, Phillip, have something the others didn't have—the fear of being buried alive." Michael's hands began to tremble. The water sloshed over the rim of the glass, spotting the papers on his desk. "I must have all three in order to study the effects of fear on the mind. Don't you see it has to be you? No one else has what I need."

"You keep talking in the present tense as if I'm going to let you continue these experiments on me." Phillip scanned the room hoping to see a way out other than the door that was behind Michael.

"Oh, you will continue with the experiments, Phillip. You see, you don't have a choice. This is my research. I will get my results." Michael slammed the glass down on the desk. The glass shattered into sharp jagged pieces. Michael didn't notice the deep gouges in his palm. Blood covered his hand, dripping down his fingers. He ran his hand through his hair, smearing the blood through the thick tangles. A single drop formed on his brow and slid down the side of his face.

"Please, Michael, just let me go. I can't do this any longer, it's too painful."

"Yes, I know. The mind creates such intense pain during moments of fear. You saw the pictures of yourself. Are they not brilliant? Did you notice the expression of panic on your face? Did you see the fear in your eyes? Here, see for yourself. If you look real close, you can actually see the fear hovering over your body. It's fantastic." Michael tossed the pictures at Phillip. They hit him in the chest, then scattered on the floor around his feet. "Your mind was lost in excruciating pain, yet you are still able to function outside of those moments. It's fascinating. God, that first night was so wonderful. I need to know how long a person's mind will last under those circumstances."

"Then what?"

"Then I must terminate the patient. What else?" Michael lunged toward Phillip. Phillip stepped to the side to avoid direct impact. His legs gave out. He fell to the floor. Fear raced through his mind as he felt Michael clawing his way up his legs. He lashed out with his free leg. His foot grazed Michael's shoulder. "It's no use fighting me, Phillip. I drugged the tea. You won't have the strength to fight me. In fact, depending on how much you drank, you might not be able to move much longer."

"Fuck you," Phillip yelled. His foot connected with Michael's chest. Phillip heard the thud from the impact. He heard the gasp as Michael fought for air. Michael's grip eased up on Phillip's foot. Phillip leaned back and kicked Michael again, this time with both feet. Michael fell backward against the couch.

Phillip tried to stand. The room spun out of control. He leaned against the bookcase, using the shelves to help pull him up. He was too slow. Michael lunged against his back, pulling him back down to the floor. He tried to kick Michael again. His legs wouldn't respond. He raised his arm to take a swing, but his drug-weakened muscles just twitched and he fell on the floor in spasms. He lay on the floor with his muscles convulsing, unable to defend himself any longer.

"That's better." Michael stood and blotted the blood from his hand with his shirt. "I'm sorry it had to be this way."

"Please, Michael, don't do this. Please—" Tears cut off Phillip's words. Unable to move, he watched as Michael lifted up the red carpeting that he himself had admired at every therapy session. Below the rug were several wooden planks of a different type of wood than the others. Phillip, unable to turn away, watched as Michael lifted the boards one by one and exposed a large opening beneath his home. Phillip could smell the familiar stench of damp rot spilling out from the hole in the floor. "Michael, you can't do this. Please, I'll do anything you want, just please don't put me down there alone."

"Oh, you won't be alone. You never were alone. I was always with you." Michael looked over at Phillip and smiled. He stood up and grabbed Phillip's feet, dragging him toward the opening. Michael stepped down into the hole and pulled Phillip in with him.

"God, no, please stop." Phillip's body wanted to move. He felt his muscles twitch, trying to respond to his commands. It was no use. His body had become limp, lifeless.

The smell of decay and death surround him. He looked around the crawl space as his head shifted back and forth from the movement of being dragged. He noticed several wooden boxes scattered below the floorboards, lying in piles of dirt. "Michael, please don't do this. I'll do anything you want. Please don't leave me down here for too long."

"Oh, you don't understand. This is the final stage of the experiment." Michael crawled over to a crate and scooted it through the dirt closer to where Phillip lay. "You see, this is where we must part ways. I won't be coming back to get you out this time, but don't worry, you won't be alone. I'll be watching you the entire time." He smiled at Phillip and brushed the sweat-dampened hair from his forehead.

Panic raced through Phillip's mind as Michael began to remove his clothing. Michael lifted Philipp, now naked, and placed him in the wooden box. He tried one last time to reason with Michael, but the fear had consumed him and taken his voice. His eyes moved back and forth trying to catch the last glimpse of life from above. He concentrated on the beam of light from the late-morning sun that crossed the floor in the office above him. The opening in the floor caught the beam of light and pulled it down with him. He heard the lid creak and watched as Michael closed the lid on him, shutting out the last bit of light he would ever see.

Phillip lay in the darkness and listened to Michael pounding nails into the lid. He closed his eyes and concentrated on his breathing to help ease the panic. His body shivered from the cold and the forced calm he tried to maintain. Phillip knew Michael would soon be watching, waiting for him to show signs of panic. Phillip was determined not to give Michael that satisfaction. If he was going to die, he was going to do it on his own terms. As his breathing slowed, his rational mind returned. He wasn't going to give up. He would just have to wait until the drugs wore off and life returned to his muscles. Then he would find a way out. He lay in the damp, dark box. He remained motionless and calm until unseen things began to crawl and slither over his skin.

WORDS TO DIE BY

S weat gathered along the edge of his hairline as he stood
pissing in the dim and dingy bathroom. The acrid, bitter
smell of his urine pricked his nose as it pierced the air. He glanced
at the white porcelain bowl long ago covered in stains of rust, piss,
and shit. Davis shook his dick and flipped it back inside his pants
as he stared at the words scrawled across the stained tiled wall. A
nervous chill ran down his spine when he noticed a response to his
posting from the night before. The chill lingered. It penetrated his
skin, sinking deeper into his muscles and bones.

There had been too many thoughts from too many voices
running through his head last night. The commotion had dulled his
creative mind, making it impossible to produce, yet he knew he had to
write something, anything to make the stop worthwhile. Davis spent
his working life as the second-shift supervisor at a manufacturing
facility in Salem. He took the position a few months after graduating
from high school. Twenty years later, his daily routines were set.
He lived in Boston, exactly 37.2 miles from where he worked. He
left work every night at exactly 11:45 p.m. and took the same route
home each time. There were three rest areas on his nightly route, and
therefore there were three stops. His illegal words from last night
were simple, straightforward, a standard among others like him.

Davis was here—August 10, 2010 12:01 a.m.

He stared at the words, not understanding why someone would
do such a thing. He had not asked a question, and he certainly did

not write it as an invitation to talk. Davis had simply stated a fact. Yet the words were there in red ink accusing him of lying. The controlled, precise penmanship of the author chilled his blood. He read the words carefully for the fifth time.

No, you were not, because I was here—August 10, 2010 12:01 a.m.

His creative mood diminished. His anger toward this stranger consumed him. *I won't let him get away with this*, he thought as he pulled his fine tip black Sharpie marker from his pocket. *I will not have my good name tarnished.* He bent down eye level with the words. He raised the pen to the wall. A soft thump came from the other side of the wall as if someone had opened the stall next to him. He paused and listened, expecting to hear footsteps or breathing. Silence echoed around him instead.

His hand that held the pen began to tremble as the feeling of being watched settled into his mind. Not wanting to make his presence known, he placed the toilet seat down without a sound and stood on top of it. His heart pounded in his chest. His temples throbbed. He leaned against the old metal wall. It wobbled against him. He brought his face up far enough so that his eyes were level with the top edge of the stall. He could smell the stale fumes from years of bleach and disinfectant. The bathroom appeared empty. He held his breath, listening for the slightest of sounds.

You do realize that in all likelihood the man is waiting for you out there, a dainty voice quivered in his mind. *It would be to your advantage to get out of here before something terrible happens to you.*

Don't say those kinds of things, he responded in his mind. *There's obviously no one there.* He stepped off the toilet and returned his attention to the wall. He studied the words one by one looking for a hidden meaning. "I'm not going to play your games with clever rhymes or verse." The words sounded hollow as they fell from his lips. He pulled the cap off with a smirk of satisfaction and began to write.

I would like to know who you think you are, and what you expect to gain from calling me a liar. What is it you want?

He leaned away from the wall, tilted his head to the left, and then added several exclamation points.

He opened the door to the stall. It groaned with agitation. The fluorescent lights flickered as he passed by the row of sinks. The mirrors that hung against the wall were tarnished and chipped. He looked into them through the streaks of dirt and grime. Shadows danced around him as the lights pulsed on and off with an electric buzz that sizzled around him. He quickened his step toward the door.

The heavy night air told of an approaching storm. The wind howled around him, billowing through his untucked shirt. He paused at the driver's door of his car and looked out across the parking lot. A car sat off in the distance. Davis knew the lot had been empty when he arrived. The car had come in while he was inside. He strained his eyes and thought he saw someone sitting in the driver's seat. "That's him," he mumbled into the darkness. "He's just waiting for me to leave so he can write something foul against me again." He unlocked his car, leaned over the front seats, and opened the glove compartment. Fumbling in the dark, his hand gripped the smooth handle of his knife.

He had purchased the knife several years ago. *You can never be too careful*, he remembered telling himself, *especially at night.* He placed the knife in his left hand and shut the door. His footsteps sounded heavy as he walked across the parking lot. He switched the blade open. He gripped the handle tighter as he neared the trunk. A voice spoke up in his mind. *The fucker is in there. We can see him. You better teach this son of a bitch a lesson.* Davis found strength in the voice. He took a deep breath and crept alongside the car. He walked up to the driver's door and knocked on the window. He waited for a response that never came. He lifted up the door handle with his right hand and pulled the door open. A foul stench rose up from the interior of the car. Blood covered the windows and dashboard. The man's lifeless, naked body fell out of the car. His head lolled backward from the thick cut across his neck. Davis's stomach knotted. He held back the sour bile that filled his throat.

Davis wanted to run. The voices in his mind screamed the

same logical action. His feet refused to listen to any of them. His ears filled with the heavy pounding of his heart. His world became blurry. The thumping of his pulse seemed hollow and distant. The voices went silent. The world swirled around him as he stared at the man's naked body. His full coat of black chest hair congealed with the drying blood. His limp cock lay in a tangle of matted pubic hair. Davis reached out and touched it. He felt an odd intimacy with the man that he couldn't explain. For just a moment he felt saddened that the man would never again have an erection or feel the pleasure of an orgasm. The man's cock lay lifeless like the rest of him. Davis pulled his eyes away from the man's cock and looked at his full body. A familiar feeling entered Davis's mind, as if he knew the man. He leaned in closer, holding his hand to his mouth and nose to block out the smell of the decaying body. The dead face stared back at him with its hollow gray eyes. Davis recognized the man. He was looking at himself.

Davis fell into a black void in his mind. Darkness surrounded him. He awoke in his bed. His body shivered from the cold, yet the thin cotton sheets stuck to his sweat-dampened body. The thick, heavy curtains caused the midday light to turn to dusk in his room. The dreams began to subside from his mind, leaving a whimper of silence.

He tossed the covers off and sat on the edge of the bed, rubbing the sleep from his eyes. He stood up and grabbed his robe from the closet, making sure he replaced the hanger in the exact spot from where he had taken it. He peered around the corner of his bedroom door. Relief washed over him as he saw the five locks of his front door still intact. Even with this added knowledge of security, he still felt as if he wasn't alone.

❖

Davis drove down highway 107 with an anxious knot in his stomach. The feeling of being watched had continued throughout his shift. Alone on the highway he felt even more uneasy about his once-familiar surroundings. The exit signs and mile markers seemed different to him tonight, somehow misplaced. His agitation grew stronger, forcing him to break his path, his system that he had lived by for most of his life. As he approached the first rest stop, he turned his head and stared at it. It stood alone in the dead of the night. His foot tapped the brake. *Old habits die hard, don't they?* A voice echoed in his head. He forced himself to pass it by. A twinge of guilt pricked his heart as if he were leaving an old friend behind.

As Davis approached the second rest stop, the voices in his head cleared, allowing him to think without all the chatter. His mind focused on the bathroom wall and the lies held in those words. His hands tightened on the steering wheel. His pulse quickened as he accelerated the car. He drove past the second rest area, not even looking in its direction. He knew a response had come. He could feel the new words from the stranger etched into the wall like a hot poker pressing into him, burning its image on his skin and scarring him for life.

The parking lot of the rest stop stood empty. Davis pulled into his usual space and sat staring at the building while the car coughed and choked. The storm grew stronger outside. The wind rustled through the trees. His car rocked from the gusts as he tried to build the courage to leave the comfort of his car and walk into the unknown. He knew he had to go inside. Walking away from this was not an option. He wanted the lies and the nightmares to stop, and the only way to stop them would be to stop this man from taunting him. He took a couple of deep breaths to calm his nerves. He opened the door and stepped out into the night.

The scent of an early fall hung in the air. Dead leaves from trees too weak to hold on to them any longer crunched under his feet. He reached into his jacket pocket and felt the comfort of his knife cradled at the bottom. *Just in case*, he thought to himself. He opened the door to the building. Under the faint smells of urine, vomit, and shit that he had become accustomed to, a different smell lingered—something new, the smell of death. Its scent was pungent and burned deep in his nose. It rushed out to greet him before drifting away in the wind. Davis took a tiny step inside the door. He listened for footsteps, breathing, or someone taking care of their private business. All he heard was the slow, steady drip from one of the faucets.

Davis stopped to look into the grimy mirrors. The shadows from the previous night had not returned. His reflection stood alone, staring back at him. He walked to the last stall and placed his hand on the door. He hesitated for a moment before opening the door. It creaked against him. He broke out in a cold sweat. His armpits became damp with nerves as he noticed the same steady penmanship as the previous night.

I am everything you desire. I am everything you fear, and what I want is you!

Davis refused to pull is eyes away from the words. The words, written in deep red ink, seemed to pulse and move in a downward flow, filling the words themselves. He placed his trembling finger against the letters. The ink was still wet. It flowed around his finger, smearing the words. He rubbed the substance between his finger and thumb. He sniffed it. The dark smell of death he had noticed earlier came off his skin. Fear seized his entire body as the door to the bathroom closed.

Davis stood paralyzed with fear and anger as he heard the man open the stall next to him. His temples throbbed. The pain in his head shattered his thoughts as if someone had driven a thousand nails into his skull. The sounds from the next stall cut through his ears. The man's zipper, the heavy stream of his piss, the splashing of the water in the toilet—everything echoed around him. Davis sat on the toilet to steady himself. He covered his ears against the deafening sounds.

He stared at the floor and noticed the man's left foot from underneath the wall. He wore dark green canvas sneakers on his large feet. As Davis stared at the man's foot, a dark spot splattered on the side of the man's shoe. Davis stared at the pattern it made as it soaked into the canvas. A second drop appeared, and then the smell of death and blood. The man was bleeding in the stall next to him. Davis wondered if it was a self-inflicted wound used to write on the wall. He heard the toilet flush, the stall door opening, and then water running in one of the sinks. Davis knew it was time to confront his tormentor.

Davis stood just outside the stall door and stared at the stranger. He appeared younger than Davis had expected. The man looked up from washing his hands. He looked at Davis through the mirror. The man had a handsome face with a heavy growth of dark whiskers across his jawline. Blood dripped from the man's small, flat nose; yet he didn't seem to notice. Davis took a few steps toward him and then stopped. The man turned off the water and shook his hands dry.

"What's your problem, man?"

"Your nose is bleeding," Davis answered in a distant voice he didn't recognize.

"What?" The man ran his finger under his nose. When his finger came back clean, he looked into the mirror to double-check. "Look, man, I don't know what you're talking about."

"The blood, it's dripping on your shoe and the floor. Why are you lying to me? I can see it." Davis walked toward him. He could smell the man's sweat mixing with the deep scent of the blood. "What did you do, punch yourself in the nose to get the blood to write with?"

"I don't want any trouble. I just came in here to take a piss."

"No, you didn't. You came in here tonight to write more foul words against me, just like you did last night." Davis felt his anger toward the man grow. "It's one thing to torment a person, it's quite another to lie about it as well. That is unforgivable. You should be man enough to admit what you've done."

"You need to back off before someone gets hurt." The man held up his hands as if protecting the space around him.

Davis gripped the knife in his pocket. His fingers rubbed the smooth granite surface of the handle. The comfort of the knife eased the pain in his head. The blade flipped open as he brought the knife out. Davis raised the knife and slashed it through the space between them. The blade cut through the palm of his stalker.

"Motherfucker!" The man cradled his cut hand. Blood flowed

from the deep cut, soaking into the man's blue dress shirt. "You're fucking crazy." He stepped to the left to give himself an escape.

Davis, full of adrenaline, blocked his path and brought the knife down across the man's chest. Davis could feel the blade cutting through the material of the shirt and entering the man's skin.

In desperation the man pushed against Davis. They both lost their balance and fell to the floor. Davis lost his grip on the knife. He heard it hit the floor behind him. He turned and crawled over to it. A foul odor rose up from the stained grout. Davis choked on the fumes.

The man stood up and kicked Davis in the stomach. He doubled over in pain, curling into a fetal position. The man's foot made contact with Davis's body again. He felt a crack in his chest and knew the man had broken a rib. Sharp pain came with every breath. Yet in the pain he found additional strength. He grabbed the man's foot as he came down for another hit and twisted it. He felt the man's bones snap and break in his hands and he tumbled to the floor next to Davis.

Davis crawled over to the knife and wrapped his bloody fingers around the handle. He stood over the stranger and watched as the man's shirt became darker with sweat and blood. Davis knelt over the man and placed the knife to his throat.

"Why are you doing this?" The man looked into Davis's eyes.

"The pain you're feeling is nothing to the pain you inflicted upon me with your words."

"I don't know what you're talking about. Please just let me go."

"Why do you insist on denying what you've done?"

"Please, I don't know what you're talking about."

"No?" Davis stood and bent over the man. "Then let me show you." Davis grabbed the man by his dirty blond hair and dragged him across the floor.

Davis kicked the door of the stall open and pulled the man in behind him. He knelt down once again and pulled the man's head up. "That's why I'm doing this." Davis pointed the knife toward the wall. "Those words hurt me. You called me a liar." The bloody tip of the knife clicked against the tile as Davis pointed out the words. "You smeared my good name with those foul, hateful words."

"I'm sorry, man. I never wrote those words. You've got to believe me!"

"Even after showing you, you still won't admit to it. Your lies are hurting me more than those words." Davis's mind became a mass of voices and images, clogging his own thoughts. Sweat dripped into his eyes, burning his vision. He had to stop the lies, the voices and the nightmares this man created. He brought the blade to the man's trembling throat and dragged it deep across the flesh from one side to the other. The man's body shook and convulsed. The words he tried to form gurgled out of the large gash. Davis watched as the man's dark, foul blood poured onto the floor. He stood up as the man took his last breath. Silence filled the bathroom as Davis walked out into the heavy air of the night.

Seventeen minutes later Davis opened the door to his apartment. His mood had lightened since the little trouble in the bathroom. It wasn't how he would normally have handled a problem situation, yet difficult times sometimes call for extreme measures. "It was his fault." He spoke to the empty room as if defending himself to a jury. "He started it. I had no choice. I had to defend my good name." With anxious hands, he set the five locks on the door. He stopped and noticed the blood that covered his hands and clothes.

He eased his feet out of his shoes and carried them across the apartment. The lights in the bathroom flickered on with the motion of his body. He set his shoes down under the pedestal sink and turned on the water to let it warm up. His face looked drawn and years older than he remembered. Dark circles appeared in heavy bags under his bloodshot eyes. His whiskers were starting to gray in spots. "It's his fault. I had to stop him." He turned off the water in the sink and decided a shower would be better to cleanse himself of the man's scent.

The bar of soap turned bright pink as he rubbed it over his chest and stomach. The lather, thick with the smell of lavender and the man's blood, developed into a deep rose as it fell over his body and down his legs. Pale red water gathered at his feet and trailed down the center of the tub before swirling down the drain. The heat of the water intensified the smell of death. It turned his stomach to think of the man in the shower with him. He turned the hot water down and let the icy cold water rinse away the last of the soap and memories.

Davis patted himself dry as he walked into his bedroom. The light of the moon cast faint shadows across the pale gray walls. His head still ached. He opened the bottle of Excedrin PM that sat on his nightstand and downed two of the pills without water. He crawled into bed and pulled the sheets up to his neck. He laid there staring at the ceiling and waited for sleep to take him.

❖

Davis stood in the bathroom of the rest area once again. The air hung over his head, thick with the stench of blood. He didn't like being here. He turned to leave. The door he had just walked through was gone, replaced with the same tiles as the rest of the walls. He was trapped with no way out. The lights flickered and hummed overhead. The faucets dripped a steady beat. His heart followed, beating in the same dull rhythm. He walked to the mirrors and watched the sweat break out against his face. He turned on one of the faucets to splash cold water on his face. The pipes vibrated and shook the sink. The faucet, opened up spraying a thick brownish-red liquid that smelled of rotten eggs and onions. The smell overpowered him. His stomach knotted. He gagged and vomited into the sink.

He heard a thump on the far side of the bathroom. He turned toward the sound. He swallowed the remains of his vomit that clung in his mouth as he walked over to the last stall. Dark pools of drying blood covered the floor. His bare feet sank into its congealing puddles. He could feel it oozing through his toes. He opened the door.

The man's dead body, drained of blood, lay in the same position as he had left it. Everything looked the same, except the man's clothes were missing. He lay in his own drying blood, bare and exposed. Davis searched his weakened mind. He couldn't recall taking the man's clothes. Voices rose in his head with feeble explanations. He studied the body. The man had a beautiful body with dark curly chest hair that ran down to his navel. A crusty white substance lay matted in the man's pubic hair. A nervous laughter escaped Davis's lips as he realized that the man had had an orgasm while Davis slit his throat. The man opened his dead eyes and look up at Davis, cutting off the laughter.

Davis screamed and fell back out of the stall. "This isn't happening. I killed you. You're dead." He backed up against the wall. It felt cool against his skin. He wanted to run. He wanted to escape this nightmare. He stood frozen. His eyes remained fixed on the dead man looking back at him. The stranger rolled over. His lifeless body thumped and slapped the cold tile floor. He dragged himself closer to Davis, smearing the blood over his grayish-blue skin.

"It's you that I want, Davis." Blood and mucus leaked out from the man's mouth. His tongue fell out and hung in a hideous angle like a dog with rabies. "Ou, Davith. Ith ou thath I wanth."

Davis covered his ears to drown out the newly formed lisp of the dead man's voice. He closed his eyes to the man, hoping to hide from him in his mind. He could feel the cold, dead body crawl over his feet. Fear paralyzed him. His skin burned from the stale touch of death. His breath came in an icy mist as he breathed. His body convulsed as he felt the dead man's body cover his.

He awoke in his own bed with the coldness of death under the covers with him. Davis took a few deep breaths to calm his mind and body. He looked around his room. Darkness surrounded him. He turned on the small lamp that sat on his nightstand. The room came aglow with a faint light. He shivered against the sweat of his body. His feet felt heavy, as if covered in socks. He tossed the sheets off his body. His eyes widened in horror as he noticed the dried blood covering his feet. He looked down, stunned to see himself fully dressed in a blue shirt and black slacks. The dress shirt, with a cut across the chest and covered in dried blood, was familiar to Davis. A torrent of visions from his dream came rushing into his head. He wore the clothes of the man he had murdered. The pain in his head returned like a railroad spike to a slab of wood. It tore into what remained of his sanity.

He stumbled into the living room. As he reached the light switch, he knew something was out of place, that something or someone stood in the room with him. He stared into the blackness trying to decipher the familiar shadows he knew so well. The pain in his head made it difficult to think. The feeling persisted. He switched on the light and stared at the words written across his living room wall.

Nice job, but you missed.

The same tight, concentrated penmanship that he had become familiar with in the bathroom stall marred his living room wall. Davis glanced at the front door. The locks were all securely in place.

Davis looked around the room. Everything appeared to be in order. His eye caught the edge of a pen sitting next to a book on the coffee table. He picked it up and went to the wall. He stared at the words, moving and vibrating against the dull white paint. The pain in his head blurred his vision. He felt sick. His muscles ached.

Where are you?

He stood back and looked at the words he had written. He no longer recognized his own handwriting. He waited for a response. The room came in and out of focus. The floors seemed to roll in waves up and down like a makeshift funhouse. He gripped the back of a chair to steady himself as red letters began to form on the wall.

Look behind you!

Davis stared at the words as they appeared before him. Fear gripped his chest. His breathing came in short, heavy puffs. Fear kept him from turning around. He could feel something behind him. A chill brushed across the back of his neck like someone caressing a lover for the last time.

He swallowed his fear and turned around. The living room was empty, yet he knew he wasn't alone. He could feel a presence around him, closing in on his space, removing the air he breathed— suffocating him. "Leave me alone!" His scream fell flat against the air. He collapsed to the floor on his hands and knees as his stomach knotted. He retched several times before spilling the contents of his stomach. He could hear scratching from all directions. The noise became clearer, like someone writing on a chalkboard with a damp piece of chalk. He looked up at the wall and wiped a string of vomit from his chin. Words formed all around him.

I am here. I am there. I am above you. I am beneath you. I sleep with you. I bathe with you. I've even fucked you.

His arms gave out. He fell against the floor. He rolled over on his back and held his hands to his ears to block out the noise around him. The words continued on the ceiling, larger and redder than the other words, as if they were screaming at him.

I am a part of you. I am on top of you. I am next to you. I am inside you!

Davis felt a searing pain racing across his stomach. A warm, wet liquid flowed around him. He tore at the shirt. His eyes widened with fear as he saw the blood pumping and gurgling from the opened wounds. In desperation he tried to squeeze the edges of the cuts together to stop the bleeding. His hands were too weak to grasp his blood-soaked skin.

As he felt his life slipping away, he noticed a shadow standing above his head. The black form moved over to the side of him. It stood motionless, watching him die. Davis tried to talk. His lips moved, but with no purpose. His mind struggled to form words. His mind failed him. The voices in his mind went silent. The sound of death was all that he heard. The shadow took a more solid form and knelt down beside him. Davis's eyes widened with the realization of who stood over him. As Davis took his final breath, he saw himself kneeling next to his dying body, grinning a devilish smile.

FEAR #2:
HIEROPHOBIA—THE FEAR OF PRIESTS

B less me, Father, for I have sinned." Gian trembled as he sat in the tiny booth. He could smell the years of frankincense and myrrh etched into the ancient wood. It surrounded him, teased him, and terrified him. "It's been over five years since my last confession." He braced himself for the priest's prayer.

"It's been a lot longer than that, Gian," Father Gregory replied.

"Why…"

"Father, how did you know it was me?" Gian wrapped his arms around his body to quiet the nerves.

"You have the voice of an angel, Gian. I knew it was you from the first word spoken. I have not seen you in church since your parents died. Why did you stay away? You should have known that this is where you belonged, among the people who love you."

"My parents made me come to church, Father." The words fell from his lips. "I am terrified of this place, of all places holy. When I was a child I felt that I would burn in hell for being a part of it. When they died, I vowed never again to set foot in the house of the Lord."

"It appears as if the fear is no longer holding you prisoner. Your presence here today proves that."

"The fear has not subsided, Father. I'm keeping my eyes closed to block out my surroundings. My nerves are shaking. I'm covered in my own sweat." Gian heard the faintest creak of old wood as if something next to him had shifted. Then a heavy breath filtered through the confessional.

"Then why come back?"

"My therapist says I must face my fears."

"So why are you confessing? Could you not just sit in the church as an act of facing what you consider to be a place of fear?"

"I'm here because of you, Father."

"Me?"

"Yes, you; and the nightmares."

"Tell me about them."

"As a child I had terrible nightmares," Gian began. "Even before I understood about Christianity I would dream that I was walking up to the altar with my parents on either side of me. We would stand before the cross to pray. When I would begin to recite the Lord's Prayer, the cross became covered in blood. I would turn to my parents for help. The people holding my hands were no longer my parents, they were the decomposing bodies of the priests. They would turn to me. Their flesh would peel from their bones, landing on me. Their skin was cold, sticky, and wet. The sickening sweet smell of rotting flesh would penetrate my nose. I would scream, running from the church with their hollow laughter chasing after me."

"Good."

"Father?"

"It's good that you are confiding in me. Do you feel I am somehow connected to these nightmares, as you call them?"

"Yes."

"Can you see the priest's face in your dreams?"

"No. The priests don't have any facial features, but I know you're there."

"You should be careful, Gian, where you lay blame."

"I was not laying blame, Father, yet you seem eager to accept it."

"You know not what you are saying, my child. This fear you have has clouded your judgment."

"It is not my judgment in question. The dreams I had as a child were the same as those of other children in this parish."

"And how would you know such a thing?"

"Children talk, Father. We confide in one another when our parents dismiss our thoughts as immature or fanciful. They were as afraid of you and this place as I was."

"I don't like the direction you are taking with this. I never..."

"I did not say that you did, Father. Their fear was real, just like mine was—still is. The difference is I'm still alive."

"The difference is your parents listened to you, unlike the others in my congregation. They believed you when you told them about the dreams. They even believed you when you told them that I was not who I pretended to be."

"They were going to leave your order, weren't they?"

"Yes. We couldn't allow it. You see, it's not just me—it's everyone here. They believe in the words of our dark Lord so much that they will do anything to protect one another, including sacrificing their own children."

"You killed my parents, didn't you?"

"You seem to have already figured that out, so there is no use in my answering that question."

"I was supposed to die with them."

"No, you were meant to live."

"Why not kill me like the others?"

"You left after you were released from the hospital."

"So you couldn't find me."

"Until now."

"I will stop you."

"No, you won't. You know this is the way it must be. Besides, as I said before, it's not just me. Take a look outside the booth. Everyone out there has waited over five years for this day. We knew you'd come back."

"Why?"

"You don't know? You are the son of our beloved saint. You were born from the blood of those sacrificed in his name."

"I don't believe you."

"Believe it or not—it doesn't matter. They are out there waiting to welcome the new priest to their church."

"I won't do it, you can't force me."

"Yes, I can. I will if I have to. It's your destiny, our destiny. Every one hundred years a new leader must rise. You shall take my place as I transcend into our Lord's realm. You will lead the congregation as I have."

"No."

"Open your eyes, Gian. Let go of the fear. See me standing before you."

"Our Father, who art in heaven…"

"Prayers will not help you, Gian. Open your eyes. See me as I am, as you will soon be. Yes, there you go. Accept the Dark Lord into your life. Feel him enter your body. Yes, allow him entrance to your soul. Yes. Take him in. Revel in his glory forever and ever. Amen."

PORTALS OF SATISFACTION

I've given up on intimacy. The constant rejections have crushed me, left me hollow and empty. One would think that after so many failed attempts I would have learned my lesson, yet I kept repeating the same scenarios, always with the same known outcome. They say that repetition is the source of insanity; if that is true, then I have already lost my mind. I fear what I know I'm becoming; a fifty-two-year-old man living alone with unmet needs. Where desire turns to desperation and desperation leads to things I'd rather not admit. My sole sexual outlet is to pry into the private lives of other men. Night after night I sit alone in the dark, peering through the self-made portals in my walls, optical glory holes of quiet contemplation—self-gratification.

It started up again when Patrick moved in. He's like all the others; beautiful, sexy, and not ashamed of the body he inhabits. Just like the others, Patrick teased me. Offered me things, dirty, seductive things with his body language. My cock became a raging vessel of desire as I sat behind my desk interviewing him. I knew he would never put out, even if his body told me otherwise—they never do. I worried about what would happen if I let another man into my home. The last one left before things got out of control. I promised myself when Kent left that I wouldn't let it happen again. Then loneliness took control of me. I placed an ad on Craigslist. That's when Patrick came into the picture. I couldn't resist the temptation. It gnawed at my groin, burning and itching until I relented and let Patrick sign the lease.

My home is a three-story Georgian-style building in the heart of Cambridge, just a few blocks from Central Square. On a clear night from my rooftop I can see the sparkling lights of Boston just across the Charles River. Life on the outside, something I'll never be a part of.

I've gone to great lengths to reconfigure my home to accommodate my growing compulsion. I've had the entire house split down the center. I have my half. My tenant has the other half. I spent months redesigning each half to mirror the other. My bathroom backs up to their bathroom. The headboard of my bed is in the exact same position as the headboard in their bedroom. I've even added a few special features throughout the house to aid in my viewing pleasure.

I sleep during the day while Patrick is at work so I can spend my nights watching him as he sleeps. The wide-angle lens that I installed just above my headboard looks down across his bed. He sleeps in the nude with no covers. His body is firm, covered in a light coating of brown hair that spills down his chest, stomach, and legs; ending at his ankles. His stomach rises and falls as he breathes in the night air. His cock is long and slender. Its head pokes out of the thick folds of skin as he sleeps, as if it's watching me watch him. He wakes every morning with an erection. Precome from his secret dreams is always dried and matted to the thick tangles of pubic hair.

I don't know how much longer I'm going to be able to take this. I want him more than I have the others. He's been my tenant for five months. With every passing day my desire to have him grows. It's consuming me to the point where I don't know who or what I am anymore. I've been watching his every move. I know what he likes to eat. I know how he sleeps. I know how he likes to have sex. He's an insatiable bottom, getting fucked by a different man numerous times throughout the week. My jealousy rages with each new man he brings home.

It's six-thirty in the evening. I awake to Patrick coming home from work. I hear the water turn on in Patrick's bathroom. I get out of bed and light a cigarette before heading into the bathroom. I open the medicine cabinet and look through the one-way glass. He's looking at himself in the mirror. His eyes sparkle. He smiles at himself—at me. His fingers run across his long face and square jawline. He caresses the dark afternoon whiskers that have broken through his otherwise smooth skin. My cock stiffens, lifting out in front of me as I look into his unwitting face. He turns around, leans in to test the water, and then begins to undress.

He unties the knot in his silver-blue tie, pulling it through his button-down collar. He removes the suit coat. I notice damp spots under his arm, discoloring the light gray dress shirt. He unbuttons his shirt and lets it slide off his smooth round shoulders. His fingers graze through his chest hair as they move down to release his pants. He kicks off his shoes. I imagine the deep masculine smell that invades the bathroom from his leather loafers. His pants and underwear come off together. He slips the black dress socks off his feet giving them a quick sniff before tossing them with the other clothes. I watch his beautiful firm ass as it disappears behind the shower curtain.

I follow him into the shower. I pull down the bench I've installed facing the back of my shower that has also been equipped with a one-way pane of glass. I stroke my swollen cock as he stands under the water. He turns, facing me as the water runs over his head. His brown hair becomes matted to his skin as the water flows down his body. I try to imagine what his body smells like after a long day at the office: stale deodorant fading alongside the Old Spice cologne he doused himself with ten hours ago. I lick my lips as the water cascades down Patrick's body and runs down the full length of his cock. It looks as if he's taking a piss. I want to be in there with him. Kneeling in front of him tasting the water infused with his body oil and sweat.

The shower curtain moves behind Patrick. Another man steps into the shower. He's taller than Patrick by several inches. His muscle-sculpted body is hairless. His arms, shoulders, and chest are covered in bright-colored tattoos. I read Patrick's lips as he greets his guest. His name is Matt. I find myself not liking him. I will him to leave. Matt doesn't listen to my mental demands. Instead he seems to taunt me. He grabs the bar of soap and rubs it over Patrick's body. Patrick leans back against him, closing his eyes. The lather runs in thick streams down Patrick's body and gathers in his pubic hair.

Patrick is getting aroused. The pink head of his cock pushes through the folds of skin as his erection grows. Matt reaches around, rubbing the head of Patrick's cock in the palm of his hand. I see Patrick's legs tremble from the caresses. I want to make Patrick feel that pleasure. I want him to shiver and moan in my arms. My balls tighten. I take another draw from my cigarette and blow the smoke into my crotch. I look down at myself watching the precome leak out of my cock and drip down my leg. I tighten the grip around my cock. I watch myself masturbate in a cloud of dull gray smoke.

There's a loud thump that startles me. I look into the mirror. Patrick's body is pressed against the glass wall. His legs are spread. He's waiting for Matt to fuck him. The dark tangles of hair in Patrick's armpits are matted to his skin in thick swirls. Steam and water drip from strands of hair that cover his body. He's pushed further against the glass. His chest hair glides across the mirror, leaving intricate designs on the steamy surface. His erect nipples flatten into dark discs against his skin. I lean in closer, running my tongue over the smooth glass, imagining his moans of pleasure as I flick his nipples with my tongue. His face presses against the glass. I kiss his lips, wanting to sink my tongue into his open mouth. He grimaces as Matt's cock stretches his ass. I reach out and caress his face, needing, wanting to touch him—knowing that I can't.

Patrick bends down to receive more of what Matt has to offer. He pounds his fist against the glass as Matt gives him what he wants—that which I cannot give. I can almost hear the shouts of painful pleasure escaping from Patrick's mouth. I can feel myself getting close to losing control. I step up on the edge of the tub. I smack my cock against Patrick's face. Precome smears across the glass—across his cheek. The urge to take Patrick burns inside me.

The come begins to build. It grows at a fevered pace. I grab the curtain rod to support myself as the first wave of pleasure explodes across Patrick's face. He licks the glass as if licking my come. Excitement rushes through me. I come three more times, covering the glass—Patrick's body.

Even though I am spent, Patrick is still in the heat of passion. I watch as the two of them fuck like animals in the next room. They're smiling and happy in the throes of passion. I become angry that it's not me in there with him. I can't stand the rejection and pain. I step out of the tub, wrapping myself in my robe. I look back. My heart disintegrates as I watch Patrick release against the window. His beautiful white come showers the glass in thick, long streaks. I turn off the light and turn my back on him. Something has to be done to stop this madness.

❖

Patrick is standing at the foot of my bed. He's a dark silhouette standing within the pale glow of the night-light. He's naked and aroused. He looks across the bed at my unclothed body. He crawls across the bed to me. I feel the impressions his hands and knees make on my mattress as he comes closer. The heat of his body engulfs me. I panic at his closeness. I can't breathe. I wake up in a cold sweat. The thin sheets are damp with my sweat. The smell of my body has penetrated the fabric. I slip my hand under the covers. My crotch is wet with cold, sticky come. I look around the room. I'm alone. Sadness sinks into my body. It burrows a deep hole into my gut. It sits there, eating me from the inside out.

The alarm clock says it's eight thirty, yet it feels much later. I roll over, peering through the lens in the headboard. Patrick's bed is stripped clean. I try to look further into the room. What I see is nothing more than a blur of shadows. I pull myself out of bed and walk over to the bathroom. I open the medicine cabinet. His bathroom is empty.

I hear a distant thud from somewhere in the house. I wait, trying to clear my sleep-deprived mind. It's my front door. I throw on a pair of jeans and a T-shirt as I head downstairs. My mind is still fuzzy from sleep. I open the door. I don't recognize the man standing in front of me. Before I can question him, he speaks to me.

"Jonathan. I hope this is a good time?" His deep voice resonates through my mind. My cock responds to his sultry tone.

"For what?"

"It's me, Patrick. Are you okay?"

"Yes, I'm fine. Did you lock yourself out or something?"

"No. Are you sure you're all right?"

"Yes. Why do you keep asking me that?"

"It's kind of hard to lock myself out of the apartment when I've never been given the key." He leans against the door. "This morning when I signed the lease you said I could come by tonight to pick up the key to the apartment. I'd like to start moving in tonight if that's okay?" He looks at me with a questioning eye. "You don't remember, do you?"

"Yes, of course I do." I'm repulsed by his insinuation of my senility. His body is taunting me again. He's dressed in a tank top and cut-off jeans. The smell of his sweat drifts into my house. The hair under his arms is damp from the night heat. His Old Spice deodorant caresses my senses, taunting me. My cock stiffens. "Sorry, come on in." I stand aside and let him enter. I close the door, locking it behind us. "The key is in the living room, straight through the kitchen." I follow him. I stare at his round, firm ass being held within the tight confines of his shorts. Yeah, he wants it bad. He's aching for a good fuck. I can smell it coming off his body. I walk through the kitchen knowing that I have to do something. I have to stop this obsession before it spirals out of control. I reach over the kitchen island, slipping a knife out of the wooden block. I hold it behind my back. My fingers twitch. I grip the cool ceramic handle tighter. I follow him into the living room.

THE MIDNIGHT BARKER

Folks say a circus is for children of all ages. That may be true for some shows, but not for mine. I don't give a rat's ass about the children—the little boys with chocolate smears, the little girls in pigtails, or their parents. That's not to say we don't give these folks a show. We're the best in the business. After all, we've had a long time to practice, and practice makes perfect—or so they say. But we don't do this for the show or for the townspeople who pay their admission fee. We do it to survive. We do it for the young men in the towns we visit. And not just any young men; many of them just won't do for my circus. The young man we want has to have a tainted heart. He has to want it, need it, desire it. Through their desires, we create our Netherworld where we make their fantasies come true. Through their fantasies, we feed. The circus is a jealous whore, a ravenous hag that sucks the vitality right out of a person, just like a bloodthirsty vampire sucks the veins dry. That's my show under the big top.

❖

My men are getting restless. Living on the road gets tiresome after a while, especially doing it as long as we have. Hard days of performing followed by private midnight shows take their toll even on us. We had high hopes for the last town. I thought we had found the right young man. He was ripe for the picking, twenty-four and beautiful. He would have tasted so good. He was a young lost soul looking for a way out. I gave him his ticket—he never came back. He betrayed us. He broke our agreement by cutting open his wrists before we could take him. His selfishness frustrated our plans. I so hate to be disappointed. It just ruins my mood. So here we are in a new town, hungry and a bit irritable.

We have set up our stage in a remote town in southern Vermont. It's a quaint little place, I suppose, if you like all the mountains, the rivers, and the friendly people living their boring, suffocating lives day in and day out. What horror! It is with deep regret that I don't get to choose the locations we visit. They choose us. There's someone here who needs us. I can feel his sadness, smell his soul. Best of all, I can taste his desire. We'll find him. It's just a matter of time. After all, the show must go on.

❖

I can hear the crowds building outside my home on wheels. It's a small RV. It has all the comforts I could ask for, including a deluxe queen-sized bed that gets a lot of use, I'm proud to say. I've had to do quite a bit of work on the rest of it, though, as I didn't see a need to keep the kitchen and bathroom. It just seemed like wasted space for someone who doesn't need to eat, and without eating…well, you get the picture. I tell a lie. I do eat, just not what anyone would find in a kitchen. So I made those spaces into my dressing room, complete with a large closet for my various outfits. I admit that each day's outfit is identical to the next: black pants, blood-red shirts, black cloaks, and the most important of all accessories—top hats. Even with this unvaryingly elegant style, you'd be amazed at how much time it takes to prepare ourselves to be seen by the outside world. It's a painstaking process, but necessary if we are to keep our identities a secret. The crowds aren't ready to know what exists on the other side of the painted set they call the world. If they ever did find out, all hell would break loose—quite literally.

I stand back, taking a long look in the mirror to make sure I haven't missed anything. I was quite an item back in my day, when

I was alive. I could get any man I wanted just with a simple wink of an eye—a nod of my head. Things haven't changed that much: I can still get any man I want; I just go about it a bit differently. I crouch down to get the full view, as my six-foot-four frame doesn't quite fit into the mirror. I bring my face closer noticing a part of my shadow that I missed. I brush on a bit more eyeliner and white grease paint to conceal it. I study the face that I've created, give myself a little wink of approval, and open up the door to the outside world.

The raucous laughter of the kids pierces my ears as I walk through the crowd. Little brats with strawberry ice in one hand and blue cotton candy in the other are enough to make me want to rip out my eyes and cut off my ears. One of the little girls sees me. I brace myself for her assault.

"Mister, mister!" she screams in a high-pitched voice as she runs over with one of those disgusting, childish grins on her face. "You look funny!" She giggles frantically. "What tricks do you do?" She begins to jump up and down. "Show me, mister, show me! I wanna see what you can do!"

"Be careful of what you wish for, little girl." I squat down in front of her. "I might just eat you alive." Her eyes grow large. The smile fades from her face as I flicker my body to give her a glimpse of my true self.

"Mommy!" she screams as she turns and runs away. "Mommy, that man over there, he scared me!"

"Now, Betsy." The woman picks up the little girl. "There's nothing to be afraid of. He's just one of the circus performers."

"But, Mommy, he has a really ugly face inside."

"You're not so cute yourself, you little bitch," I mutter under my breath. I tip my hat to the two of them, flashing one of my killer smiles.

I cross the midway on my way to the big top. The noise is deafening. My carnies make the most of doing what they do best: yelling and shouting to kids and their parents, convincing them to shell out dollar after dollar for a chance to win the prize. Then there are the shrieks at the games, the toy guns shooting blanks, the engines of the rides, the kids beseeching their parents for more money, and of course the loud, awful music. It's enough to drive a sane person crazy. I guess it's a good thing I lost my sanity as long ago as my virginity.

The big top looms over the midway and our little caravan of trucks, RVs, and trailers. Its bright white canvas billows up and down as it stretches over the large ring and bleachers underneath. The peaks and edges are accented with red. It reminds me of the face of a clown—a pale white clown, with red lips and bloodstained teeth. The wind whips at the tent, animating it. It's hungry, ready to devour. I can feel the familiar shift between the two worlds. I take a deep breath of the night air. The young man's scent hangs within it. My cock thickens in anticipation of what's to come. Or who.

The crowds begin making their way into the tent; their voices become muted by the stale air that hovers just below the thick canvas roof. I stand in the center of the ring—a silent observer. The lights are off down here. I'm surrounded in their darkness, yet able to see everything with great clarity. The organ begins. One long, low note followed by another. The spotlight comes on. I'm standing in a perfect circle of radiant white light. Showtime!

"Ladies and gentlemen." I throw my voice in all directions to confuse and disorient my guests. "Welcome to my humble home. I am Nathaniel, your host for the evening. Please, sit back and relax while you still can, for tonight you will witness terrifying acts that thrill and amaze the young and the old alike. You will see things in this ring that you've only imagined in your darkest of dreams. Before the night is over, you will encounter creatures that you thought—that you hoped—moved only in myths and tales to scare your children. I'm here to tell you that they are real, and they will walk among you tonight."

I pause as the two worlds shift again. I feel flushed, electrified, and incredibly horny. My cock pulses with life, his life, our life. The young man is dreaming. I can feel his night sweat on my skin. His sheets are damp. They trap his body heat around him. His scent is taking control of my emotions.

The music of the organ shatters the divide that has split my mind. I clear my throat and proceed with my spiel. "Without any more delays, I am proud to present to you Joseph and the Wheel of Death." The crowd goes wild with applause. The noise sickens me in my fevered state. I step out of the circle of light. My body is damp with his sweat. I can still smell him around me.

Joseph looks over at me as the wheel comes out of the back and moves to the center of the ring. I nod at him to assure him that everything is fine. I watch him walk out into the swirling lights. The audience gasps, some with excitement, others with shock: He stands before them in nothing more than a very small, black leather thong. It leaves nothing to the imagination—trust me.

Joseph is the perfect image of a man. His large, muscular frame is painted a golden hue to simulate sun-drenched skin. His dark hair and deep green eyes can pierce a stone-cold heart and shatter it like a piece of glass. He loves his body, and loves even more to show it off. I've tried to get him to cover himself up; it's been of no use, a complete waste of my time. He says clothes reduce his pleasure in the wheel. So I've given up that battle. It's one I won't win.

I watch as Joseph steps into the wheel and the large metal door is locked behind him. The crowd's curious anticipation fills the air. The wheel, a large circular cage, shines as the colored lights glint on its metal surface. Inside is where the fun is. Inside the frame welded at various angles and positions are large razor-sharp daggers. The wheel, brought over from our world, has a mind of its own. It begins to turn and roll. I can see Joseph smiling.

He balances himself at first, following the flow of the wheel with careful footsteps. The wheel spins faster and his body is tossed from one side of the cage to the other. The audience gasps in horror as he falls against the blades. Joseph is in pure ecstasy as the first of the blades sinks into him. He lets himself go, no longer trying to keep his footing. He's thrown from one side to the other, blades cutting and slicing as he falls.

This audience, like so many before, doesn't know what to believe—or to feel. Their eyes are discs of disbelief. Their mouths are agape. And yet they can't look away. They're caught in our web of two realities. Their narrow minds are closed to what their eyes must somehow see: No blood flows from Joseph's wounds.

I see Joseph looking at me. I can feel his pleasure mounting. I'm aroused by his own circumstances, knowing that he will soon be in the height of ecstasy. I want to join him, to become one with his body during these final moments. I flicker, shifting my body into its natural form. I slip into the intermittent shadows of the ring that the strobe lights offer. My body blends with the shadows. I enter his body. We become one. I feel what he feels, taste what he tastes, and see what he sees. His desire mounts as I settle in. His body begins to tremble. I can feel him reaching the end. My presence inside him ignites his senses and mine. The warmth of his growing orgasm rushes through me, through us. It flows through his cock, warming us. We're thrown against several more daggers. The unexpected invasion of the blades makes the release more powerful than expected. I'm spun out from his body. I lie in the shadows and watch as he continues to release himself.

The wheel stops. It knows that the act has finished. Joseph steps out of the cage. His body in this reality is shimmering with sweat. It glistens in the light. The audience goes wild with excitement. They stand and cheer. The noise is too much for my ears. I slip away into the dark recesses of the tent and flicker back into this reality. He takes his final bows and runs toward me.

"You've never entered my body like that before." He kisses me. "That was amazing."

"I wanted to know what you felt during those final moments." I can feel the energy inside him as the orgasm fades away. My time inside Joseph's body has heightened my senses. I become light-headed. The realities shift. I can feel the young man again. His name is Derek. His dreams are calling out to me.

"You're shifting, aren't you?"

"Yes. It's time. I need to go to him. Can you introduce the next few acts?"

"Of course."

"I'll be back before the final act."

"You had better. You're the only one who can handle those animals." He smiles at me before walking back out into the ring.

The crowd, fueled by blood and desire, roars as the anticipation builds for the next act. The voices fade from my ears as I leave the tent, heading back to my RV. I strip the clothes off my body and slip into bed. I close my eyes, concentrating on the young man's desires. I feel the shift again. Instead of holding back, I enter it.

Derek is in his bed. A thin, pale blue sheet covers his body. I study him. His sweat-dampened blond hair is matted to his head from lying on the pillow. There's a light shadow of whiskers along the square lines of his jaw, chin, and upper lip. His lips are thin. They quiver from his dreams. His eyes move back and forth under his eyelids. He has long, dark lashes. They flutter with the movement of his eyes. I watch the rise and fall of the sheet as he breathes in his sleep. He looks peaceful as he slumbers. I feel his dreams. They torment him, as they do so many other young men. What he desires, he feels he cannot have.

I pull the sheet off the bed, exposing his body. His warm scent escapes into the air. I take a deep breath of him. I can smell his desire mixed with the wonderful coarse scent of his dampened pubic hair. I become lost in his nakedness, a state of being I can no longer have. His chest is covered with blond hair that reaches up to his neck. I run my fingers through it. It's soft, silky, and damp. His nipples are firm and poke out through the blanket of hair.

My eyes follow the movement of my fingers downward. Derek's skin twitches and quivers from my touch. I miss the feel of another man's body—the smell, the taste. It is the one thing that I miss of my former self. It still torments my darkened heart to this day. How I long for these moments of silent pleasure with the one who shall be taken. It is during these moments of sleep that their innocence comes through, and it's that unblemished soul that gives me the most joy and pleasure—or as much pleasure as I can have.

His cock is long and thick. It lies against his stomach in a pool of precome. I run my finger through it. The blond hair swirls through the sticky liquid adhering to his skin. I bring my finger into my mouth, licking his sweetness from it. His precome is warm and a bit tart. It flows through my body like electricity in water. My senses are heightened. I want more of him. My hunger grows. My need to take him consumes me.

I lean down, running my tongue over his stomach, lapping up his precome like a rabid dog looking for something to quench his thirst. I drain the excess fluid that had fallen into his navel. I shift my tongue into a narrow, thin strip, letting it slip into his piss slit. I extract the stale piss and come from Derek's earlier bedtime activities. His body squirms. His cock thickens as I pull my tongue out of him. My tongue reshapes itself. The movement causes more precome to be released. I lick it up as well. These are my most private moments. These moments mark the first and last time these young men will ever enjoy the pleasures that they denied themselves. The last time they will ever feel anything in their human form. Those moments offer the most pleasurable experience any human can have. Unfortunately, once Derek learns of these pleasures, it will be too late for him to do anything more about them. By then, he will have become one of us.

I will not let this one go, like I did the last. By the time I am done with Derek, he'll beg for the one-way ticket out of this maddening reality that he calls home. If he dares to break our agreement, I will rip his heart out with my bare hands. I will feed upon him until there is nothing left of him but a bloody stain on the carpet. Ah, I won't worry about that now. No, no, I shouldn't get ahead of myself like that. It's not good for my mood. I run my fingers over his cock, feeling the desire and the blood running through the veins. I tilt my head from one side to the other, looking at his tender young body. I should be gentle with him. He looks so restful, so innocent. Yes, gentle is the way to go with him. I need to remember that.

I enter his mind as my shadow spreads out against him. The heat of his body warms my cold form. I wrap my arms around him, pressing myself against him. My own desire builds. I can feel the form of my cock growing and thickening between us.

"Who are you?" His mind speaks to me in his dreamlike state.

"I am Nathaniel. Please call me Uncle Nate."

"No, who are you really?"

"I am everything you desire. I am everything you fear." I stand before him in his dream, while my shadow's form lies next to him in his world. His body heat increases as his desire for me rises. I can smell his fear, his lust. His scent is intoxicating.

"I'm not afraid of anything, not even you," his mind replies.

"It's not me you fear. It's the desire you feel for me. The desire you feel for other men. That's the emotion that runs through your veins, that's the secret that you hide. It's the passion and sexual urges you want to take a razor to—slicing and ripping into your veins, hoping to cut it out of you. Letting yourself bleed in hopes the secret will pour out of you in your blood, cleansing yourself in the process."

"I don't know what you're talking about."

"No?" I run my hand down his sleeping body. It shivers against my form. I trace the shaft of his cock with my finger. His body moves closer to me. A soft moan escapes between his trembling lips. "Tell me that it doesn't feel good. Tell me that you don't want me."

"I…I don't…" He looks at me. He doesn't say anything.

"You can't say it, can you?" I move between his legs and bring his warm, hairy balls into me. They fill my mouth with their size and weight. I roll them around. My tongue caresses and licks each testicle. "Say it! Beg me for it!" I release his swollen balls and sink my form further into his bed. I slip my tongue between his damp cheeks, find his tight virgin hole, and enter his moist ass. "You know you want it. Tell me what you want. Give into your desires. Tell me to fuck you."

"I…I can't help it," his mind replies. "Yes. Please…"

"Please what?"

"I want you to take me. I will do anything you ask. Just please don't stop what you're doing."

"Do you know what you're asking?" I walk up to him in his mind. I lick his neck. I taste the desire in his sweat. His hot breath beats against mine. "There's no turning back. I do this for you, and you will be mine forever."

"Yes, I understand. I'll do anything you ask, just please don't stop."

"Then you know what to do." I come out of his sleeping mind

and out of his bed. His body is soaked with sweat. His cock, thick and full of need, expels more precome. I want to taste him again. I resist. I know it is not the time. I place the ticket to the midnight showing on his pillow. I lean down and kiss his trembling lips. "Come," I whisper as the two worlds shift. A smile appears on my face as I awaken in my own bed. I can see him in my mind. He's awake, sitting in his bed holding the ticket. He looks confused, yet there's a sense of calm about him. He'll come. I can feel it. He's ours now. I get out of bed and prepare for the last act.

I find Joseph standing off in the darkness of the tent watching as Benjamin completes his act. The audience cheers as he's lowered to the ground. He loves the attention. He goes into a small encore as the crowd continues to applaud.

"Are we all set?" Joseph asks without looking at me.

"Yes, he will come."

"Good. I'm feeling a bit weak. We all need to feed again."

"And a good feed it will be." I turn to face Joseph. "While I'm doing the final act, gather everyone and prepare for the feast. At midnight he will come for me."

I walk out into the center of the ring as Benjamin leaves. The applause dies down as I stand before them. "And now, I will deliver to you what I promised at the beginning of the show." I pause for a moment, waiting with very little patience in me for a screaming child to shut up. "There are animals in the world that you may have heard of that you didn't think were real. I stand here to tell you that they are not imaginary creatures of myth and folklore. These creatures are quite real. Given a chance, they will rip and devour everyone sitting out there tonight." The fear builds in the air. I inhale it, letting it fill me. "Please, do not be alarmed. I've been working with these creatures for many years. I know how to control them. You must remain calm. They feed on your fear. The more fear they can smell, the wilder they become." Yes, that did it. They're scared, some even terrified. I can smell their fear as the sweat breaks from their pores. The men in the audience smell especially delicious. This is going to be a fun crowd.

"Ladies and gentlemen, I give you the Chupacabras!" I lead the creature out from the shadows. The audience gasps. It stands erect and leers at the audience. It's taller than I am, rearing up on two strong legs with hoofed feet. Its arms are short, less than a foot in length. Its body is covered in green scales that are razor sharp. Its spine runs outside the skin of its back.

"The Chupacabras, the goat sucker, uses its forked tongue and large fangs to penetrate the skin and drink the blood of its victims. Do not let the name fool you. Released from my control, it would drain each and every one of you before you could flee this tent."

The creature is getting restless. It tugs and pulls at the thick chains. They rattle. The audience goes silent in fear as they watch me struggle with it. It wants to feed as much as I do. "I apologize for its behavior. It seems to be hungry tonight." I lean in closer to its head, as if listening. "What? What's that? You see someone that looks tasty?" I look out at the audience. They've gone dead silent on me. "Let's walk closer to them so you can point the one out to me." I bring the Chupacabras over to the edge of the ring. We're within a few feet of the first row of bleachers. The audience looks terrified. Fear has frozen their bodies. No one moves. No one breathes.

The creature's long, crooked fingers wiggle in the air, then point to a husky man sitting in the third row. "That's him? That's the one you want for dinner?" The Chupacabras nods his grotesque head in response. It smiles and runs its long, forked tongue over its lips. Saliva drips from the fangs. It licks the saliva and spits it at the man, hitting him in the neck. "Naughty Chupacabras," I remark. "I am so sorry for that, sir. Please forgive us." He smiles at me as he wipes the slimy spit from his neck. If he only knew that he'd just been marked, that the Chupacabras follows its own scent and feeds upon its prey while they sleep. I hurry the Chupacabras out of the ring and hand it to my assistant, Leo. I turn back into the light.

"Let's hope the next one has better manners than that." A few giggles and strained laughs come from the audience. Their fears still hang in the stale air of the tent. I bring out a much smaller creature for the final show. It stands just two feet high. It resembles the humans in many ways, but has an enlarged nose, ears, and hands. It appears to waddle as it walks, giving the audience an illusion of innocence. It plays its role perfectly.

"Standing before you is our final act of the evening. You may look at this tiny creature and think that we have gone soft, presenting something as harmless as this little fellow. Trust me when I tell you that the Pukwudgie is one of the most violent and evil creatures to walk the earth.

"They originated in these parts of the United States and were first sighted and feared by the Wampanoag Nation. Since then they have grown in numbers and acquired certain powers of dark magic." The audience leans forward as the creature moves closer to them. He gurgles words that are inaudible and sneers at them. "They can appear and disappear at will, leaving the human mind incapable of remembering them. They paralyze their victims with poisonous arrows and feed up on them while they're still alive. They are also known to possess the souls of all they kill and have developed the ability to appear as their victim."

The crowd becomes restless as the gray-washed skin of the Pukwudgie begins to glow and shimmer. I tug on the leash, trying to hold it back. I can feel the old frayed leather giving way. It starts to growl and then to moan. The sound vibrates against the tent. It's an agonizing sound to the crowd, but music to my ears. The leather cord snaps. The Pukwudgie leaps into the air. The audience screams and begins to scatter. Without warning, without notice the Pukwudgie disappears. There is silence in the air except for the heavy breathing from the terrified onlookers. I'm glowing with pride at my little pet. He always makes such a grand exit.

"Thank you all for coming." I move back and forth in the center of the ring, throwing my voice again to disorient the already confused circusgoers. "I hope that we've given you everything that we promised. Perhaps the next time you hear the tale of a strange animal, you'll think twice before dismissing it as a myth." I pause, expecting some type of gratitude for all of my hard work. Applause, cheering, or even booing would be better than this silence. Did I do so great a job that I've left them speechless? Could I possibly be that magnificent? Those are all rhetorical questions. Of course I am all those things and so much more. The clapping begins to grow, one by one, as they come out of their dazed state of mind. Soon the tent is filled with applause and cheering.

"Thank you! Thank you!" I take a couple of bows to acknowledge the adoration of my fans before leaving them to their boring, pathetic lives.

I make my way back to the RV and wait for Derek. It's nearing midnight. The night air is thick with humidity. His scent reaches my nose. He's nervous. There's fear in it, yet an excited curiosity as well. His mind is racing with questions, questions I suppose I shall have to answer. He's closer. I can feel his heart thumping. It vibrates like the beating of a distant drum, almost inaudible, yet I can feel it over my skin.

I look out across the field and see a dark silhouette emerging through the dense pocket of trees. The moon is full. Its pale light illuminates the field and casts a delicate shade of off-white across Derek's body. His entire being intoxicates me. My cock stretches as I remember his nude body, hidden underneath his jeans and T-shirt. I've seen him as no one else has. That thought alone makes me wish that he were all mine, that I didn't have to share him with the others. The soft hair that lies across his chest still lingers on my fingers. I lick my lips and can still taste his ass.

"I'm glad you came."

"I'm not sure why I did."

"You know why." I let his baritone voice linger in my ears.

"Don't I know you?" He looks at me with questioning eyes.

"Yes, we met for a brief interlude earlier this evening." I move up next to him. I can feel the heat of his body. I bend down and inhale him. He took a shower before coming to meet me, as if going out on a date. I want to laugh at his innocence. I can smell his deodorant working to quell his nerves. His fresh sweat is like nectar to me.

"You were in my dream." He steps away from me as if I've crossed some invisible line of safety. "Who are you?"

"My name is Nathaniel." I lean down to him again. "But please, I insist you call me Uncle Nate."

"No, who are you really?"

"I am everything you desire." I brush my face against his. He's unshaven. "I am everything you fear." I run my fingers through his hair. I smell it: lavender and lemon. "I am the passion you want. I am the pleasure you long for. I am the pain that you cannot escape."

"I don't think I should have come here." He takes a few steps back.

"You're not going anywhere." I grab his arm and pull him to me. His back is against my chest. I wrap my arm around his torso. The muscles in his stomach tighten against my grip. I can feel his heart pulsing against my body. "You cannot deny it any longer. Give in to your desires." I lean down and brush my lips to his ear. "You know you want it. I can feel it." I lick his neck. "I can even taste it."

"What if I've changed my mind?" His voice quivers.

"Then, my love," I begin as I tighten my grip around his body, "then I will rip your heart out with my bare hands and have it as a midnight snack." I take a deep breath to calm myself. I pat his head and smooth out the tangles of dampened hair upon his forehead. I run my fingers down his cheek. He lets out a soft moan. "Why fight it? Give in, and let yourself go. Know true passion as no other human will ever experience it."

I turn him around to face me. There's a tear rolling down his face. His eyes look up at me. They move back and forth as if looking for an answer to some unknown question. He raises his head upward. I meet him halfway. Our lips touch. His are softer than anything that has ever crossed my lips. They are salty from his sweat with a hint of lingering peppermint. I press into them as they tremble before parting. I slip my tongue inside him. I can feel the swell of his cock against my groin. I reach between us. It lengthens from my touch. His moans vibrate in the back of my throat. I force myself to pull back before I ravage him and take the breath from his body.

"Are you ready?" My hunger grows, as does my desire for his body.

"I won't be back, will I?"

"No, not in this form anyway."

"Will it hurt?"

"The pain you will feel is that of exquisite, unending pleasure." I place his hand in mine. "Brace yourself. You'll be moving between realities, and the shift may feel as if your body is being pulled apart. It's quick, but painful nonetheless." The shift blurs my vision. I hear Derek groan as if someone hit him in the gut. My world, our world comes into focus. I look at him waiting for his reaction.

"Fuck! What happened to you?" he shouts as he looks upon my featureless face. My long, billowing black hair blends against my shadow. The single feature that still exists from his reality is my ice blue eyes, which stare back at him.

"Don't be alarmed. What you saw in your world is an illusion of who I once was. You are seeing me as I am in this reality. We are shadowers. Our bodies are solid for the most part, yet we don't have any features to speak of. We cannot be seen in your world as we are. Therefore, we have to make ourselves up to look like we did when we were alive."

His uneasy eyes look away from me for the first time. "Is this it, just a damp cavern?"

"No, of course not. There's a whole world above and beyond these granite walls. A world you will have the rest of your life to explore, with me as your guide."

We walk down the damp, dimly lit hallway in silence. The voices of my clan drift down the empty corridor in front of us. Derek's grip tightens around my hand as we walk through a stone archway that opens up into a large arena. The torches are lit and hang upon the wall. My men are standing around a large white bed that sits in the center of the room. The wrought-iron frame is covered with a thin, sheer fabric that hangs and billows in the underground breeze.

"What are all these other men doing here?"

"They're here to feed as well."

"To feed?"

"Yes, we have to feed in order to survive, and the only thing that brings us eternal life is the souls of young men such as yourself."

"I thought you brought me here to have sex with you, that somehow I would live with you here in repayment for the use of my body."

"I—or, rather, we—do need your body in order to feed. The people in your world wouldn't understand. They're too uptight about sex and pleasure to even begin to enjoy it. The soul of a man is connected to his sexuality. In fact, it's a part of who he is sexually. Every time a man has an orgasm, a small piece of his soul escapes. It is through his orgasm that we feed until there is nothing left of him."

"What happens to his...to my body?"

"Your body will just cease to exist. As your soul escapes, you will gradually fade away until all that is left is your shadow self."

I turn to Derek. His eyes are large discs of green staring back at me. I unbutton his shirt. The soft hair of his chest caresses my fingers. I can feel his heart slamming against his chest. It's good that he's scared. With fear there is more blood racing through his veins, which means his orgasm will be stronger, and the stronger the orgasm, the better the feed. He's terrified of what he has wished for, but even through the fear, there is a desire waiting to be unleashed. His shirt falls to the ground.

I lead him to the edge of the bed and lay myself down upon it. The men gather around us. Derek slips his feet out of his tennis shoes and unbuttons his pants. He pulls the jeans and his boxers off with one tug. He looks around at the others. His lips quiver. He touches his body, running his trembling fingers through the hair on his chest and down into the mass of curls around his erect cock. He looks down at himself for the last time. He crawls into bed with me. The warmth of his human body engulfs me.

I kiss him. He gives in to his desires. I hear the soft moans of the others around us. I roll over on top of Derek and raise his legs in the air. The thick form of my cock stretches and hardens at the sight of Derek's tight ass. It's covered in the same blond hair as the rest of his body. I lower myself between his legs and let my tongue stroll up and down his sweat-dampened crack. The muscles in his ass tighten as my tongue enters him. I shift my tongue to thicken, hoping to ease the pressure that he'll feel when my cock enters him.

Others join us on the bed, two at a time. They cradle his head and kiss his lips as his body succumbs to the pleasure. I pull my tongue out of him. The scent of his ass lingers on my lips. His cock is thick and has showered his stomach with precome.

I place his legs over my shoulders and enter him without warning. He gasps as my cock opens him up for the first time. The heat of his ass wraps around my aching cock. I fuck him. Our bodies rock upon each other. The pain in his face has turned to pleasure as my cock swells within him.

I lean down and suck his cock into my mouth. It's wet with his precome. I let the warm, salty liquid slide down my throat. My stomach churns with the flavors. It wants more. I become ravenous. I thrust my cock in and out of his ass as I suck the building level of moisture out of his shaft. I can feel his cock swelling in my throat. His breathing is short and heavy. The others caress and stroke his chest and stomach. He throws his head from side to side as the pleasure of my cock continues to build inside him. My mouth is soon flooded with the thick, creamy release of his cock. I swallow every drop with greed and urgency, sucking more and more of his warm, young soul into my throat to satisfy my hunger.

Without giving Derek time to pause, I slip myself under his body. He rests his back against my chest. I wrap my arms around his torso. My cock slips back inside him. I begin to fuck him again. His cock grows thick and solid once more. The first of my men climbs around us and positions himself between our legs. He licks the remains of Derek's first orgasm off his shaft before slipping the entire length of Derek's cock into his mouth. I fuck Derek's ass, with deliberate action, waiting for another one of his orgasms to feed us.

One by one, hour after hour, the members of my clan crawl into bed with us and wait to be fed. Derek had already fed twenty-three of us. There are nine more to go. Derek has slipped in and out of consciousness for the past four or five feeds. The human body does not know how to process the state of ecstasy that they endure in our world. They simply short-circuit as the process continues.

I watch as his sweat-soaked body begins to fade. The beautiful golden hair covering his chest dims and then disappears as if it never existed. He's in pure ecstasy at the moment and doesn't notice that his human body is dying. That he's losing his features. I feel a strange twinge in my chest. For the first time in 193 years, I think I may be mourning the loss of a body other than my own. Derek's body was like no other. It was perfect in every way. A body neither he nor I shall ever see again.

I push the weak feelings away. They serve no purpose here in my world, because the circus must go on. I am, after all, the Midnight Barker.

FROM WITHIN THE ALE HOUSE HE CAME

My son, I have come to hear your confession as appointed by the magistrate." Father Fitzpatrick knelt on the dirt floor in front of the cell. "Almighty Father, I pray that you shall hear the words of this condemned man on this, the twenty-fourth day of April in the year of our sovereign Lord seventeen hundred and twenty-six. I beg—"

"Silence, Father. I have no confessions I wish to bestow on you, nor do I wish to hear your prayers to save the soul you feel is so unfit." Bradford sat in the corner of his cell. The only light came from small cracks in the walls of the prison. Its dirt floors stank of the hundreds of men that came before him, all of them tried and convicted of the same crime as he. He could feel their presence around him as if they were reaching out to him from their rotting graves.

"Bradford, I have known you all your years. You must confess to the crimes of which you have been convicted and plead to the almighty Lord for his forgiveness, lest you never be allowed to enter his kingdom."

"I am innocent of the charges of sodomy that the court has placed upon my head."

"Do you deny the circumstances in which these charges were brought against you?"

"I have done what I am accused of; that I have already admitted to."

"Are you intentionally trying to confuse me, Bradford? If you say you have done what you are accused of, then how can you be innocent?" Father Fitzpatrick moved to the left. "Bradford, please come out from the dark corner so that I may see you."

Bradford stood and with the aid of the cell wall limped over to where the priest knelt. His nightshirt, the one article of clothing he was allowed to keep upon his body, was stained with dirt, vomit, and dried blood. He swayed on weakened knees, grasping the cell bars for support. For the first time in his life, he faced the man of God without fear. "The court and your almighty Lord shall not hear an apology uttered from my lips. My body is my own to do with, as I desire. If I seek pleasure for my body with that of another man, then that is my private bidding. I will not be beaten or made to feel ashamed for the glorious pleasures I have received from others like me."

"Do you not fear the wrath of God?"

"Fear God? Look at me, Father." Bradford sank down to the ground with his hands curled around the iron bars. "Do you see fear in these eyes?" Bradford waited for a reply that never came. "What is left in me to fear when death is my future? What? Did you think that I did not know of my own fate?" Bradford sat staring at the man of the cloth, the man he had known for most of his twenty-eight years, and he looked upon him as a stranger. "I am sentenced to imprisonment for a period of two years before I shall be hanged in public view, and that is only if I survive the rot and disease that permeates these cells, so tell me, Father, what can your God do for me—the same God who has sentenced me to die?"

"What I see before me is a terrified man. Perhaps your fate could be less of a burden to you in your finals days if you share with me the events that brought you to Newgate Prison."

"It is not what that has taken my life. It is who. The treacherous bitch of a man, Thomas Newton, is the reason I am here. For he is just as I, perhaps even worse, as he sold his body to men in order to earn his living, yet he is out there while I am in here like so many of my intimates before me."

"Did he flee before he could be caught?"

"They sent him on his way. He is untouchable."

"I do not understand how this could be."

"He has sold his soul to the devil. He has turned against the same men who he once sought pleasure from."

"If you could find it in yourself to share this with me, perhaps I could make known this man to the constables and..."

"You are a fool to think that this man works alone." Bradford looked down in disgust as he plucked several spiders that had nested in the hair of his leg. "The devil of which I speak of is the constable himself and the Society for the Reformation of Manners to which he belongs. Thomas is their spy."

"They know of his..." Father Fitzpatrick paused as a guard approached carrying a tray.

"I hope for your sake, Father, that this prisoner's confession is taking longer than expected, for I would hope that you are not one to take up a conversation with a sodomite."

"I shall stay as long as I see fit. I am here doing God's work."

"You're wasting your breath, father. There is nothing here worth saving." The guard dropped the tray on the dirt floor, kicking it sideways underneath the bars. He cleared his throat. He spat. His foul-smelling mucus hit the side of Bradford's face.

"What kind of treatment is that?" Father Fitzpatrick, stood facing the guard. "Have you no decency?" He looked down at the tray, shaking his head. "Surely you do not expect him to eat the rotten flesh of meat that you have given him?"

"He should feel blessed to still have his life. The man is a filthy sinner. He deserves nothing more than the scraps of food from the waste pile out back." He walked away with his final words echoing through the prison halls. "The sooner he dies, the better off we shall be."

"Father, do not defend me in front of others." Bradford reached through the bars, grabbing the priest's cassock. "If they believe you are aligned with me, it will secure your death. I cannot have your blood on my hands." Bradford pulled the tray of food toward him with his foot, leaned against the wall with a pained grimace, and sighed.

"Please tell me that you are not planning on eating that tainted meat. It will send you to an early grave."

"That is a good one, Father," Bradford chortled, "as if I should be afraid of death from the rancid food." Bradford dug out a maggot that had burrowed into the meat before tearing into the rotting flesh with his teeth. "Look around you, Father. I'm lying on a dirt floor in my own excrement. The pile of straw that I call a bed, I share with the countless diseased men that slept here before me. I doubt that my well-being is any more in danger from consuming this food."

"Please, my son. Tell me how you came to this." Father Fitzpatrick sat down next to the bars, resting his back against one of the stone pillars. "It will help you pass the time, if nothing more."

"Very well, Father." Bradford swallowed the tough meat before taking another bite. "Your company tonight will be a pleasant retreat from the other nights I have endured here alone."

❖

"I visited Plump Nelly's house the Saturday before last." Bradford paused, "Sorry, Father. Plump Nelly's is an ale house, near Moorfield Garden. It's where gentlemen go to be with other like-minded men." Bradford licked his dry, cracked lips. "The clock had just struck midnight. There were at least fifteen or twenty men enjoying each other's company. As I took my drink, I saw Thomas Newton swaying his hips as if he were a woman, enticing the men with promises of his body."

"Is this not the way all sodomites carry themselves?"

"Some men can carry it off quite well. Thomas is too much of a man, too masculine to carry on as a woman. He is a rough young man from the streets. I've bedded with him on numerous occasions. He is quite skilled with his body. He knows how to please a man proper. His rugged, masculine ways are what I have found so enticing in the past. The feminine persona he carried that night did not appeal to me, nor did it bring me to any heights of passion."

"What about the others?"

"Most were drunk on ale by the time I had arrived. They were quite vocal about their approval of Thomas's manners." Bradford grabbed his stomach and groaned. He heaved, straining his parched throat. The rancid meat fell from his mouth in a pool of reddish-brown sludge. "My apologies for my condition, Father." Bradford lifted his torn, dirty shirt to whip his mouth. In doing so he exposed more of his body to Father Fitzpatrick than he wanted to.

"Bradford, you are bare under your nightshirt. Did they not let you keep your undergarments?"

"There was nothing left of my trousers or undergarments by the time they had finished with me."

"Finished with you?"

"Please, Father all this talk makes me weary. Let me finish. You shall learn the truth about the men of your country and of your God.

"When Thomas witnessed me watching him, he took it to believe that I was looking to fuck as we had many times before. He made his way through the groping hands of the drunken men and stumbled into my arms. He laid quick kisses upon my lips and neck while he placed my hand inside his trousers. His lean prick, stiff with need, pulsed as my fingers grazed the sensitive skin. Thomas worked himself into a fit using my hand.

"I told him that my purpose that evening was not a sexual one, and even if it were I had been put off by his womanly manners. My words insulted him. He threw my hand off his prick. He slapped my face, telling me that I was not acting as a gentleman should to a proper lady.

"Having enough of his prancing, I took my leave. I walked through the Moorfields on my way home. I stopped to make water near the footbridge. As I stood relieving myself, I noticed the silhouette of a man coming toward me from the ale house. When the figure approached I became familiar with it, knowing it to be Thomas. He leaned against the wall of the bridge, eyeing my exposed prick. With his cold hand he gripped my prick, holding me while I continued my business. He smiled at me. His mannerisms had changed back to those of the rough young man I so desired.

"As my prick emptied itself, it began to stiffen in his hand. He fondled me, raising my desire so much so that I thought I would expel my seed right there on the footbridge. He nibbled my neck. His rough whiskers tickled my skin until I began to shudder from his attention. His grip tightened around me to the point that my prick began to ache. With my trousers around my ankles and my prick in his hand, Thomas shouted into the darkness. They came at me from all sides. Between the flush of passion, the sudden activity that surrounded us, my judgment was clouded. I could not get away from them."

"So their rough handling of you caused your injuries?"

"Rough? Father, they beat me senseless. They tortured me before bringing me before the court." Bradford lifted his shirt, exposing the dark red lesions and black bruises covering his body. He looked at the priest's shocked expression. He lowered his garment.

"Why were the actions of these men not mentioned at your trial?"

"What purpose would it have had? They can torture a man, shove a branch up his arse, and fuck him with it till he's torn inside out, left raw and bleeding, and their actions are not against the laws of this land, yet we are given these treatments for loving another man." Bradford cleared his dry throat. He coughed. Blood sprayed from his mouth. He wiped his lips with the back of his hand. "They will go on doing as they please to my intimates who have yet to be captured, with Thomas Newton, the worst of them all, leading the way."

"I cannot stand to see you suffer. Tell me what I can do to ease your pain."

"Father, there is nothing you can do for the physical abuse I have endured. The mental anguish over what awaits my friends is by far more severe. If you could get word to them about Thomas

Newton, perhaps a few of them could be spared what I have gone through."

"What you are asking me to do goes against the laws of this country, the church—of God."

"I know what I am asking you to do is great. Would not your God look upon you with kindness for saving even one man this type of punishment?"

"Not if that man is a sodomite." Father Fitzpatrick lowered his head, crossing himself. "I'm sorry, my son, may the Lord have pity and mercy on your soul." He stood, looking down upon Bradford.

"Fuck your Lord, Father." Bradford wrapped his swollen fingers around the bars, pulling himself up to face Father Fitzpatrick. "You are no better than the men who tortured me. Would you like to take your turn on me as well?"

"I can do nothing more here." Father Fitzpatrick walked down the hallway without looking back.

"Go ahead, Father," Bradford shouted. "Find something solid. Shove it up my arse. Your refusal to help me or my fellow intimates hurts me no less than if you were the one fucking me with the tree limb." Bradford took a deep breath that set off a new round of coughing. His lungs felt heavy. His ribs, sore from the beating, throbbed against his coughs. Bradford's hands ached from the tight grip on the metal bars. He slid down to the dirt floor.

His mind wandered in and out of consciousness as he crawled over to the darkened corner of the cell. He struggled to pull off his bloodstained shirt, folded it and used it as a pillow against the dry, brittle straw that made up his bed.

Bradford closed his eyes. He inhaled as deeply as he could to relax his mind. The stale scent of sweat mixed with piss from the men that slept there before him surrounded him. He welcomed their lingering presence, taking comfort in the fact that he wasn't alone. As sleep consumed him, his mind drifted into dreams.

Bradford stood in the main room of Plump Nelly's, surrounded by the familiar faces of his bedmates. They laughed. They fondled one another, speaking of marrying in the back room. Samuel, outfitted in one of his wife's dresses, sat on another gentleman's lap. The man's pants were about his ankles. The rocking motion of the two men gave evidence to their action.

Bradford felt a shift in the air as he walked around the room. His longtime friends, even his past intimates, seemed to ignore his presence. Bradford began to wonder if he or they were there at all. The door to the back room or what the men liked to call the chapel opened on its own. Bradford walked across the threshold. Samuel lay in the bed with a thin sheet covering his body. Bradford turned around. He looked back through the main room of the ale house. It stood empty, dark.

"Please, come in and shut the door so the others will not intrude on our time together. I've been waiting for you."

"The others?" Bradford questioned as he shut the door. "There is no one out there. The room is deserted."

"We are not alone anymore."

"I don't understand. Why are you here?"

"I wanted to see you one last time." Samuel tossed the thin sheet off the bed, exposing his naked body to Bradford. "Come, lie with me. Let us marry before it's too late."

"Late for what?" Bradford let his eyes wander over Samuel's body. His chest and stomach were covered in a thick mat of black hair. His prick, thick with need, rose out over the folds of skin. It lay nestled in a mound of tight curled hair. Bradford became heavy with need as he removed his clothing.

"They know of us and where we meet."

"Who?"

"The Society for the Reformation of Manners. They and the constables have vowed to seek us out. They mean to execute us all." Samuel patted the mattress. "Please, no more of this ugly talk. Lie with me. Let me upon you one final time."

Bradford let himself be drawn down on top of Samuel. Their pricks swelled with the heat of desire. Bradford rolled over upon his back, bringing Samuel on top of him. He closed his eyes to the forbidden pleasures as he felt Samuel's tongue glide down his smooth chest. His prick, already damp with his urge, grew with renewed heat as he felt Samuel's mouth surround it.

The pleasure of his bedmate began to change as a painful pressure raced through his body. He opened his eyes and looked down his body at the man between his legs. Samuel was no longer his bedmate. Thomas was between his legs, gripping his prick with the strength of a vise.

Bradford sat up on his elbows meaning to speak. His words were cut short when he noticed the butcher knife lying next to them. The room blurred in his vision, slowing their movement and his voice. With shock and horror running through his mind, he watched as Thomas picked up the knife. As if time did not exist, Bradford watched as Thomas brought down the knife, severing his swollen prick.

Bradford's screams of pain woke him from his troubled sleep. He grabbed his prick, reassuring himself that the painful visions had been a dream. He sat up against the cold, damp wall, fearing that sleep might take him again, and with sleep would come the dreams. He stared off into the darkness of the prison cell, listening to the agonizing sounds of the other prisoners until the first light of day shattered the night.

"Come on, get up," a voice called in Bradford's mind. "We need to get you to the pillory, so you can stand in judgment before the entire city." The guard kicked Bradford, waking him from a restless sleep. "I said get up," the guard bellowed as he kicked Bradford in the groin.

Bradford doubled over from the pain, covering his prick with his hands. He tried to stand. His legs wouldn't hold his thinning weight. He reached out for assistance; the guard backed away from his plea. Bradford, realizing he wasn't going to get any help from the guard, steadied himself on his hands and knees. Using one hand as a guide, he pulled himself up along the wall. He leaned against the wall to brace his body, enjoying the cooling effects of the stones on his fevered skin.

The guard pushed Bradford away from the wall. Bradford

stumbled. His weak legs could no longer support him. He fell to the ground. A bone snapped in his hand. Hot, searing pain shot through his arm. He winced, biting his lip to avoid a scream that he knew would all too well please the guard. Bradford crawled over to the opened gate. He used his one good hand to grasp the bars to pull himself up.

He guided himself down the long corridor, holding on to the bars of each cell he passed. As they reached the entrance of the prison, the light of the day blinded Bradford's vision. He stopped, feeling the warmth of the sun against his skin. A feeling he had almost forgotten. He took a deep breath of the fresh morning air, letting his lungs absorb as much of it as it would allow. He closed his eyes, taking another breath, raising his face to greet the morning sun. His moment of happiness vanished as the guard pushed him into the courtyard.

Dust blew up around Bradford as his body hit the dry, brittle ground. He looked out across the vast yard. The pillory erected on the far side of the square stood in the shadows of the buildings awaiting his arrival. His stomach knotted. His body shook with nerves. The guard kicked him, demanding that he get up. Bradford ignored him, hoping for a few more moments in the warming sun.

Bradford's enjoyment of the sun was cut short when his feet were raised off the ground. He looked behind him as the guard lifted his legs by the metal shackles and began dragging him across the road. Bradford dug his fingers into the dry soil, trying to fight the pull of the guard. He coughed and choked on the dust that flew up around him before coming to a stop in front of the pillory.

Bradford gave up fighting. The exertion had weakened him further. He knew if he was going to survive the public display, he would have to give in, keeping his body at rest. Bradford turned his face from the crowd as the guards pulled him up on the wooden platform. They lowered his head down to rest it upon the rough, splintered wood of the stock. His wrists were placed in position before the heavy wooden beam was lowered and locked into place. The brace had been connected to a large wooden pole that had been secured to the center of the platform. Bradford looked out at the crowd. He could see his naked body in their expressions. They wore their disgust on their faces as he began to walk with his body affixed to the rotating stockade.

As the morning grew on, people continued to gather, shouting profanities and wishes of death. Bradford kept his head up, facing each of them as he continued to walk around the platform. Women with their children carried satchels of stones. The crowds eagerly spent two shillings per stone to throw them at Bradford. To his shock, even the children who were too young to know the purpose of their activity joined the brutal assault, laughing as if they were playing street games.

Bradford grimaced, clenching his teeth as each stone struck his body. People first took aim at his face. It wasn't long before their target became swollen beyond human recognition. They moved on to other parts of his body, including his limp, shriveled prick. His groin ached beyond anything he had already sustained; yet when he thought it could hurt no more, a large stone took direct aim at his enlarged bloody nut sack, sending a fresh rush of nausea through his body.

Through the one eye Bradford could still see out of, he met the stare of Thomas Newton who stood off at a distance. Thomas leaned against a stone gate, smoking a pipe. The clothing he wore was no longer the old tattered cloth that he had once lived in. Today, Bradford saw Thomas standing in the rich fabrics of purple, red, and black that were reserved for the elite of London, as the commoners could not afford such luxuries. Bradford renewed his anger toward Thomas as he realized the full implications of his actions. Thomas was able to save his own life, while at the same time getting financially rewarded for his hateful testimony against his former intimates.

The vicious actions of the onlookers increased as the day progressed. People no longer limited themselves to the purchase of stones; they assaulted Bradford with rotting fruit, lumber, or even large stones taken from the foundations of buildings. Men would cautiously approach the pillory, taking hammers to Bradford's toes until there was nothing left but loose bags of flesh dragging beneath each foot. By late afternoon, Bradford was unable to walk the pillory; succumbing to the pain, he slipped in and out of consciousness. While he was removed from the stocks to be returned to his prison cell, the townspeople followed him, shouting profanities he could no longer comprehend. The hundreds of voices that still shouted at him blurred into one inaudible noise.

Bradford felt his body being dragged back down the dirt floor of the prison corridor. He welcomed the silence the prison walls offered as his limp, broken body reentered the cell. He heard the prison guards laugh as they stood over him. He wanted to rise from the floor in defiance. He resisted, knowing that even if he had the strength to do so, the guards would have beaten him further. So he took their laughs. He accepted their bitter words, hoping they would soon depart, leaving him to die in peace.

As the night grew on and Bradford's body weakened more, he began to hear voices of his former companions. Their voices soothed his mind as he remembered their loving touches, their words of endearment. He held on to their voices, wishing to die with the memories of their time shared together.

With the words subsiding, he felt a presence near him. He opened his eye with a great deal of effort to witness the silhouette of a man standing in front of his cell. "Father?" Bradford whispered between his swollen, bloody lips.

"No, it is I, Thomas, who stands before you."

Bradford withdrew from the deep familiar voice. "Did you come to gloat?" His weakened voice held a bitter tone that even surprised him.

"I knew I would not be able to rest without seeing you. There is so much I wish to say."

"Spare me your reasons." Bradford coughed, spraying blood across the dirt floor. He raised his head against the pain to look upon the man who had betrayed him. "Have you not done enough? Do you wish me to see your treacherous lying face as I take my last breath?" Bradford lowered his head. He closed his eyes. He waited, not for more words from Thomas—for death, as it closed in around him.

He wanted the pain and agony to go away. The ugliness and hatred of the world he lived in was too much for him to bear witness to. He began to pray for death. In his weakened state, he heard another voice echoing down the hall.

"Thomas, open the cell door. Help him."

"Father, it is too late."

Bradford held on to the words as he let go of his life.

"He knows, does he not?" the priest questioned.

"No, I did not have a chance to tell him."

"For God's sake, allow him to die with dignity. Tell him that the judge has ordered his reprieve. He has granted Bradford his freedom."

Bradford took his last breath as he heard the cell door open and the words that the father spoke.

FELONIOUS BEHAVIOR

Nine-one-one, what's your emergency?"
"I've been hit." Jack didn't recognize his own voice. The words sounded distant and strange, as if they hadn't come from him.

"Hit how, sir?" the deep, husky voice asked.

"Hit how? By a car, how do you think?" He felt his temper rising. It rushed to the surface as it always did. He closed his eyes and took a deep breath to steady his nerves. "I'm sorry, I didn't mean to snap at you. It's just that I'm in a lot of pain."

"It's okay, sir. Can you tell me where you are?"

"Please, don't call me 'sir.'" Jack knew it was a stupid request given his current situation, but he couldn't help it. He hated when people addressed him as sir. His father was a sir, and at twenty-eight he wasn't ready to be compared to his father. "My name is Jack, Jack Stevens. I'm at the intersection of Brattle and Ash."

"Okay, sir...Mr. Stevens. I have the police and ambulance on the way. May I speak to the driver of the car who hit you?"

"The driver didn't stop." Jack heard several low beeps in his ear. He looked at the screen. He'd lost his connection. "Fuck." He started to redial, then flipped his phone shut. Sirens echoed in the distance. The side of his head throbbed. He reached up and touched the area. Pain exploded through his head. His fingers came away red. Nausea swirled through his stomach at the sight of his own blood. He tried to concentrate on other things—the chirping crickets, the birds singing their evening lullabies, even the approaching sirens—but his mind couldn't let go of the blood and the pain. Despite the mild spring temperatures, gooseflesh began to cover his arms. He closed his eyes and waited for help.

Lights soon began to flash through Jack's eyelids. Relief washed over him as he heard a door shut, followed by the sound of footsteps. He opened his eyes to a cop towering over him. From Jack's position the cop looked twisted and disfigured. The cop knelt down next to him. Jack could smell coffee on the man's breath. His stomach groaned with the thought of a mocha latte. "The ambulance is on its way. Just try to relax. My name is Officer Adams. Can you tell me your name?"

"Jack Stevens." Jack stared up at the cop and saw the lines of age on his pale, pudgy face.

"Where's the driver who hit you?"

"He slowed down right after he hit me. He took off down Brattle." Jack reached out and held the officer's hand. "Sorry, I just…"

"No need to apologize." The cop smiled at Jack. "Did you by chance notice any details about the car that might help us locate the driver?"

"It was a dark-colored car, small, like a Toyota Corolla or something similar. The license plate, I think, started with 5XC. I couldn't see the rest of it."

"Are you sure about that?"

"That's what I remember."

"Okay, well, you just try to stay calm while I go make a call." The officer wrapped his hand around Jack's arm and gave it a gentle squeeze. "Hang in there. We'll see what we can do." The officer stood up as the paramedics arrived. Lights of blue, yellow, and red flashed in the dark, casting odd shadows across everything that was once familiar to Jack but now felt foreign and unfriendly.

One of the paramedics checked Jack's vital signs while the other wrapped his head in gauze. Without warning, they lifted Jack up on a gurney and shoved him into the back of the ambulance. Jack's head spun from the quick movements. He felt the urge to vomit nearing the surface and closed his eyes in hopes of settling his stomach. A sharp pain pricked his arm. He looked down just as the needle slipped below the surface of his skin. He turned his head from the sight of it sliding into his vein. He felt the needle move deeper under the skin, swelling, stretching just under the surface. The ambulance began to blur in his vision, the pain eased as he slipped into unconsciousness.

Jack woke up in a drug-induced fog. Machines beeped and pulsed on all sides of him. He looked around the strange room, bare and antiseptic. The morning light filtered through the small window, which was covered with heavy curtains. A fir tree sat dying in the corner from lack of light. Its faded needles clashed with the pale green paint of the room. A television hung from a metal arm attached to the wall. Through the darkened screen, Jack saw his reflection. Memories of the previous night flashed on and off in his brain as if he was watching a replay of the event on television.

"How are you feeling this morning, Jack?" The thick New England accent of the cop brought him further out of the dissipating fog.

"Like shit." Jack didn't feel like small talk. He wanted answers. "Did you get the bastard that hit me?"

"Yes, we did." He pulled up a stool and sat down next to the bed.

"So he's locked up, right?" Jack studied the cop's face. "So what happens next? Do I need to press charges or something formal like that?"

"Look, Jack. Why don't you just worry about getting better and getting out of here? Put this all behind you and get on with your life."

"Put it behind me? Are you serious?" Jack groped around to find the button that would raise the head of the bed. "I know I should be grateful that I wasn't hurt worse. Have you spoken to the doctor?" Jack didn't wait for a response. "See these stitches?" Jack pointed to the side of his head. "I'm going to have a six-inch scar down the side of my face because of him. The doctor said even though my leg and hip will heal, because of the damage that I sustained, I'm going to have some mobility problems. My stage career is over. I won't be able to be on my feet for extended periods of time."

"I'm sorry, I didn't know." The officer looked around the empty room. "Look, you have every right to press formal charges. I just want you to know that you'll be better off just dropping it."

"Why would I do that?" Jack watched the movement in the officer's eyes. He couldn't look Jack in the face.

"I need to go. I shouldn't be here."

"Wait." Jack grabbed hold of the cop's arm. "What's going on?"

"The guy who hit you…he's already out."

"What do you mean, already out?"

"Jack, please let it go."

"Don't give me that shit. You came here for a reason this morning. What aren't you telling me?" Jack could feel his temperature rising. It didn't mix well with the drugs the machines were pumping into his body. His heart thumped in his chest.

"The guy who hit you, his family, they have a lot of influence and money. They made some calls. They got him out within the hour. The truth is, even if you were to press charges, there is no way he'll do any time for what he's done."

"Excuse me, Mr. Stevens?" Jack leaned to the right to peer around Officer Adams. A man in a three-piece suit walked into the room. His confident, strong stance carried his tall frame and broad shoulders. His straight midlength black hair fell around his smooth, rectangular face. He didn't smile. Jack wondered if he even knew how. His cologne filled the air as he approached the bed. Jack noticed the cop didn't look in the man's direction.

"Yeah, that's me. Who are you?"

"Who I am is of no importance to you." The man walked to the side of the bed and pulled an envelope out of his inside breast pocket. "This is from my client. They believe this should be a sufficient payment for your silence around the unfortunate incident last night."

"Is that what they're calling it?" Jack could feel the heat coming off his body as the anger crept up his neck and face. Jack noticed the man's eyes flinch with anger. Jack figured the man wasn't use to having someone talk back to him.

"They've been more than generous, as you will see." He flipped a manila envelope onto the bed next to Jack. "You'll do well to accept their apology. Trust me, you don't want to piss them off by being ungrateful. That would require another visit from me, and next time I won't be so pleasant." The stranger didn't wait for a response. He turned and left the room with the same purposeful stride he had when he arrived.

Jack looked at Officer Adams, then at the plump envelope. He opened it. His eyes expanded in disbelief as he thumbed through the contents. "Shit, there's at least two hundred thousand in here."

"Now do you believe me?" He placed his hand on Jack's arm. "Just let this go. They're not kidding around. Next time you'll end up in worse condition than you are now."

"Fuck it." Jack tossed the envelope on the bedside table.

"Good, I'm glad that's over with."

"No, it's not over. I want to press charges. I want to see this through. I'll use their money to hire a lawyer."

"Jack…"

"No, you don't understand. All my life I've backed down from difficult things because I didn't have the confidence to fight back. I'm not going to back down from this. They want a fight, they've got one."

"You'll lose." Officer Adams stood up. "You'll lose just like everyone does."

"I just need one thing from you."

"What's that?"

"I need to know the name of the guy who hit me."

"No, Jack. I can't get involved any more than I already am. I'll file the paperwork. After that you're on your own." He stood up and placed his hand on Jack's shoulder. "Take care of yourself, Jack. Please reconsider. You don't want to fuck with this family. Trust me, I know."

❖

Jack opened the door to his apartment for the first time since the accident. He stood in the doorway, staring at the contents of his old life, and thought how much had changed in eight short days. His small, stylish apartment in Beacon Hill still held his creative touches and theatrical personality. His life at the moment felt anything but his own. His once familiar surroundings felt strange, as if he no longer fit into the life he had been building for himself.

Jack hadn't seen nor heard from Officer Adams since the first day in the hospital and had given up hope that the paperwork had been filed as promised. He wanted to get past it, to move on with his life. He couldn't get over the feeling of failure. He decided to try one last time. He would call Officer Adams in the morning. For now, he would try to rest and clear his mind of everything related to the accident. He pulled off his shoes, sat down on the couch, and began flipping through the two hundred channels. His eyes felt heavy. They closed, then fluttered opened, then closed again. Jack gave up the fight and laid his head back against the couch and drifted off to sleep. He awoke several hours later to a knock at his door.

Jack grabbed his crutch and maneuvered his way around the furniture, trying to wipe the sleep from his mind. As he reached the entryway, the knock came again—this time louder.

"Hang on. I'm coming." Jack snapped the door open in agitation.

"Jack Stevens?" a man asked in a gruff, raspy voice. He stood with his hands behind his back. He wore a pair of dark dress slacks and a black turtleneck shirt that showed off his solid build.

Jack figured the guy had a military background. "Yeah, what do you want?" Before Jack had time to react the man pushed his way through the door. He wrapped his large hand around Jack's neck and kicked the door closed. Jack tried to break free from the man's grip, but he was too strong. Jack's body made contact with the wall. Jack felt the drywall crack with the force. "Who the fuck…" Jack lost his breath as the man's fist slammed into his gut. He doubled over and collapsed on the floor. He laid his head on the cool ceramic tile as he watched the polished black leather shoes walk around him.

"You were told to drop it." The man squatted down behind Jack and turned him over onto his back. "If you would have only listened to my colleague in the hospital, you and I wouldn't have to be having this little talk now."

Jack knew he wasn't going to be able to defend himself without some sort of weapon. He saw his crutch just a few feet from where he lay. He reached out. His fingers touched the metal surface. The man's foot came down on Jack's wrist. "I wouldn't do that if I were you." The man grabbed Jack's outstretched arm and tossed him into the living room as if Jack's 140-pound mass was a cardboard box. "You don't want to piss me off, you little fuck." The man reached down and picked Jack up by the shirt and threw him on the couch. "You're lucky my clients are such understanding people. You'd be dead by now if it were up to me."

"Get the fuck out of my house." Jack's tone surprised even him.

"That's no way to speak to a guest. Such terrible manners you have." The man reached behind his back and pulled out a .44 and pointed it at Jack's temple. "Maybe this will teach you some manners."

Jack felt sick. A dead weight blanketed him, suffocating and hot. Sweat saturated his clothing. He wondered if this was how everyone felt when they were moments away from dying. His bowels gave out. A rancid, hot liquid sprayed from his ass, soaking through his gym pants and running down his legs.

"Nice, do you always shit yourself on the first date?"

Jack wanted to respond, but before he could muster the words, the man snapped the gun away from his head and slipped it back into the waistband of his pants. A wave of emotions shook Jack's body. The hot sweat against his skin turned icy cold.

"Consider this your final warning, kid." The man tossed an envelope on the coffee table. "Buy yourself some clean clothes." He pulled the gun out again. "Next time, there won't be any conversation or pleasantries. You'll be dead before you have time to shit yourself." He turned and walked out of the apartment.

Jack felt numb. His entire life had caved in around him in less than two weeks. He felt tears well up behind his eyes. Emotions swelled inside him. He heard his dead father's voice criticizing, and ridiculing him. It was as if his father was standing behind the couch. *You're a pathetic excuse for a son, and an even worse excuse for a man.* Something snapped inside Jack as he heard his father's words again. Determination forced its way through the flood of emotions. He wasn't going to lose this fight. For once he was going to win and prove his father wrong. A calm feeling settled into his mind. For the first time, everything seemed clear. He knew what he had to do. He stood up, removed his soiled clothes, and began planning his next move.

Jack stood in the shower washing the shit and sweat from his body. He felt secure and at ease even after his unexpected visitor. He knew his old life was lost to him. He would never be able to go back to the way things were before the accident. His one hope of moving forward and finding a new life was to close this one and never look back. Yet in order to close it, he would have to finish what the police and the court system couldn't do—make the guy pay for running him down.

Jack wiped the steam from the bathroom mirror and looked at himself through the streaks of moisture. Droplets of water fell onto his chest, dampening the dark, curly hair that lay across it. He studied his body, looking for evidence of a struggle to show Officer Adams. His visitor had known what he was doing—there wasn't a mark anywhere on his body.

He opened the vanity drawer and shuffled around until he found his Swiss army knife. He opened the blade and held it to his chest, watching the reverse motion of his reflection in the mirror. He hesitated. His hand trembled. He pressed the knife against his skin. Jack took a deep breath and clenched his teeth as he applied more pressure. He felt the tip of the blade sink into his skin. He dug deeper, moving the blade down and across his chest. He dropped the bloody knife into the sink and held on to the edge of the countertop. His fingers became white from the tight grip as he waited for the pain to subside and the flow of the blood to slow.

Jack washed the knife and tidied up the bathroom as if nothing out of the ordinary had happened. The initial pain had ended. A dull throb was all that remained. He tossed the knife into the back of his linen closet and covered it with several boxes of half-used containers of deodorants, shampoos, and colognes. He closed the linen closet and stood in front of the mirror. He smiled at a face he no longer recognized. It was time to make the call.

"This is Adams."

"Officer Adams, thank God you answered. You have to help me, please."

"Jack, what's happened? Are you okay?"

"You were right. They sent someone else to my home. Can you come over?"

"Jack, I told you at the hospital, I can't get involved."

"Please. You don't have to come on official business. You were right. I'm through with it all. I just thought..."

"I'll be there in ten."

Jack placed the phone down next to him as the line went dead. His bloody handprint was on the unit. He smiled through the pain and waited for Officer Adams to arrive. He removed the towel from around his waist and blotted the blood on his chest. Jack felt like he was in control for the first time in his life. He liked the feeling.

He closed his eyes and rested his head against the arm of the couch, listening to the ticking of the clock. Soon he heard the downstairs door open. Heavy footsteps ascended the stairs.

"Jack?" Officer Adams moved his head inside the opened door. "Are you okay?" He ran over to Jack and knelt beside him.

"Thanks for coming." Jack reached out to Officer Adams. "I didn't know who else to call."

"It's okay. How bad are you hurt?" He pulled the towel from Jack's hand and looked at the cut. "It doesn't look that deep. We should still get you to the hospital."

"No." Jack raised his voice. "No, it's okay. If we go to the hospital they'll ask a lot of questions, questions I don't want to have to answer. I just want to lie down. Can you help me get to my bedroom?"

"Sure." Officer Adams reached down and picked up Jack's crutch before wrapping Jack's arm around his neck. "Okay, here we go." Officer Adams braced Jack's weight against his own.

"The bedroom is down the hall." Jack motioned with a nod of his head. He couldn't help smiling at how easily his plan was going to work.

"It's kind of odd." Jack broke the silence that had fallen around them.

"What is?" Officer Adams questioned as he laid Jack on the bed.

"After everything that's happened, I don't even know your first name." He noticed Officer Adams's eyes glancing back and forth over his naked body.

"It's Carl. So what happened? Was it the same guy from the hospital?"

"No, it was someone else, though this guy had pretty much had the same message as the first one. Listen, I don't want to talk about it. I'm finished with it."

"I'm glad to hear that. Are you sure…?"

"Yeah, I'm okay." Jack smiled and placed his hand on Carl's leg. "I'm just glad you're here."

"I need to go, I shouldn't…"

"Stay with me." Jack leaned up on his elbow. He could feel the anxiety pulsing off Carl's body. He leaned in and kissed him.

"Jack, stop this." He pulled away. "I don't know what you were expecting from me, but I'm married and have a teenage daughter. I thought you were seriously hurt. Is this what you called me for tonight?"

"Please, after everything that has happened this past week, I just need to feel something again, even if it's not real."

"I'm sorry I can't."

"Please, I can feel something between us. I know you want this as much as I do. Please be with me, just this one time." He looked into Carl's eyes and kissed him again. This time Carl didn't pull away. Jack fell back against the bed as Carl unbuttoned his shirt.

❖

Jack lay in bed with Carl cuddled up next to him. The sex had been at best mediocre. Carl's body was unattractive and clumsy. Yet somehow he managed to pull it off and give Carl what Jack believed to be the best fuck of the man's life. Jack couldn't wait to give Carl something else. Jack tossed off the covers and stood up.

"Where are you going?"

"I'm getting dressed, as should you. I don't want you to get in trouble for being away from the station for too long."

"Shit, what time is it?"

"It's a little before eleven. You've been here for a couple of hours." Jack pulled on a pair of gray sweatpants. Jack came around to Carl's side of the bed, leaned over, and kissed his lips. Carl's breath was stale and pungent. "You should probably get dressed and back to the station." Jack took a roll of gauze bandages and wrapped his self-inflicted wounds as he watched Carl dress. "You don't have dress with your back to me. I've already seen everything you have to offer."

"This was a mistake." Carl buttoned up his shirt and zipped his pants up. "Nothing against you, Jack, it's me. I shouldn't have done this."

"I'm sorry if I did anything to upset you. I really thought you wanted me." Jack followed Carl to the front door.

"Good-bye, Jack."

"See you." Jack shut the front door, then headed back to the bedroom. He grabbed a sweatshirt off the floor and pulled it over his head as he rearranged several framed pictures on the dresser. He turned the video camera around and pushed the replay button. He watched as the night with Carl replayed on the small screen. "That should do the trick." Jack slipped a tape in the camera and recorded a copy. "It's time to pay Carl another visit."

The police station was quiet. A few officers nodded and smiled as Jack walked up to the counter.

"Can I help you?" asked an older uniformed woman.

"I need to see Officer Adams."

"Your name?"

"Jack Stevens. Officer Adams was the one who responded to my accident. I just have a couple of quick questions for him."

"Let me call him for you."

"Thank you." Jack leaned on the counter and watched the woman make the call.

"Carl, this is Jill. There's a young man up here to see you, he says he has some questions for you about his accident...Yes, that's right...Jack Stevens. Okay, thanks." She sat the phone down in its cradle. "He's on his way up."

"Thanks." Jack backed up and looked down the hallway. He couldn't help but smile when he saw the scared look on Carl's face as he walked up to meet him. "Officer Adams, thanks for seeing me."

"Let's go down the hallway so we can talk."

"Sure." Jack glanced back at Jill. "Thank you for your help." He smiled and nodded as she looked up from her desk. Jack followed close behind Carl as they made their way down the hallway.

"In here." Office Adams opened a door that led into a large open office area. As they walked through the sea of desks, Jack noticed a pair of handcuffs lying on the back of one of the chairs. He scooped them up and slipped them in his pocket. Carl's desk sat at the far end of a large open area. Carl sat down behind his desk.

"Jack, what in the hell are you doing?"

"It's nice to see you again too." Jack smiled. "Nice-looking family," Jack said as he held up the pictures of Carl's wife and daughter. "Was this your first time fucking a guy?"

"Keep your voice down." Carl looked around the room. "What kind of game are you playing with me? You want money, don't you?"

"I'm insulted. I don't want your money. I want the file of the man who hit me."

"Jack, I told you before..."

"I know, but that was before this." Jack pulled the camera out of his coat pocket and pushed the Replay button. He watched Carl's face redden and his expression change. "Do you think you might be able to help me out a little?"

"You're in way over your head, Jack. I hope you know that."

"Maybe, but I still want the file."

"Jack, I could get suspended if anyone found out that I gave you the guy's file. I can't risk it, not with you going around all half-cocked."

"You could also find yourself in divorce court if you don't give me what I want. I wouldn't think that would go over too well here either."

"Fine, I give up." He pulled a manila folder out of a stack of papers. "This is what you want." He handed the file to Jack.

"Thanks. I thought you'd see it my way."

"Don't you have something for me?" Carl walked around to the front of the desk.

"I thought I gave that to you earlier tonight." Jack smiled. "Oh, you mean the tape. Sure take it." Jack popped the tape out of the camera. "I have another copy back home anyway. You never know when I may need something else from you." Jack slipped the file into the waistband of his sweats and pulled the T-shirt over it. "Thanks again for the fuck." Jack turned and left without looking back.

It was nearing eleven when Jack arrived home. He knew sleep was out of the question. His body was flushed with adrenaline. He sat down at the kitchen table and poured himself a shot of tequila. He downed the cold, smoky liquid and opened the file.

Jack's heart stopped as he came face-to-face with the guy who hit him. His name was Reginald Lamb. The deep green eyes from the color photo looked up at him. There was innocence in Reginald's face that he hadn't expected to find. According to the documents Reginald was twenty-five. He had graduated with honors at MIT three years ago. There was no mention of employment. He found Reginald's current address a few pages in. He was surprised to learn that Reginald lived in one of the more run-down parts of the city.

He wondered why someone who came from such a wealthy family would settle for living in a more modest environment. He closed the file and downed another shot before heading out to find Reginald.

❖

Jack sat in his car on the darkened street, staring at the third-floor condo where Reginald lived. Jack could see the silhouette of a man moving from room to room behind the closed curtains. The lights went out in the upper floor. A few moments later Reginald walked out of the house and headed down the street.

Jack got out of his car, reached across the seat, and grabbed his backpack and crutch. His leg was bothering him after the long walk back from the police station, and he had no idea how long a walk he was embarking on this time. He shut the door and followed Reginald down Massachusetts Avenue toward the MIT campus. The street was alive with activity. Groups of college students hung outside the bars, smoking between drinks. A few homeless people yelled profanities as Jack passed by. Jack's plan took a new path as he watched Reginald walk into Paradise, the only gay club in Cambridge. He waited for a few moments before heading inside.

The light in the club was dim. The windows, coated with black paint, closed the club off to the outside world. Jack looked around the few scattered men and found Reginald sitting off in a corner by himself. Reginald caught Jack looking at him. Jack smiled and nodded before heading over to the bar to order a drink.

Jack turned around. He met Reginald's stare as he downed the shot of tequila. Reginald's thick black hair hung around his square face. Long strands of hair fell over his forehead, covering a portion of his right eye. His facial features were masculine, and sultry. If Jack had met him under different circumstances he would have considered Reginald quite a find. Jack ordered another shot and then walked over and set his drink down on the small wooden table. He sat down without speaking and leaned the crutch against the table.

"How do you know I'm not waiting for someone?" Reginald questioned Jack's directness. His voice was flat, deep, and sensual.

"Are you?"

"No."

"I didn't think so." Jack finished the cold liquid. "Besides, I can give you what you need." Jack's heart raced with adrenaline.

"What happened to you?" Reginald nodded toward the crutch.

"A hit-and-run," Jack answered. He waited for a response that never came. "Yeah, the guy hit me and just took off." He stared at Reginald's face, looking for a twitch in his eyes or a glimmer of recognition. There was nothing but a blank stare.

"So what is it that you think I need?"

"What you need isn't going to come from idle conversation. Why don't you take me back to your place and let me show you." Jack wanted to reach over the table and rip the guy's eyes out. His anger twitched in his face. He forced a smile in hopes of concealing it.

"You are direct, I'll give you that."

"I don't believe in games. They're a waste of time and effort. I'd rather spend my energy on more pleasurable things." He could feel the agitation and restlessness gnawing inside him. He knew he had to stay calm in order to keep his plan on track. He took a deep breath to calm his nerves. He wasn't going to let his emotions get the better of him, not when he was this close. "So, are you going to take me home or do I need to find someone else in here who knows what they want?" Jack stood up. He grabbed his crutch and backpack and stared at Reginald.

"This should be interesting." Reginald stood and walked up to Jack. "I'm about to take you home with me and I don't even know your name. I'm Daniel."

"Jack." He stared at Reginald and wondered why he was using a fake name. "Well then, Daniel. Let's go."

Reginald's place was not at all what Jack had expected. While the place was spotless in its appearance, the furniture was old and tattered. One would never know by the look and feel of the place that Reginald came from a wealthy family. "Nice place you have here," Jack lied.

"Thanks for saying so. It's okay, though, you don't have to lie."

Reginald kicked off his shoes. "I know it's a shithole. It's all I can afford at the moment." He walked up to Jack and ran his hand across Jack's chest. "Now, what's this about giving me what I need?" He leaned in and kissed Jack.

Jack's stomach soured from the touch of Reginald. He forced back the disgust and allowed Reginald's tongue to enter his mouth. He could taste a bitter, stale flavor in Reginald's mouth mixed with the earlier beers. Jack's body tensed up as he felt Reginald's hands exploring his body. Jack knew he had to act fast; he couldn't stand to be touched by him any longer.

Jack reached around the corner of the entryway from where they came in. He had seen a table against the wall. Reginald's hand slipped between them and fondled Jack's crotch. Jack's stomach churned. His fingers touched something square and smooth. He strained his fingers and wrapped his hand around the base of something. He lifted it. The weight felt good in his grasp. He raised his arm and brought the object down. The edge of the base made contact with Reginald's head.

Their kiss broke. Reginald pulled away and stared at Jack in disbelief. Jack raised his hand again. He looked into Reginald's eyes as he brought the heavy object down a second time, hitting Reginald in the forehead. Reginald collapsed on the floor. Jack stood over the body. His heart raced. Blood pulsed through his veins, energizing him. He studied the square marble base he held in his hands, wondering what other purpose it could have, other than a weapon to bash in someone's head. He smiled at the thought of Reginald buying it, unaware of its future use against him. He dropped it on the floor and watched Reginald breathe in and out. He swung his backpack on his shoulder and grabbed Reginald's hands, dragging him across the living room floor.

The place was small, so finding the bedroom didn't take any time; however, moving Reginald was another story. Jack set his backpack down and pulled and tugged and finally managed to get Reginald up on the bed. Jack straddled Reginald and pulled the shirt up and over his head. Jack ran his hand over the soft, black hair that covered Reginald's chest. He scooted down the bed and unbuttoned his pants. He removed the rest of Reginald's clothes, then stood up and looked at his naked body lying in a strange, lifeless state. He looked at peace. He wouldn't for long. A sense of pride flooded Jack's body as he realized the control he held over another person. Reginald began to moan. Jack pulled the handcuffs out of his backpack, snapping one cuff around Reginald's wrist and the other to the bed's metal headboard.

Jack unzipped his pants and pulled his dick out. He stood next to the bed with a full bladder and waited for the first stream to escape. After a little coaxing he let the warm, salty piss spray over Reginald's face. "That should help wake you up." The urge to piss grew as he watched Reginald's hair become saturated with his urine. He grimaced as he held back.

"Wha…what the fuck!" Reginald woke to a surge of confusion and panic. He tried to get up. The handcuff pulled against his arm and wrist. "What in the fuck are you doing?"

"Taking a piss, what does it look…or should I say taste like." Jack relaxed his muscles and let the heavy flow of his urine spread over Reginald's body and face. Jack pissed into Reginald's open mouth, cutting off the words he didn't want to hear. Reginald spat and choked. Jack shook his dick as the last of the piss dribbled across the bed and floor. He zipped himself up. "So, you were saying?"

Reginald stared at Jack and spit the last of the piss from his mouth. "Why are you doing this?"

"It's payback, you fuck! Why do you think?"

"Payback for what?"

"Let's see, how did your family word it?" Jack paused, enjoying the growing fear he saw in Reginald's face. "That unfortunate incident, I believe is what they called it."

"My family? What do they have to do with this? What incident are you talking about?"

"About two weeks ago at the corner of Ash and Brattle?" Jack waited for some sign of recognition. "You hit me in your car and left me lying on the street. Remember?"

"Look, man, I don't know what you're talking about. I never hit anyone."

"Lying to me is not going to help matters any." Jack crawled onto the bed. His own piss soaked into the knees of his jeans. He reached into his back pocket and pulled out his Swiss knife and drew the blade. Reginald's eyes grew in fear. The light in the room glinted on the steel blade. Jack ran the blade down Reginald's cheek and neck. His desire for control seized him, darkening his emotions. He became aroused by the situation he had created. He felt his dick thicken in his pants. He wondered if this was what his father had tried to teach him. Jack wished he had listened to his father sooner.

"Please, I swear, it wasn't me."

"No?" Jack crawled off the bed and opened up his backpack. "Well I have a police file here that states different facts." Jack tossed the file on the bed. "Go ahead take a look."

Reginald opened up the file with his free hand. "There's got to be a mistake. I swear to you, I didn't hit you."

"Liar," Jack screamed as he stormed the bed. His fist made contact with Reginald's jaw. He heard Reginald's teeth smash against one another. Reginald swung his clinched fist. It hit Jack in the chest. He winced as he felt the cut reopen. Jack pulled a second pair of handcuffs out of his back pocket and placed it around Reginald's wrist. He slammed his fist against Reginald's jaw again to quiet him down and snapped the cuff to the headboard.

Reginald pulled and tugged against the metal restraints. His body twitched. His skin glistened with sweat. "What do you want from me?"

"I want to teach you a lesson." Jack stood over the bed. His eyes traced the slim, naked figure lying helpless on the bed. "What's this?" Jack moved his hand down Reginald's stomach. He could feel the nerves pulse under his fingertips. "You're getting hard." Jack laughed at the thought. "So you like it rough, do you?"

"Fuck off."

"Fuck off? Fuck off?" Jack ran the blade of his knife down Reginald's quivering stomach. "Don't you mean 'fuck me'?" He ran the tip of the knife through the tangle of black pubic hair and up over the shaft of Reginald's dick. "Do you think fucking me will somehow make up for what you did?"

"I'm telling you I didn't hit you, you have to believe me." Reginald's chest heaved and trembled. Jack ran the knife down Reginald's shaft and pushed the tip of it into his tightened nut sack. "God, please don't." He dug the tip deeper into the skin. "Please, I'll do anything you want, just please stop."

Jack released the pressure of the knife. "Anything?" Jack placed the knife on the nightstand. "Well, maybe a fuck isn't out of the question." Jack kicked his shoes off and unbuttoned his pants. He pulled his underwear and pants down to his ankles and then stepped out of them. He pulled his shirt over his head. The bandage stuck to his shirt. It pulled at the tender, red skin of the cut. Jack grimaced and tossed the shirt on top of his other clothes. A fresh spot of blood began forming on the bandage. He stood naked and aroused as he stared at the fear in Reginald's face. "You better not let me down again if you know what's good for you." He climbed onto the bed and felt the heat of Reginald's body against his. Jack closed his eyes and took a deep breath, enjoying the feel of domination and control. He settled his ass down over Reginald's dick and found it swollen and hard. "Damn, you do like it rough, don't you."

"I'll do anything you want, just don't kill me."

Jack rose up off Reginald's body and grasped the firmness at the base of his cock. He settled down over the head, opened up, and let the thickness slide into him. "Come on. Fuck me, you bastard." He grabbed the knife and held it against Reginald's neck. "Don't go soft on me now." Jack grunted as he squeezed the deflating cock inside him. "Come on. You're the one who likes it rough. You're the one whose life depends on it."

"I'm sorry, I can't do this."

Jack sat up and felt the softness sink out of him. He sat there looking down at Reginald. He gripped the knife with a trembling hand and held it to Reginald's face. "See this cut on the side of my face?" Jack turned his head to the left and leaned toward Reginald. "See it? Answer me."

"Yes, yes, I see it." Reginald's voice broke from the tears welling up inside him.

"You did this the night you hit me." Jack dug the knife into Reginald's temple and pulled it down across his face.

Reginald screamed as the blade ripped through his skin. He pulled against the handcuffs. Blood flowed from the cut, staining the pillowcase a deep, burgundy red. Reginald arched his body in an attempt to throw Jack off balance. He bent his legs to give himself more leverage and tried again. Jack lunged forward. Reginald brought his chin to his chest and threw his head toward Jack's face. His forehead smashed into Jack's nose. The cartilage gave an audible snap.

Jack yelled in agony and brought his hands to his face. Blood spilled from his nose, soaking his hands and fingers. He looked down at Reginald. "You fuck." He raised the knife and plunged it into Reginald's throat. He grimaced and dug the blade deeper, leaning into the blade with the full weight of his body. Blood squirted from Reginald's throat, spraying Jack's face and chest. He held the knife deep in place as Reginald's body twitched and jittered against his. Reginald's arms flailed against the handcuffs. His frantic words gurgled and sprayed from his mouth. His body tensed, then fell lifeless.

Jack heard slow, steady clapping from behind him. He turned around, still straddling Reginald's lifeless body.

"Very nice." The man from the hospital stood in the room. He was wearing the same familiar three-piece suit. For the first time Jack saw a smile on the man's face. "If you wouldn't mind I'd appreciate it if you would climb down off the body and put your pants on. Your current state of undress is quite a distraction."

Jack pulled himself off the bed and slipped back into his pants. "Who are you?" Jack held the T-shirt to his nose to soak up the blood.

"I'm sorry my manners aren't what they use to be." The man walked up to Jack and reached his hand out. "I'm Reginald Lamb."

Jack turned and looked at the lifeless body lying on the bed, then back at the man in the three-piece suit. His heart was racing. The pulse of his blood pounded in his ears, deafening and confusing his mind.

"Yes, that's right. I'm the one who hit you."

"That's not possible. The police file…"

"Ah, you can thank Officer Adams for that. He does earn his pay." Reginald's smile grew as he watched the horror and shock on Jack's face. "It was all his doing. You see, the day I visited you in the hospital I knew you were going to make trouble. I could see it in your eyes, and I couldn't let that happen." He walked over to the bed and stared at the lifeless body. "Officer Adams was paid a lot of money to find someone to take my place." He turned around and looked at Jack. "His name was Daniel."

"What?"

"The guy you just murdered. His name was Daniel. His family disowned him after he came out to them. He was pretty much a loner. He seemed like the perfect person to take the fall for me. I had no idea that you would go all Freddy Krueger on me and kill the poor guy."

"You fucker." Jack rushed Reginald. It was like hitting a steel wall. Reginald stood without flinching and grabbed Jack by the neck and threw him up against the wall. Reginald's large hand squeezed Jack's neck and raised him off the floor. Jack kicked his feet, trying to get Reginald to release him. Reginald tightened his grip even more.

"Don't piss me off, you little shit." His face was inches from Jack's face. "You should have taken Officer Adams's advice and left everything alone. All of this is your fault." Spit sprayed from Reginald's lips and landed on Jack's face. "Now I'm going to have to get myself dirty once again and clean up the mess that you created."

Jack reached out and dug his nails into Reginald's face. Skin curled under Jack's nails. The scratches were deep and brought blood to the surface.

Reginald's face grew red with fury. He grabbed Jack and threw his head against the wall. The drywall caved under the force. Jack's head spun with pain as his head landed against the wall a second time.

Jack's body went limp. The energy and control he'd felt earlier faded away as if someone had opened up a drain. Without warning his body was airborne. He landed several feet away from Reginald.

"It's about time you got here."

Jack turned his head and saw Officer Adams standing in the doorway. Jack saw Carl look over at the blood-soaked bed, then down at Jack. Their eyes met. For a second, Jack thought he saw a glimmer of compassion in Carl's eyes. "Please, help me."

"I'm done with this mess," Reginald said as he walked up to Carl.

"Don't worry, Reggie, I'll take care of it."

"I don't want to have to tell Mother and Father that you couldn't handle the job."

"You won't." Carl glanced over at Jack, then back at Reginald. "Get out of here. I'll take care of this."

Reginald bent down next to Jack and pulled Jack's head up by his hair. "It's too bad. You're kind of cute." He kissed Jack, then let Jack's head fall back to the floor. He walked out of the room without turning back.

Jack took a deep raspy breath of air as a calm settled over him. "I can't believe you're here."

"Jack, don't. I told you to let it go. You wouldn't listen." Officer Adams took the gun that Reginald had left and pointed it at Jack. "I'm sorry, kid, you should have listened to me." He pulled the trigger. He flinched as Jack's body jerked from the impact of the bullet to his head. He stood and watched the life drain out of Jack.

"This is Officer Adams." His radio snapped and crackled. "I've got a murder-suicide on my hands, requesting backup."

Fear #3:
Clinophobia—The Fear of Going to Bed

Harold stood in the doorway of the bathroom and stared at his empty bed sitting in the middle of his small rented room. The covers were the way he'd left them that morning, tossed to one side and wrinkled. His flannel boxers hung from the bedpost, another reminder of a moment in life that was lost. He walked toward the bed with uneasy steps. His body shivered despite the hot August night.

The antique mantel clock that hung on the wall opposite his bed chimed eleven. Each note echoed through the house with its slow, steady beat. He took another step toward the bed and stretched out his hand, grasping his boxers between the tips of two fingers. He slipped them over his naked body. The soft, worn material was a small comfort, but one he welcomed.

Harold crouched down with his hands on his knees and turned his head sideways to peer under the bed. The view from the awkward angle was never enough to convince him of his safety, yet each night he repeated the failed attempt in hopes of not having to get on his hands and knees. He let out an aggravated sigh and assumed his position on the floor. He bent his head down between his hands to get a better view. Out of the corner of his eye he saw something move within the shadows beneath his bed.

His heart pounded in his chest. Sweat formed within the recesses of his armpits. He took a deep breath and laid his head on the floor. He scanned the space beneath the bed. He thought he had felt someone or something under the bed staring back at him, but the space was empty. He leaned in closer to the edge of the cheap metal frame, determined to put his mind at ease. The air under the bed was stale and heavy with dust. He sneezed. Dust billowed out around him. It was then that he saw it again. Something moved to his left as if it were trying to sneak up on him. He felt it looking at him. Then a sound seeped out from the darkness. The faint clicking noise grew until Harold realized it was the sound of gnashing teeth. Fear raced through his mind. He jumped up from his crouched position as he heard what sounded like nails tapping against the wood floors. He climbed up on the bed and waited for it to reach out from under the mattress and pull him down into hell.

Harold reached toward the nightstand and turned on the small lamp that sat behind his alarm clock. The room glowed with the soft, pale light. He let out a sigh and let his feet and legs stretch out in front of him. He pulled the covers up to his waist. His fingers twitched as he laid them in his lap. He sat motionless, moving his eyes from left to right and back again looking for the slightest movement, shadow, or sound from within his room.

Thunder rumbled in the distance. The clock ticked the seconds away. Harold heard the gears of the old clock spin in anticipation of another hour passing. He counted the chimes in his head. *One...two...three...* Lightning flashed, illuminating the sky. Thunder shook the windows in their frames. *Four...five...six...* The wind began to howl outside. The storm was coming in off the ocean with enough force to swallow the town. *Seven...eight...nine...ten...eleven...twelve...* Thunder crashed louder. Harold could feel the vibration shake the bed. The lights flickered off and on in rapid succession. Harold panicked as the lights flickered one final time before dying. Darkness settled in around him.

The ticking of the clock seemed louder in the dark, suffocating the other, weaker sounds. Harold peered over the bed, wondering if it was safe to leave in search of a flashlight or candle. He pulled the covers back and moved his left leg over the edge. His toes touched the cool, smooth surface of the floor. Before he could bring his other foot in line with his left, he felt something cold run over the top of his foot. He screamed and pulled his foot up. He held it in his hands as he peered over the edge. Lightning flashed. In the split seconds of vision, he saw what appeared to be a finger slip back under the bed.

The storm outside continued to batter the town. Harold slipped down into the bed and pulled the covers up to his neck. Each time lightning exploded in the sky, shadows danced across the walls and furniture in his room. In the pulsing light, he could not distinguish which, if any, of the shadows were moving toward his bed.

A sudden rush of cool air ruffled the thin cotton sheet and glided over Harold's body. The air billowed up in his face. The smell was stale and earthy. Goose bumps rose across his skin. The sheet rustled down by his feet. Terror filled his mind. He froze as he felt something cold and wet lick the bottom of his foot. He tried to pull his foot away. He couldn't move it. Something was holding his leg from below. The dampness continued to move up his arch to the ball of his foot before licking the crevices between each toe. The long tongue-like thing snaked its way around each toe before slithering over the top of his foot toward his ankle.

Harold's fragmented mind grasped the fleeting image of the cigarettes in his top dresser drawer. He knew he wasn't supposed to smoke in the house. He didn't care. He needed something to work with. Harold opened the drawer and pulled out the pack of Camels. His hands were shaking. He placed a cigarette in his mouth and fumbled with the lighter several times before the embers began to burn. The presence coiled around his ankle. Harold inhaled the cigarette. The ember sizzled and burned, glowing brighter in its orange hue.

He tossed the covers off and brought the lit end of the cigarette against his leg where he felt the pressure. The smell of burnt hair from his leg drifted over the bed. His skin smoldered as the burning ember scarred his skin. Harold felt the pressure from his leg ease. He lifted the cigarette and pushed it into his ankle. His teeth ground together. He held the scream in his throat to fight off the pain. The invisible hand that held his leg lifted. He kicked and pulled his leg back toward him. He flicked the lighter on and held it out in front of him. The foot of his bed was empty.

Sitting with his back against the headboard, Harold wrapped his arms around his knees and stared off into the dark. He drew on the cigarette and let the smoke smolder out of his mouth and nose. The smell of burnt skin and hair hung in the air. He rocked himself back and forth in sync to the soothing sound of the clock. His thoughts were fragmented. Every sound, every wink of a shadow sent his mind on another path of fear.

The clock fell silent. Harold stopped rocking. Something stirred around him. He couldn't determine where the shift came from. Fear paralyzed him as he waited for the unknown. The sound of scraping nails against the wooden floor seeped up from under the bed. Something shifted, this time from underneath the bed. His fingers trembled. Ashes from his cigarette fell onto his foot. He didn't notice the hot embers settling between his toes. His heart skipped as he felt something thud below him, as if it were coming up through the mattress.

He scooted around on his hands and knees and pounded his fists against the mattress. "Go away and leave me alone," he screamed. He tore the thin bed sheet and exposed the mattress. "Where in the fuck are you?" Adrenaline and fear rushed through his body as he dug his fingers into the old, frayed mattress lining. Rusted, jagged wires pierced the tips of his fingers. He pulled open the small tear in the mattress. He stopped dead in his tracks when he saw what lay within the mattress.

His eyes locked upon the hollow sockets of a skull. He reached into the mattress to touch it. His bloody fingers trembled as they grazed the smooth surface of the bone. He felt something move somewhere within the mix of bones and mattress padding. Suddenly he felt the cold, clammy fingers of a hand tighten around his wrist. He pulled against it. The grip was too strong. He strained his body and braced himself against the mattress, and yet the grip continued to pull him further into the bed. His face brushed up against the skull. It was cool and damp against his skin.

Something snapped in his shoulder as the pull shifted directions. The pain, sudden and hot, swelled through his neck and arm. He dropped down through the rot and bone. His mind went blank. He fell deeper into the void. His screams for help were muffled as his body disappeared into the mattress. The room fell silent except for the ticking of the clock.

As the sun rose the next morning over the horizon, a sign hung in the window of the small room. It read: *Room for Rent—Immediate Occupancy.*

DOWNTOWN CROSSING

I can't tell if he wants to fuck me, or beat the shit out of me. It doesn't matter—I have nowhere to run to, even if I wanted to get away. It's late, later than normal for me to be riding in the bowels of the city. This time of night a cab is my preferred mode of transportation. Tonight, for some reason, I chose to live life on the edge. An edge I now feel I'm hanging over, waiting to fall, or worse yet, waiting for someone to push me into the bottomless pit.

The car is empty except for the two of us and a few drunk or incoherent people. I feel something churn in the pit of my stomach. I'm aroused more than I should be, given my surroundings. The bulge in my jeans is getting larger, more noticeable. My cock expels a spasm of precome. It soaks into my underwear. It's cold, tacky, and somehow comforting. There's something hidden behind the arousal. It's deep, raw, and powerful. The feeling hits me again, moving deeper into my gut. I recognize the feeling—it's fear. The sour, bitter, invisible liquid burns my throat. Perhaps it's a warning not to trespass. A prediction of what's to come if I continue on this path. His dark ember eyes smolder as they glare at me. They're cold, dangerous, yet hot and erotic.

He's wearing faded baggy jeans. The edges are frayed; frayed like I feel this night has become. Tan work boots cover his large feet. A part of me wonders how they will feel kicking me in the stomach as I'm lying on some darkened alley in downtown Boston. The other part of me wonders what it would be like to be down on my knees removing his boots, touching his sweaty white socks, and smelling his scent. My body twitches as another spasm of precome reaches the surface.

His white T-shirt hugs his strong, muscular chest and arms. Black lines form nondescript designs through the fabric. I stare at them, trying to make out a pattern. I see a skull with dark, hollow eye sockets that stare back at me—another warning sign. The skull moves as he breathes, twisting and contorting against him. It pulls me in. I want to look away. I can't. The image just draws me closer to him. I hear my own heartbeat in my ears. It drowns out the drone of the subway car. My eyes move up his body.

His hair is tar-black and cut short. Its color complements his strong facial features and mocha-colored skin. For the first time I wonder what his ethnicity is. My guess is Hispanic with a bit of Mayan Indian, based on the high cheekbones and strong nose and jawline.

His lips are dark, thick, soft. I want to kiss them. I want to feel them pressing against my lips. Our eyes make contact for the first time. My heart stalls. I look away. I feel his eyes upon my body. They're penetrating my skin, burning deep into my soul. I'm light-headed from the intense attraction toward him and the overpowering fear held in that desire.

I want to look over at him to see his face again, to lose myself in his presence. I glance to the left without moving my head. His eyes are dark and mysterious, with a spark of brutality. They're still looking at me. I look down at my feet to concentrate on something other than him.

The car rocks without warning. In my peripheral vision I see him stand. My chest hurts from the steady hammering of my pulse. I don't dare look in his direction. I force myself to keep my eyes looking elsewhere, anywhere except where they want to be. He walks toward me. He's taller than I imagined, several inches over six feet. He towers over me, holding on to the rubber strap that hangs from the metal railing.

My eyes are at his crotch. His jeans are loose. I notice movement beneath them as the train rocks back and forth. I decide he's wearing boxers. I imagine his large, sweaty balls swaying between his legs, his cock dangling in front of them—in front of me.

His T-shirt has lifted above the waistband of his pants. The thick black elastic band of his underwear is showing. There are white letters imprinted into the fabric. Only the top half of the stitched letters is exposed. I recognize the name. I watch the rise and fall of his stomach as he breathes. I follow the motion, mesmerized by the peaks and valleys of his abs. He has a thick line of black hair that falls below his navel and scatters outward as it disappears behind the waistband of his Joe Boxers. I imagine his treasure trail as being the last thing I see as he kicks the life out of me. I want to run my tongue through the hair, to taste his body, his sweat. My fingers twitch, desperate to reach out to him. I lock my fingers together.

I allow my eyes to wander discreetly, so as not to be noticed. His hands are large. His thick, long fingers grip the rubber handle. I wonder what they will feel like around my neck as he chokes me to death. It's becoming harder for me to breathe. His biceps, which are larger than my neck, flex as the train shifts. His armpits are damp. Long, dark hairs poke out of the short sleeves. I want to lick them. I want to bury my face in the sweaty recesses of his body. He's close enough that I can smell him. His scent is deep, musky, and masculine. It hangs in the air around us. I take a deep breath to bring him into me.

The rocking of the car stops. He sits down across from me. I look over at him. He's staring at me. His face is void of all emotions. All I see is a deep, dark emptiness looking back at me.

I begin to sweat. It's not the overheated kind. It's the nervous kind. It's thick and pungent. It soaks the armpits of my green T-shirt. What's not absorbed into the fabric runs down the sides of my body. The blood that races through my body goes straight for my dick. It pulses with excitement. I realize that I have to get away from him before I do something I'll regret. I decide to get off at the next stop, still on the Boston side of the Charles River and still in the downtown area.

The train begins to slow. The stop is sudden and rough. I look over my shoulder to see where we stopped. The station is Downtown

Crossing, eight stops away from the safety of my home. I stand up. My legs are weak, unstable. I walk toward the door, holding on to the metal railing for support. I step off the train. I feel his presence follow me onto the platform.

I walk through the underground station. Damp air from the tunnel chills my overheated body. My shoes are silent against the tiled floor. I try to listen over the noise of the train to hear if someone is behind me. I hear footsteps, the kind that large, tan work boots would make.

I want to be on the train with movement, people, and hope. I turn back. He's standing just a few feet away, standing between me and the safety of the car I just exited. We look at each other. A sour liquid crawls up my throat. My entire body fills with fear, yet a sullen longing lies deep inside me, as if I've been marked and belong to him.

I watch as the train pulls away and disappears into the tunnel. I feel alone, isolated and vulnerable. A small grin appears on his face. I wonder if he sees my fear, or perhaps smells it like a wild animal on the scent of his prey. His broad shoulders and muscular frame ignite something in me that I don't recognize. He could snap my scrawny body in two without breaking a sweat, yet the sight of him thrills me more than I care to admit. My dick aches. Blood rushes through the veins. It swells in my jeans. I turn away to hide my desire from him.

I walk over to the escalator and let it carry me up to the city. The streets are dark and deserted, as if the world has ended during my time underground. I look around for any signs of life. I feel disconnected from my world. I'm lost in the very city I call home. There's someone behind me. I know it's him. I hear him breathing. He's closer than before.

I continue walking without any direction or plan. All I know is that I have to keep moving. I have to keep the distance between us. I turn the corner and walk down Washington Street. The buildings are dark, stone mausoleums, a symbol of death for the day that has ended. The streetlights cast an orange glow across the cobblestone streets. I see his elongated shadow stretch across the sidewalk behind me. It gets closer. I watch with anticipation as it inches toward me. It devours everything in its path. I feel it touch me. My body tingles with desire as his shadow covers mine. We become one. It's then that I realize he's gaining on me. I want to stop dead in my tracks and let him take me, end this game of cat and mouse. I want to give into his advances, whatever the outcome; whether it's to fuck me or to slit my throat. The fear keeps the pursuit moving.

I make a left onto Avenue de Lafayette, hoping to see a light on in a window or to see someone else walking the streets in the dead of night. It's void of life, just like the rest of the city. I feel the vibrations of an occasional truck or car as it speeds along the interstate below me. I hold on to the brief, distant feeling of security that it offers.

I stop and listen. It's silent behind me. I turn around, ready to face the inevitable. I expect his fist to meet my face or the razor-sharp edge of a knife to sink into my gut. The street behind me is empty.

I'm alone. The beating of my heart echoes in my head. Relief rushes through me, but with this calm there's a strange feeling of regret. I walk back the way I came, retracing my steps back to the subway station. I see an alley to my right. I look down the darkened path and see the bright red sign of the station. I hesitate. The fear begins to build again as I contemplate my next move. I turn and enter the alley.

The old, decaying brick walls of the buildings seem to close in around me. My heavy breathing bounces off the walls. I'm halfway down the alley, halfway to safety when I hear something behind me. Fear paralyzes me. I hear the sound of heavy boots approaching from behind. I close my eyes to block out the life that I fear I might lose. The footsteps stop. His hot breath touches my neck. My body tightens into a knot, waiting for his next move. He covers my mouth with his right hand while his left wraps around my torso. He lifts me off the ground. He throws me up against the cold, damp brick wall. His body mass crushes me.

I feel something stiff and solid pressing into me. I want it to be his dick. I want him to be as aroused as I am. My twisted mind tells a different story involving a knife and my death. Tears form in my eyes, not from pain, from panic as I hear him speak.

"You shouldn't be out here by yourself this time of night," he whispers in my ear. His voice is deep, hypnotic, and tinged with a slight accent. "There are bad people out here that might want to hurt you." He thrusts himself against me.

My face brushes across the rough surface of the bricks. Blood trickles down from my cheek. His breath is stale, hot. I want to kiss him. I want to taste the bitterness on his tongue. His face is against mine. The sharp blades of his whiskers pierce my skin.

A sudden yet brief moment of hope rushes into me as his hand moves between us. I wait for him to caress my ass. Hope fades as he goes for my wallet. His large, thick fingers dig into my back pocket. I take the moment to relish his fingers grazing my ass as he manages to grasp the trifold. His heart beats against my back. It quickens as if he's getting angry.

"This is all you have, thirty dollars?"

"I...take my cards and..." His fist slams into my lower back, cutting off my words.

"I don't want your fucking cards." Spit splatters across my face as he speaks.

Thoughts scatter through my mind. I can't retain anything long enough to react to it. I should be worried about my life. I'm not. What is on my mind is his spit sliding down my face. I want it. I want to taste his saliva in my mouth. Disregarding the consequences, my tongue darts out between my parched lips and licks the spit that has slid down to the side of my mouth. The flavors rush through my body. It's tart, bitter with sweet undertones like a wild blueberry that's not quite ripe. My head spins as if I've just taken a hit of some hallucinogenic drug. With one taste of him I become an addict. I want more of him, and I'm willing to risk anything to get it.

"You just fucking tasted my spit!" His tone becomes darker. "You want more?" He spits again. "Go on, take it. Lick it off your lips."

I don't resist. I taste him again. The flavors invade my senses.

Another hit, another rush. My mind is a blur of images as thoughts of sex with this man or my possible death dance a dark tango. My head swirls again as he turns me around to face him. He pushes me against the wall. His hot breath batters my face.

"Looks like I found myself a cocksucker tonight." A twisted smile crosses his lips as he notices the large bulge in my pants. His hand covers my swollen dick and squeezes. I realize my balls are in his vise grip as well. Tears form in the corner of my eyes as the pain rips through my body. "You like this, don't you?"

I move my lips. Words won't form in my mind. I try again. I feel the words reaching the surface. They spill out of me before I have a chance to stop them. "Kiss me." My heart sinks as I hear the words that stumble from my quivering lips.

"Kiss you?" He leans in closer to me. Our noses almost touch. "What do you think this is, some sort of fucking date?" He grabs my chin and shoves my head against the wall. Colorful dots blink in and out of my vision from the impact.

His eyes are like the hollow eye sockets on his shirt that I saw staring back at me on the subway. They burrow into me, burning me with their black embers. "You're lucky I don't fucking gut you right now." He reaches into his back pocket and produces a knife. The blade flips up. He brings it closer and rests the cold steel blade against my cheek. "Kiss you, huh?" His eyes are pockets of emotion. He brings the knife to my throat as his lips touch mine.

His lips are hot and thick and taste of dirt and sweat. His large hand grasps my head. His fingers lock onto my hair. His mouth opens up. His tongue pushes through my lips. I open up to receive him. He enters my mouth with such force that my lips slip open. The steel blade of the knife presses against my skin. I feel faint, as if all the blood has left my body. He devours me as he sucks the very breath from me.

"Get on your knees," he pants as he pulls our mouths apart. "I want to see what else you can do with that mouth." The knife disappears into his back pocket. He shoves me to the ground. My knees land hard against the cobblestones.

His crotch is in front of me. I feel as if I'm back on the subway, desperate to touch him, fearing what will happen if I do. His dick is swelling beneath the denim fabric. He's aroused. I hope it's me that is bringing about this change. I fear, however, that his arousal is coming from a different place—a place of violence. A place I'm finding myself in the middle of with no hope of getting out. The outline of the head of his dick presses against the denim. I reach out to touch it. My fingers tremble. The tip of my finger caresses the bulge. It moves in response.

"Remove my belt."

I look up at him. The angle of my view distorts his face much like the lines and images on his shirt. I reach up and pull the end of his belt through the buckle. My fingers shake from fear, desire, and a cold chill that has settled into my body. I tug the thick leather, pulling it through the hoops. I set it down on the ground.

"No. Put it around your neck."

"What?"

"You heard me. Wrap it around your fucking neck." His fist slams into my jaw. I feel something snap in my mouth. Warmth, then pain rushes to the surface. I taste blood. He towers over me with an expressionless face. "Do it now." He reaches for his back pocket.

I take his belt and wrap it around my neck before he brings out the knife again. The smell the old, damp leather invades my nose. He grabs hold of the end and yanks on it, tightening it around my neck.

The bulge in his jeans is growing. My eyes trace the outline of his cock as it hangs down his right leg. I see a wet spot forming in the material. I want to taste it, to suck the precome off the denim. I reach up and run my hand down the length of his cock. He knocks my hand away and reaches for his zipper.

The belt is tight around my neck. I watch with growing anticipation as he lowers his zipper. His fly opens to expose his black boxers. His thick fingers slip inside, fishing for his dick. Long, curly black hair escapes the confines of his crotch. He tugs and pulls on his dick until it falls from the opening. It hangs in front of me. Long, thick, and tantalizing. Precome forms and hangs from the folds of his foreskin.

He grasps the base of his dick and slaps my face with it. The precome smears across my cheek. I open my mouth, hoping to taste it. He shakes more precome onto my face, as if he's shaking his dick after a long, hard piss. He slips the head of his dick in my mouth. My jaw doesn't want to cooperate. The pain intensifies as he grabs the back of my head and shoves his dick down my throat. My nose disappears into the thick mass of his pubic hair. His dick fills my mouth and throat, forcing me to breathe through my nose. I take in his scent. It's pungent and sharp. He pushes my head further into him. The zipper's cold metal teeth dig into my skin. My gag reflex kicks in. I force the bitter liquid back down my throat along with his precome.

"You like that cock, don't you?" The force of his thrusts causes me to lose my balance. I grab his calves for support. They're like steel beams, thick and solid. My jaw is on fire, swollen and burning from his thickness. The edges of my mouth feel as if they're going to split open, and still he keeps fucking me as if he's never going to stop.

Spit and precome covers my face and chin. He grabs the back of my head and thrusts one final time, holding me against his crotch. The thick layers of his foreskin dangle in the back of my throat. I use my muscles to milk it. I swallow the warm salty liquid that he releases. He pulls up on the belt, cutting off my breath. I become light-headed. The alley blurs and spins around me. The world blinks in and out as I feel the pulse of his dick beating down my throat. Air rushes into my body. He releases the belt and pushes me off his dick. I fall to the wet pavement gasping for air. I look up at him. He stands motionless, lumbering over me. His dick hangs wet and heavy in front of him. In the dim light I watch as a thick thread of precome hangs off the tip. It wiggles and shimmers as it releases and falls to the ground.

My thoughts from the subway rush back into my mind. It's

exactly how I pictured it. He's standing above me with those tan work boots poised and ready to kick the life out of me. My clothes are wet from lying on the rain-soaked pavement. I raise myself up.

"Stay down." His right foot pushes against my chest. "I haven't decided what I'm going to do with you yet."

The pressure from his foot weighs heavy against my chest. I watch from below as he strokes his dick. My balls have become a shrunken sack of pain from the desire and urges I can't release. I want to touch myself, to release the pressure. I know he won't let me. This isn't about me anymore, if it ever has been. It's about him. The rain begins to fall again.

"Unlace my boot," he demands as he pulls his white shirt up over his head. His large, solid chest is smooth except for the puffs of dark hair around each nipple and the treasure trail leading into his pants. The rain runs down his half-naked body. His mocha skin glistens in the orange light of the alley. He uses his shirt to wipe the rain from his face and hair. His armpits are dark, furry, and wet. I am lost in the desire of his body. "I said unlace my fucking boot!"

I shake my head as if coming out of a dream. My fingers rush to the boot. I pull and tug on the nylon laces. They resist. My hands tremble as I fight with the laces. They give in. I've won that battle at least. I feel the pressure of his foot release from my chest. I place one hand on the heel and the other hand under the ball of his foot and pull. His foot slips out of the boot with ease. The scent of his damp, sweaty foot is overpowering. My cock begins to spasm as I hold his musky foot in my hands. I bring it closer to me. He kicks his foot free of my grasp.

He rests his foot on my chest. Heat radiates from it. I take a deep breath of it. The musty, wet leather smell mixing with his sweat and dirt drives me over the edge. I feel the heat of his foot against my body as the cold rain chills the outline around it. I want to hold it again, to feel the heat of it in my hands and against my face.

"Get up." He eases his foot off my chest. "I said get the fuck up!" He kicks my face, leaving the scent of his sweaty sock on my cheek.

I'm once again staring into the eyes of my deepest desire and darkest fear. His eyes are empty, yet somehow full of life. He leans to one side and slips the sock off his foot. I watch as he bundles it up and brings it to my mouth. He pulls the hair on the back of my head. I open my mouth and he shoves his sweaty sock into it.

"Suck on that for a while." He slaps my face hard. I can feel the imprint his fingers made as the skin reddens. "Drop your pants and turn around." He pulls on the belt cutting off what little foul-tasting air I'm getting through his sock.

I unbutton my jeans and let them fall to the ground. I tug the underwear down and let my swollen dick fall between us. It smacks against his. The brief connection sends a bolt of painful pleasure through my body. I want to bite his nipple, to bring it into my mouth and suck on it before turning my attention and my mouth to his hairy armpit. I turn around before he has a chance to use the belt again. He pushes me against the brick wall.

"Now you're going know what it's like to be fucked by a real man." His hand tightens around the belt as if he's pulling on the reins of a horse.

I feel the head of his dick against my ass. I move my hands against the wall to brace myself against his assault. I know it's coming hard and fast; he doesn't know any other way. I want him, yet fear him at the same time. The length and thickness of his dick will rip into my tight ass. My ass that usually gets nothing more than a vibrator or cock the size of a carrot will have to take a dick the size of the handle of a sledgehammer.

The muscles in my ass resist as he pushes the head of his dick against me. A searing heat explodes through me as he forces his dick into me. My stomach clenches. I cough as if I'm going to vomit. His entire length is inside me. I feel as if I might pass out from the pain and pleasure I'm simultaneously experiencing. His cock moves, adjusts, and grows inside me as the blood pulses through the large veins. Then it begins.

He pulls on the belt and fucks me. I dig my fingernails into the brick wall, hoping to find another outlet for the pain. A fingernail cracks, splinters, and breaks off. I barely notice the pain and blood. I look down at my cock swaying back and forth from his thrusts. It's swollen and blood-red from the pressure that continues to build with no relief in sight. I grab it. It's wet with precome. I stroke myself with long, slow movements. I soon find myself picking up speed, trying to match the quick and forceful thrusts of his dick inside me.

A knot burns in my stomach. It swirls as it moves into my groin. My balls tighten. My cock expands. I want to yell to release the tension that continues to consume me. His sock, still shoved deep in my mouth, muffles my words, and my voice. My orgasm builds. It burns in my groin as it's stoked and fueled even further by the massive dick inside me.

My body tenses. I reach my breaking point. I tremble, shake, and then convulse. I release the first searing jet of come. It sprays across the red brick wall. A second and third explosion erupt from my cock. The thick white liquid clings to the rough surface of the wall. I continue to stroke myself and release a final time. My dick deflates in my hand as he continues to fuck me.

The pressure in my ass subsides. I feel hollow, stretched as if my ass will never be the same. He turns me around and pushes me down to the ground. He strokes his dick over my face. His large, hairy balls hang low between his thick, muscled legs.

He tightens his grip on the belt. His breathing is getting louder. He begins to grunt. His strokes become short bursts up and down the shaft of his dick. The head of his dick swells. It plays peek-a-boo with me, coming in and out of the folds of foreskin. His piss slit expands. He releases his come. It's warm, almost hot against the cold skin of my face. He shoots another load, then a third. It's thick and glides down my face and neck. I remove his sock from my mouth. I feel another load land across my mouth. I lick it off my lips. It's salty and warm. My stomach growls for more. I open my mouth and he slides his dick inside. I slip my tongue inside his foreskin and lick his dick clean of any remaining come. He pulls out and pushes me to the ground.

Our bodies are wet with rain. My T-shirt clings to my body. I look up at him. The familiar emptiness is looking back at me. He pulls up his pants and picks up his T-shirt from the wet ground. He looks at me one final time with a crooked grin on his face. He shakes his head as he removes the belt from my neck. I'm naked and wet. I don't move for fear he'll come back. I watch him walk down the alley and disappear around the corner.

❖

I step out of the shower and wrap a towel around my waist. My entire body aches from the assault. I stare at my reflection through the steam built up on the mirror. The man staring back at me is almost unrecognizable. I take pride in that thought and hope that one day there will be nothing left of him. My concentration is broken by a knock at the door. I open it without even looking through the peephole. I know who it is.

His clothes are still wet. A blank expression covers his face.

"Come on in." I stand to the side and let him pass.

"I hope everything was to your satisfaction tonight? I would hate to think we didn't create the perfect fantasy for you."

"I enjoyed it very much." I hand him five hundred dollars. "That's why I keep using your company. I never know what kind of evening they're going to plan for me."

"I'm glad to hear that. Perhaps I'll be asked to provide another fantasy for you in the future." He slips the money in his pocket. "Good night, Mr. Donaldson." He turns and walks out of the apartment, closing the door behind him.

I stand for a moment lost in my thoughts. I turn off the lights and crawl into bed with the painful reminders of my night and visions of his body to rock me to sleep.

SUMMERLAND

I can't believe you talked me into this," Adam whispered as he turned on the flashlight.

"You didn't have to come." Sean reached into the backseat of the car for his backpack. "But I'm glad you did. Besides what else were you planning on doing at one in the morning?"

"I know this sounds strange—I was actually thinking about getting some sleep tonight." Adam smiled at Sean. "But it's not often that I get asked out to a cemetery."

"You deserve only the best." Sean smiled as he tossed the backpack over his right shoulder. "You ready?"

"Let's just get this over with." Adam threw the beam of light into the darkness that surrounded them. The light fluttered with shadows as a swarm of midsummer bugs raced toward it.

They looked out across the empty road more out of habit than expecting to see anything. The distant traffic lights blinked amber, casting odd shades of yellow across the silhouette of the sleeping neighborhood. The sound of the men's footsteps across the pavement seemed too loud for the night. Something stirred in an old elm tree as they crossed the road. They stood facing the closed entrance of the cemetery.

"What, did you expect the place to be open this time of night?" Adam aimed the beam of light through the wrought-iron gate. The visitor's center, an aged stone structure, stood out against the wooded landscape behind it.

"Of course not," Sean whispered. "Come on, let's follow the

fence toward the back. There has to be a missing piece to squeeze through or a tree we can climb up to get in."

"What's up with you?"

"What do you mean?"

"Look, Sean…would you stop for a minute?" Adam stopped, waiting for Sean to get the hint. "We've been friends since kindergarten, so, what, twenty-four years? This isn't like you. You call me up in the middle of the night, or near to it as possible. You tell me to be ready in ten minutes and for what, to break into a cemetery? What's this all about?"

"Art." Sean turned, disappearing around a curve.

"Art?" Adam picked up his pace. "You're fucking kidding me, right? We couldn't have done this during the day when the cemetery is open?"

"No, it wouldn't have been the same." Sean stopped. "Here, I think I found an opening. Shine your light over here."

The beam illuminated a section of the fence that was missing two bars. "It's the essence of death I want to capture in this piece." Sean paused, tossing his backpack through the opening before slipping his left leg into the gap and pulling the rest of his body through. "What better way to capture that than doing so in the dead of night." Sean held out his hand to help guide Adam through the opening. "Besides, it's illegal to do what we're about to do."

"What is it that we're about to do?" Adam threw the beam of light toward Sean. Dark shadows fell across Sean's face, highlighting his strong cheekbones and hollowing his eyes.

"We're going to do a grave rubbing," Sean replied as if it was the most natural thing to do.

"You're kidding, right?"

"No, I've never been more serious."

"You're a photographer. A damn good one, I might add. Why the switch?"

"I don't know. A couple of months ago I stopped by a yard sale and found this." Sean reached into his backpack and pulled out a stained white linen cloth. He unfolded it, holding it out to Adam.

"Sean, it's an old, dirty rag. Please tell me you didn't buy this thing. I have a ton of them in my cleaning supplies at home. I would have been happy to give you one." He looked at the excitement in Sean's eyes. "You didn't?"

"Yeah, I did. I paid twenty dollars for it."

"Have you lost your mind? You paid twenty dollars for a piece of cloth just to carry it around with you for all these months?"

"I can't explain it. You know how it is when you see something in a store or a piece of art in a gallery? It just speaks to you. It gets into you. No matter how ridiculous it seems, you just know you have to have it."

"I get the art thing, but this isn't art. It's an old piece of cloth that no one wanted."

"I know. That's part of the charm. Who owned it? What was it used for? There are stories held within the fibers. It has a history. It had a life. Yet someone sold it as if the memories meant nothing. Every piece of trash or unwanted junk can be art. You just have to be inspired to do something with it."

"Okay, buddy, you seriously need to get a life, or perhaps a boyfriend. This here is just a little too weird."

"Adam, don't start with the boyfriend thing. We've been through this before."

"Yeah, yeah, you don't want to get involved with me because you're afraid it will ruin our friendship. You have to know how I feel about you."

"I do know."

"I don't think you do. We spend almost every day together. We know each other better than we know ourselves. I just want…"

"Adam, please. You know I love you, I just don't want anything to fuck up our friendship."

"Fine, okay, I'll drop it." Adam turned away and read a few of the headstones while nursing his wounded heart. He knew it was pointless. He just didn't want to let go of the hope that one day, Sean would see him as something other than a friend. "Here's an old headstone right here. Let's get this over with so I can go home."

"It can't be just any headstone. It needs to speak to me. I need to feel something like I did with the cloth."

"Of course it does. How stupid of me." Adam moved the beam of light off to their right. Rows of headstones caught the light, reflecting the ghostly white into the old twisted trees.

An uneasy feeling crept through Adam the further they walked. He flashed the light across the headstones, glancing at the names and dates of strangers. He wondered how many were the resting places of the forgotten. The silence, the loneliness settled around him as he remembered his mother. He made a silent promise to visit her grave soon. A chill ran through him. He began to feel as if he was disturbing their rest or violating their space. He stopped as Sean took a sharp left toward a clearing.

"Where are you going?"

"Come over here with your light." Sean pointed out the area. "I saw something over there just a minute ago when you threw your light over here. Wait. Go back. That's it. I found it, right there."

"Found what?" Adam walked over to where Sean stood looking down at his feet. The one-foot by two-foot headstone lay flat against the ground. Grass mixed with dying weeds concealed most of it from their view. "What's so special about this one? It's all by itself out here. Whoever's buried here couldn't have been all that important."

"That's just it, don't you see." Sean knelt down, pulling the overgrown weeds out by their roots. "They've been cast out, buried outside of the boundaries of the cemetery plots. It's like it doesn't belong."

"Yeah, well, neither do we." Adam crossed his arms.

"Shit, look at the carvings on this headstone. This will be an amazing rub." Sean brushed the dirt off the surface of the marble, running his fingers across the surface. "It looks like an eye."

"What?" Adam squatted down next to Sean.

"Yeah, look at this." Sean traced the outline of two half circles that didn't quite touch at the ends. In the center of the arches were two smaller round curves. The granite inside the smaller circle was a lighter shade of gray than the rest of the headstone. "Damn, that looks like black onyx." Sean ran his finger over the smooth surface of the stone set within the center of the eye.

"What are these?" Adam pointed to a series of small circles etched into the corners of the headstone. "Gerald Brink."

"What?"

"That's the guy's name, look down here. The impression is small." Adam pulled back more of the overgrown grass exposing the small lettering along the bottom edge. "Well, now you at least have a name to go with your etching." Adam brushed off his jeans as he stood.

"The placement and size of the name is so unusual, I love it."

"Sean, everything about this night is unusual, including the fact that there are no dates on the headstone." Adam heard rustling in the grass behind them. He aimed the light out across the cemetery, illuminating the night. He looked out into the darkness. The wind continued to carry the sounds. Shadows appeared between the headstones and then disappeared behind the trees. The sounds along with the movements seemed oddly choreographed. Adam rubbed his arms as a chill fell around him. "Just do your rubbing so we can get the fuck out of here."

"All right, just give me a few minutes." Sean unzipped his backpack. He shook a can of air, and then turned the spray toward the ground. Using long, slow moments, he cleaned the dirt and debris from each engraved crevice. "I'm going to need you to hold the cloth for me." Sean snapped the lid back on the can. Adam knelt down next to him. "Here." Sean handed Adam the piece of cloth. "Just unfold this and place it on the headstone. Make sure you stretch the cloth so it's tight against the surface of the headstone. We only have one chance to get this right."

Sean rubbed slate-gray wax in long, slow strokes over the thin cloth to cover the entire piece in a light coating. His strokes became firmer, more concentrated in specific areas, highlighting the intricate carvings of the headstone. Sean rubbed the man's name last. Letter by letter, the name came through the cloth in a bold dark imprint.

"There, it's done," Sean whispered. "What do you think?"

"I think you should have stayed with photography is what I think. Now can we please go?" Adam looked up, meeting Sean's eyes. "Are you okay?"

"Yeah, I'm fine. I'm just a little light-headed. I guess it's from keeping my head down while working on the piece." Sean held the cloth up at the top corners. The breeze brushed against the fabric, causing the designs to ripple. "It's by far my best piece ever."

"If you say so." Adam turned away, picking up Sean's tools and shoving them inside the backpack. "Come on, let's go."

"Are you sure you got everything?" Sean looked around the headstone. "Thanks, Gerald. I hope we didn't disturb you too much."

"Good Lord, come on. I doubt Gerald even knew we were here." Adam moved his flashlight out in front of them as they made their way back through the cemetery.

"Do you mind driving?" Sean pulled the keys out of his pocket.

"Not at all. Are you still not feeling well?"

"I'm fine, just a little nauseous. Besides, I want to keep the cloth flat so the waxed areas don't crease or crack." Sean tossed the keys toward Adam. They flew up over Adam's head, landing several feet behind him.

"Thanks." Adam bent down to pick up the keys from the pavement. A sudden gust of wind howled around him. He straightened, looking down the empty road. He tilted his head against the wind. Adam thought he heard the gentle humming of a song.

"Come on!" Sean shouted.

"Wait." Adam held out his hand to quiet Sean. He listened again. The sound was faint, but the musical notes were being carried in the air. It moved in closer. A male voice drifted around him, yet he couldn't tell which direction it came from. The faceless voice faded, as did the wind. Adam walked back to the car with a chill running down his spine.

"What was that all about?"

"Nothing." Adam looked back out into the street. "I just thought I heard something." Two loud beeps echoed through the air as Adam unlocked the car. "Let's go." Adam opened the door, sliding into the driver's seat. He paused, looked out across the street one final time before starting the car. He closed the door and pulled out of the parking lot.

"So I guess I'll drive to my place. You can head home from there?" Adam broke the silence. "Sean? Hello?"

"No, I want you to help me get this hung tonight."

"Sean, it's almost two thirty in the morning. By the time we do all that and you get me back to my place, the sun will be coming up."

"Who said anything about taking you home? Just stay at my place tonight." Sean turned his attention back to the rubbing. His left forefinger traced over the cloth, following the flow of the circles.

"I don't think…"

"That's good," Sean replied, still concentrating on the cloth. "Sometimes you think too much."

"So you've told me before." Adam pulled into the driveway. The silence of the night fell around them as they walked up the outside stairs to Sean's third-floor condo.

Sean unlocked the door. "Let me go get the frame so we can hang this." Sean kicked off his shoes as he flipped the light switch. "I can't wait to see how this looks in the bedroom."

"You're not serious about putting that in the bedroom?" Adam slipped his feet out of his sandals and headed down the hallway toward the bedroom. "Besides, I don't see any room in here for it." Adam strolled around the room looking at the hundreds of photographs that documented Sean's professional life.

"We'll make room," Sean responded as he walked into the room. He set the frame and rubbing on the bed. He stared at each wall, tilting his head in one direction, then the other before facing a different wall. He walked up to the wall opposite the bed, removing six black-and-white photographs. A smile crossed his face as he stared at the bare wall. "This is the spot. It will be perfect here."

"Why would you want to face this thing while you sleep? It gives me the creeps." Adam stopped looking over Sean's shoulder and decided to keep quiet. He knew better than to get in the way when Sean was creating. The last thing he wanted was an argument this late at night. He leaned against the door frame and watched as Sean placed the cloth between the panes of glass.

Sean stood up and held it up to the wall. "Perfect. Can you come over here and hold the frame for me?"

"Sure." Adam walked up next to Sean. He reached for the frame.

Sean grabbed the hammer he had cradled in his armpit. He pulled the nails from the barren wall, took one, centered it, and then pounded it into the old plaster. Sean dropped the hammer and took the frame from Adam. He slid it down the wall until he felt the nail catch. He leaned back, shifting the frame to the right. "Damn, now that's what I call a thing of beauty."

"If you say so." Adam stared at Sean's newest piece. He couldn't understand the attraction toward it. Sean had always been very judgmental of his own work. He never felt it was good enough. Tonight Adam saw a different side of Sean. He seemed excited about the piece, almost captivated by it. Adam couldn't find anything inspiring about it: It looked old, dark, and depressing.

Adam turned away, heading toward the hallway. "Now that that's done, if you don't mind, I'm going to get some sleep."

"Where are you going?"

"To get an extra pillow and blanket for the couch."

"Don't be ridiculous, you can sleep in here with me." Sean looked over at Adam standing in the doorway. His eyes moved back at the rubbing. "It must be the lighting in here."

"What?"

"The lighting in this room, it must be casting different shadows against the glass. I keep noticing things in the rubbing that I hadn't noticed before. It happened in the car on the way home as well."

"Good night, Sean."

"Don't you want to see this?"

"It's okay. I'll take your word for it." Adam waited for a response that never came. He walked down the hallway, pulling bedding from the linen closet on the way. He tossed the bedding on the couch, pulled his shirt up over his head, slipped his jeans down his legs, and crawled under the blanket. He could hear Sean moving around in the other room. Adam listened to the creaking boards, following Sean in his mind. The footsteps stopped. The light on Sean's nightstand went out. The condo fell silent. Adam stared off into the darkness, trying to identify the objects in the living room by the shape of their shadows. As his eyelids became heavy with sleep, the shadows blurred and shifted. His mind gave in, letting the shadows and sleep take him.

Adam awoke to the clock chiming four. He lay on the couch facing the back cushions with his eyes closed, hoping he could slip back to sleep. When that didn't work, he rolled over on his back. He opened his eyes. A dark shadow formed in his sleep-fogged mind. He focused his eyes. It wasn't in his mind. The shadow moved. It stood at the end of the couch looking at him. His heart pummeled his chest. He kicked his feet under the blanket to push himself to a sitting position.

"Jesus Christ. Sean what in the fuck…" His words trailed off. The shadow was gone. He listened for movement or a noise from the other room. The only sound was his beating heart. "Sean?" He whispered into the dark as he stood up. There was no response. He took a few steps toward the end of the couch, and then stopped when he heard the creaking of a door. "Sean, what are you doing?" He stepped to the end of the couch and peered around the wall. The hallway was empty. He looked for a light coming from Sean's closed door, but there was only darkness.

Adam walked down the hall toward Sean's room. He opened the door. The same creaking he had heard earlier filled the air. Adam looked through the dim light of the moon. Sean was curled up in his bed asleep. Adam's eyes moved over to the grave rubbing. It hung in the shadows, standing alone against the wall. Sean mumbled incoherent words as he tossed and turned in his bed. Adam's mind turned to the shadow that had been staring at him from the edge of the couch. An icy finger slid down his spine, lingering in the small of his back.

"No, please don't," Sean yelled out in his sleep. "Please…Yes, I do…Sunshine?"

"Sean?" Adam walked across the room and sat on the edge

of the bed. The thin sheet covering Sean's body felt damp. "Sean, wake up." Adam reached out, touching Sean's shoulder. Perspiration covered his fevered skin. "Sean?" Adam shook his arm.

"No," Sean screamed.

"Sean, it's okay. It's just me." Adam could see the fear in Sean's eyes as they scanned the room before focusing on Adam. A tear rolled down Sean's cheek. Adam brushed it away with his thumb.

"Adam?" Sean's face broke into a small smile. Trembling, he wrapped his arms around Adam burying his face into Adam's shoulder. "God, you feel so good."

"Are you okay?" Adam held Sean in his arms, stroking the back of Sean's head. "It's okay, it was just a dream."

"No, you don't understand." He spoke into Adam's neck, muffling his words.

"Shh, just relax. I'm here. It was just a dream." Adam broke their embrace. The fear in Sean's face remained.

"Please, don't leave me," Sean whispered.

"Why are you whispering?" Adam looked around the room, following Sean's eyes.

"Please. I don't want to be alone."

"I'm not going anywhere. I'll just be in the other room." Adam hesitated as Sean moved closer to him. A quiet awkwardness settled between them. Their eyes locked. Before Adam knew what was happening, Sean leaned in and kissed him. Adam felt the nerves twitching through Sean's lips as they pressed into his. Adam broke the kiss. "Are you okay?"

"Yeah, just please stay here with me. I just need to feel you next to me tonight." Sean's eyes pleaded with Adam. "I need you, Adam. I don't know what I would do without you."

"You don't have to worry about that. I'm not going anywhere." Adam slipped under the covers with Sean. Adam raised his arm to let Sean move in closer. Their bodies intertwined. Sean's head rested on Adam's chest. "Do you want to talk about the dream?" Adam whispered as he settled into a comfortable position.

"No." Sean ran his fingers through the fine brown hair that covered Adam's chest. "I just want you to hold me."

Adam wrapped his arms around Sean. He kissed the top of Sean's head. "You got it. Try to get some rest now." He stared off into the darkness and listened to the soft, gentle breathing as Sean fell back to sleep. Adam tried to stay awake, but he gave up fighting and let his eyelids close.

❖

The morning sun filtered in through the blinds, hitting Adam across the face. He awoke with Sean still nestled in his arm but awake. "Good morning."

"Morning." Sean smiled. "Thank you."

"For what?"

"For everything. I know I can be pretty stubborn about us, and our friendship, but you still stick by me. I don't know. After those dreams last night, I...I realized just how important you are..."

"Sean, what's wrong? You look a little pale." Adam placed the back of his hand against Sean's forehead. "You're burning up."

"I don't feel so good..." Sean suddenly grabbed his stomach and sat up. "I think I'm going to be sick." He crawled out of bed and stumbled into the bathroom.

Adam sat on the edge of the bed listening to Sean vomit. The toilet flushed several times before Sean appeared, leaning against the door frame. Adam went to him. The sour air of the bathroom struck his nose with a heavy blow.

"Come on, let's get you back to bed." Adam slipped himself under Sean's arm and guided him across the room. He pulled the sheets up over Sean. Adam sat on the edge of the bed, wiping hair away from Sean's forehead. "Just lay there, I'll be right back."

"Where are you going?" Sean reached out. He grabbed Adam's arm. "Don't leave."

"I'm just going into the kitchen to get you some ginger ale. It will help settle your stomach." Adam leaned down and kissed Sean's forehead. "I'll be right back."

When Adam looked back from the hallway, Sean had shifted on his side to face the door. Adam walked into the living room. His clothes lay piled on the floor next to the couch. He pulled his boxers out of the leg of his jeans. He slipped them on before heading into the kitchen. The cold air of the refrigerator brought gooseflesh to Adam's skin. He shuffled through the plastic containers of leftovers and half-empty bottles of condiments until he found the cans of ginger ale. Grabbing a glass out of the cupboard, Adam headed back down the hallway, pouring the drink as he went.

"Here you go. If nothing else, it will take that nasty aftertaste out of your mouth." Adam crawled under the covers as Sean propped himself up against the pillows.

"Thanks." Sean sipped the cold drink. "That tastes good."

"Care to tell me about this dream that seems to have you so rattled?"

"That's just it. It didn't feel like a dream." Sean took another sip. He looked over at Adam. "You know how some dreams are chaotic, vague, and senseless? This one wasn't like that."

"What happened?" Adam wrapped his arm around Sean's shoulder, pulling Sean into him.

"I was in my bed asleep. I woke up to someone singing or humming. I looked around the room, thinking I saw a shadow move in the darkness." Sean paused looking at Adam. "What?"

"Nothing, I just got a chill, that's all." Adam pulled the covers up as he thought back to the shadow he thought he had seen last night standing over the couch.

"I thought it was you, so I called out your name." Sean took a drink from his glass. "You never answered, so I got up to pee. When I came back into the room a man came out of the darkness. He covered my mouth with his hand."

"Did you recognize him?"

"He was behind me the whole time. He pulled me over against the wall. His body had a strange odor to it, like damp, moldy mothballs. His breath smelled like a public toilet. His hand was cold. Now that I think about it, his entire body felt cold against mine. It's what he said that scared me more than anything else."

"What?"

"He asked me if I liked sunshine. When I didn't answer he

flipped out a knife. I felt the cold blade against my throat. I asked him what he wanted. He said, 'What everyone wants. A chance to live.' He told me that I needed to get rid of my fuck buddy sleeping on the couch so that he and I could get down to business."

"Jesus." Adam poured the rest of the ginger ale into Sean's glass. "Then what happened?"

"Nothing. I found myself back in bed. I remember looking around the room. I was alone."

"Is that when I woke you up?"

"I don't think so. You know when you're dreaming and someone wakes you up? It's a sudden jolt of reality? I didn't feel that. When you called my name, it felt like a natural extension of the dream, like the next logical step."

"Well, that's all it was, you know—a dream." Adam rested his head on Sean's shoulder. He looked out across the room. His eyes fell upon the grave rubbing hanging askew on the wall. "You said this guy pushed you up against a wall. Which wall?"

"It was that one." Sean pointed in the direction of the picture. "Why?"

"No reason." Adam stared at the framed cloth. The center eye seemed to stare back at him. "Why don't you try to get some sleep?"

"You're not going to leave, are you?"

"No, I'll be in the living room checking my e-mail." Adam kissed Sean's forehead. "Just get some rest." Adam pulled the covers up over Sean. He looked back at Sean settling under the covers, making sure to leave the door cracked partway open.

He picked up his clothes from the living room floor and walked into the bathroom. He stood staring at himself in the mirror as the shower heated up. He stepped into the tub, letting the warm water cascade down his body. As he lathered up with soap, he thought he heard someone come into the bathroom.

"Sean?" He waited for an answer that never came. He poked his head out of the curtain. No one was there. He finished rinsing, turned off the water, and grabbed a towel to wrap around his waist. He walked across the hall to the half-closed door. The sounds of

Sean's snoring drifted through the opening. He walked back into the bathroom to finish getting ready. Dressed with yesterday's clothes, he grabbed his wallet and Sean's car keys. He hurried out the door, hoping to be back before Sean woke up.

❖

Adam returned ninety minutes later. As he opened the front door, a putrid smell hit him. He dropped the bags of groceries by the front door and followed the growing stench down the hallway. He heard whispers coming from Sean's room. He opened the door. Sean sat in the middle of the bed, rocking, with his knees pulled close to his chest. A mix of shit and vomit covered his body.

"Jesus, Sean. Are you okay?" Adam ran to the bed. "What happened?"

"He came back."

"Who did?"

"The man from my dream last night, he was here again. Didn't you hear me calling you?"

"Sean, there's no one here. It was just another dream." Adam looked down at the soiled sheets. "Come on, we need to get you cleaned up." Adam bent down, placing Sean's arm around his neck. He took Sean's weight against his own. They walked into the bathroom. "Just stand here for a minute while I get the shower started." Adam turned on the water, waited, and then adjusted the temperature. He grabbed the roll of toilet paper from the holder. "Turn around, we need to get as much of this wiped off as we can." Adam rolled the toilet paper around his hand. He wiped the shit from Sean's body.

Adam leaned across the toilet to flush it. He stood up, unbuttoned his shirt, and tossed it to the floor. He looked up at Sean, who stood motionless, looking at him with a blank stare. Adam unzipped his pants, pulled them off with his underwear, opened the shower curtain, and helped Sean into the tub before getting in himself.

Adam grabbed the bar of soap, running it between his hands. Starting at Sean's neck he rubbed the lather over Sean's shoulders and slipped his hands in and out of Sean's armpits before making his way down Sean's back. He knelt down behind Sean. He rubbed the warm soapy water over Sean's ass. The heavy suds clung to the thick blanket of hair that covered Sean's body from the waist down. Adam ran the soap through the crack of Sean's ass before moving his hands between Sean's legs. To Adam's surprise he found Sean's cock erect. He heard a slight moan from Sean as he ran his fingers through the mass of tight, curly pubic hair. Adam found himself hesitating as his fingers wrapped around the base of Sean's cock. He shook the thoughts from his mind and stood up. He rinsed Sean and then reached behind them to turn the water off. He pulled back the curtain and grabbed a towel.

"Let's get you dried off and into something warm." Sean's expression was blank, yet his eyes shifted as if watching every move Adam made. "Why don't you get into your robe? You can sit on the couch while I wash the sheets." Adam wrapped the damp towel around his own waist before walking Sean into the living room. "Can I get you anything?"

"No." Sean's voice was lifeless, and distant.

"Just sit here. I'll only be a minute, then I'll make us some soup." Adam finished drying off as he rummaged through Sean's closet for some clothes to wear. He pulled the sheets off the bed. The sour, pungent smell hit him in the face. Adam held his breath as he bundled up the sheets and took them to the laundry room. "Are you hungry?" Adam shouted as he turned the washer on. There was no response. He walked into the living room. "Sean, what's wrong?"

"Where did you go?" Sean looked up at Adam. "You promised not to leave me."

"Sean, I was just in the other room." Adam squatted down in front of Sean, resting his hands on Sean's knees. "Are you hungry?"

"No, I don't think so."

"Why don't you just lie down and rest?" Adam moved the pillows he had used the night before to the opposite end of the couch. He pulled the blanket off the back, tossing it over Sean. "I'll make the soup anyway, that way it will be ready when you get hungry."

"Don't go again. I told you I don't want to be alone."

"Sean, I'll be right over there in the kitchen." Adam pointed across the living room. "You can see me from where you're at. I won't be out of your sight." He kissed Sean on the cheek, tucking the blanket under Sean's shoulder. He grabbed the groceries by the door and took them into the kitchen. By the time he finished the soup, Sean was snoring in the other room. The light filtering through the windows blanketed Sean in a soft glow. Adam stretched. His back cracked. He took a seat in the recliner across from Sean. He pulled back the leg rest, scooted down in the chair, and watched the steady rise and fall of Sean's stomach. Adam's eyes became heavy with sleep. He drifted off to the soft murmurs of Sean dreaming.

❖

Adam stirred in and out of sleep. He opened his eyes and looked over at the cable box. It was nearing five in the afternoon. He closed his eyes and tried to concentrate on the blackness behind his eyelids to help quiet his mind. Just as sleep began to consume him again, a shadow crossed in front of him, causing the light to shift. Adam's eyes popped open. "Damn, Sean, you scared the hell out of me." Sean leaned against the edge of the footrest. He didn't move, he just stared down at Adam with his head tilted to the left. "Sean, are you okay?" Adam lowered the footrest. The recliner slipped back and forth from the release. "What's wrong?"

"Why did you do that to me?"

"What are you talking about?"

"This." Sean slipped the robe off his body. He grabbed his erect cock. "Why didn't you? I thought you loved me."

"I don't know what you're talking about, Sean." Adam stood up.

"Don't fucking lie to me," Sean screamed, pushing Adam back into the recliner. "Poor love-starved Adam. Always wanting what he can't have."

"Sean, stop this…"

"Shut the fuck up." Sean leaned into the recliner, placing a hand on either side of Adam. He brought his face within inches of Adam's. "You are nothing but a fucking tease, you know that?" Spit flew from Sean's lips, splattering Adam's face. "You get me naked in the shower. I let you touch me. I finally give into your pathetic whining about being more than a friend. I let you get me aroused, then nothing. You turn off the water and turn your back on me."

"Sean, you need to stop this. I don't know what's wrong with you, but you have to let me up so I can help you."

"Let you up? Let you up?" Sean raised his hands in the air. "Fine, I'll let you get up." Sean grabbed Adam's arm, pulling him up with such force, Adam lost his balance and fell to the floor. "You are such a slut, lying there on my floor with your legs spread. You think I'm going to just drop my pants any old place for you? Oh, no. If we're going to do this, we're going to do it right."

"Sean, stop this." Adam yelled as Sean dragged him across the carpeting. Adam twisted his body. He kicked his legs, hoping to throw Sean off balance. He felt the burn of the carpeting against his legs as Sean pulled him down the hallway.

"Sean, God damn it," Adam shouted. It was then that they stopped. Adam looked up. He didn't recognize his childhood friend.

"Sean, please, you have to…" Adam was lifted off the ground as if he weighed no more than a sack of potatoes. "Fucking put me down." Adam pounded his fist into Sean's back. Sean didn't flinch. Adam was thrown on the bed.

"Now we're getting somewhere." Sean crawled on top of Adam. "You want me? Well, now you're going to get me. I'll teach you to start something and not finish it."

"Fuck off," Adam screamed. He curled his legs underneath Sean. He pushed as hard as he could, sending Sean tumbling off the bed and into the wall. Adam jumped off the bed and ran down the hallway. He froze at the front door as he heard a deep guttural laugh coming from the bedroom. The voice he heard wasn't Sean's. The laughter died. What followed terrified Adam even more. The song he had heard the night at the cemetery—"You Are My Sunshine"—came drifting from Sean's room. Adam turned around.

A tall, muscular shadow stood at the far end of the hallway. The song drifted through the room, turning Adam's blood cold.

He opened the door and ran out of the house. He stopped as he reached the street and looked up to the third-floor condo. Sean stood in front of the living room window with his forehead pressed against the glass. The fingers of his left hand curled up and down as if a child was learning how to wave good-bye.

Adam walked to Sean's car and opened the door. He looked up. Sean stood motionless in the window. Adam hesitated. The promise he made to Sean rang through his mind. "Fuck." He slid into the driver's seat, turned the ignition on, and backed the car out of the driveway.

Adam raced through the narrow streets of the city, hoping he could make it back to Sean before anything else happened. His phone rang. He ran through a red light as he flipped it up. "Hello?"

"Why did you leave me, Adam?" Sean's voice broke through the tears.

"Sean, I'll be right back, I just needed to pick up a few things at work." Adam pulled into the parking lot of the strip mall. He opened the car door and ran across the lot. "Sean, please just hold on. I'll be back as soon as I can."

"You promised never to leave me. He gets angry when you're here with me, but he can't do anything until you're gone. Please come home."

"Who gets angry?"

"The man from my dreams. He says that we can't get down to business with you around. I don't like being alone with him, Adam. He scares me when I'm alone. Please come back."

"Sean, just keep talking to me. Don't hang up the phone, okay?" Adam ran into the drugstore, ignoring his coworkers waving and shouting greetings as if his vacation hadn't started just two days before. "As long as we're talking, you'll be okay." To Adam's relief, the pharmacy was quiet. "Sean, talk to me, buddy."

"Uh-oh. Need to go. Bye-bye."

"Sean, don't hang up the phone," Adam yelled as he ran back to one of the computers. "Fuck!" Adam dialed Sean's phone number.

It went to voice mail. "Shit." Adam flipped the phone closed. He dropped it into his pocket. Keeping an eye on his coworkers, Adam created two prescriptions for Sean, and then dispensed the diazepam and Xanax tablets into the palm of his hand. He knew he had to do something to keep Sean leveled out, and if that meant forging a few prescriptions, then he could live with that. Adam slipped his hand into his pants pocket and left through the back of the store, hoping to avoid polite conversations or, worse yet, questions.

Adam tried Sean's phone several times on the way back, and each time his call went unanswered. He pulled into the driveway, opening the car door before he turned off the ignition. He ran up the stairs, stopped, and took a deep breath to prepare himself for whatever awaited him inside.

"Sean?" Adam questioned as he walked into the quiet room. "Sean, where are you?" He walked down the hallway. A light flickered under the closed bedroom door. Adam put his hand on the doorknob. He paused. A faint voice carried under the door. He turned the knob and opened the door.

"Come out, come out, wherever you are," Sean whispered as he sat cross-legged in the middle of the bed in only his underwear. He clutched a kitchen knife in his right hand.

"Sean, it's okay. I'm back. No one is going to hurt you." Adam caught his breath as he noticed the self-inflicted cuts across Sean's body. "Sean, give me the knife."

"Nope, don't want to. I need it. I need to cut him out of me. Slow, careful cuts, like this." Sean took the tip of the knife and brought it up to his chest just below his nipple. "Nice shallow cuts are the way to do it." He dug the tip into his skin, bringing the tip up and over his nipple in a half circle. A thin line of blood formed at the incision. "Nope, not in there."

"Sean, give me the knife." Adam crawled up on the bed. "Sean, it's okay. I'm here." Adam reached out with one hand.

"Be careful, you might get hurt." Sean flicked the knife at Adam. The blade fell, cutting into Adam's left arm.

"Shit." Adam pulled off his T-shirt and wrapped it around his arm. Blood seeped through the white cloth.

"I'm sorry." Sean looked up with tears running down his face. "I didn't mean to...it's not...I'm sorry."

"It's okay. It's not deep. Just give me the knife."

"You'll regret it, you know?"

"Regret what?"

"Leaving me. Just like that song says. You'll regret it all someday. You know the song. You are my sunshine..."

"Sean, please don't sing that song."

"You don't like my voice?"

"No, you have a nice voice. I just don't like that song. Sing something else for me."

"I don't want to."

"Why?"

"Because the sunshine song is his song. He likes to have it sung to him."

"Whose song?"

"Gerald. It makes him happy. You don't want to be around when Gerald isn't happy. He does bad things to people when he's unhappy."

"You mean Gerald Brink from the cemetery?"

"He wasn't ready." Sean nodded toward the wall.

"Ready for what?"

"To die." Sean looked around the room as if looking for someone. "Please don't leave me again." He whispered, "It's not safe when you're gone." Sean dropped the knife on the bed. "He wants to you to leave. He doesn't want you here." He wrapped his arms around Adam and began to sob like a little boy.

"I'm not going anywhere, Sean. I promise." Adam held Sean in his arms. Sean's tears ran down Adam's shoulder. "Come on. Let's get these cuts cleaned up, then we'll go sit in the living room, okay?"

"I hurt you." Sean lifted Adam's arm. His sobs shook his voice.

"It's okay. I'll be fine." Adam scooted across the bed, stood up, and held out his hand for Sean. "Come on." Adam washed the cuts with warm soap and water and bandaged the ones he could before helping Sean into some clean clothes. "There, that's better." They walked down the hallway and into the living room. "I have something to help you relax." Adam pulled the pills out of his pocket. "I want you to take these for me."

"Will it keep him away?"

"Yes, Sean, it will keep Gerald away." Adam handed Sean the pills. A half-empty bottle of water sat on the coffee table. "Here you go." He sat down, wrapping his arm around Sean's shoulders. They sat without talking while waiting for the medication to take hold. Adam soon heard Sean's slow, heavy breathing as he slept. He stretched Sean out on the couch, tossing a blanket over him. "Sleep tight." Adam leaned down and kissed Sean's temple. He walked into the other room to make a call.

"Dad...yeah...it's me." Adam hated to ask his father for anything, especially after the way his father had treated him when he came out to the family ten years ago.

His father, the chief of police, couldn't accept that his only child was gay. He told Adam to leave the house immediately, that he was no longer a part of the family. Adam packed his bags and left that night. It was Sean who took him in and got him on his feet. It was time his father made up for that night.

"I need your help." Adam paced the hallway, stopping every few minutes to peek around the corner to check on Sean. "Don't start, Dad...Do you have any idea what it took for me to call you tonight?...I wouldn't ask if it wasn't important...Jesus, Dad, you owe me this...I need you to find out anything you can about a guy named Gerald Brink...Yes, B-r-i-n-k...Do you have to know why? Can't you just do this one thing for me without the third degree?... No, I'm not in any trouble...Thank you...Yes, call me back on my cell phone...Tonight." Adam walked back into the living room and turned on Sean's computer.

The glow of the monitor tinted the living room a translucent bluish-white. Adam double clicked on the browser icon. He glanced over at Sean as he waited for the search engine to load. He typed in the name "Gerald Brink" followed by "Mount Auburn Cemetery": no results. He ran a search for the home page of the cemetery and found it. Searching through the website, he found a link to their registry, which listed everyone buried within the grounds. He scrolled through the listing of famous residents: Mary Baker Eddy, Oliver Wendell Holmes, Henry Wadsworth Longfellow. At the bottom of the list he found the search box. He typed in Gerald's name—no results. He tried last name first and received the same response.

Adam stared at the empty screen. The phone buzzed in his pocket. He jumped from the sudden vibration. "Dad, thanks for calling me... Why, what did you find?" Adam looked over at Sean sleeping. "No, I'm not at home. I'm over at Sean's...2645 Fayweather, number 3... Sure." Adam hung up the phone. He walked into the bathroom to bandage his arm before his father arrived. He removed the rolled up T-shirt. The cut had already begun to seal with the dried blood. He pulled the rest of the gauze out of the box and wrapped his arm with it, then took a long-sleeve shirt from Sean's closet and pulled it over his head. As his head popped through the opening, his eyes were drawn to the grave rubbing hanging on the wall. He walked over to it. The replicated eyes from the headstone stared back at him with their gray deathlike glare. A cold chill ran down his spine. Adam walked out of the bedroom, closing the door behind him.

He poured himself a bourbon and Coke. He leaned against the kitchen counter, savoring the smoky flavor while he waited for his father. The bourbon calmed his nerves. He took another gulp. A car door shut in the distance. Footsteps rose on the outside stairs and approached the front door. There was a moment of silence. Adam wondered if his father was having second thoughts. He opened the door before his father had time to back out.

"Hi, Dad. Come on in."

"You owe me some answers, Adam." His father towered over Adam's five foot eleven frame. He noticed Sean sleeping on the couch. He lowered his voice. "What in the hell are you needing this man's file for?"

"So he has a police record?" Adam shut the door and motioned for his father to follow him down the hallway. "What's it say?" Adam asked as he sat on the edge of Sean's bed.

"Not so fast. Why are you so curious about this man?"

"Look, Sean believes he's being harassed by someone who claims to be Gerald."

"That's impossible. Gerald's been dead for forty years."

"Yeah, we know he's dead. We sort of stumbled upon his grave last night at Mount Auburn. I just want to know more about him."

"Why not just report the harassment to the police?"

"You have to ask? Your precious reputation might get tarnished if they figure out that one of the gay men filing a report is your son." Adam stood up. "Now, will you just give me the file?"

"You shouldn't get messed up in this, Adam. If the guy who is harassing Sean is anything like Gerald, you need to let the police handle it."

"What do you mean?"

"Gerald was a dangerous man, a psychopath who lured young men back to his apartment. He would be so full of guilt and anger after having sex with these men that he would beat, torture, and murder them. He blamed them for his temptations, said they were the devil's whores out to undermine society and the righteous people. During the investigation they found most of the body parts stored in large freezers in his house. There were pieces of the men missing, a few fingers, the eyes, and various internal organs. It's all in his file, including the statement from the young man who escaped. It was his testimony that led to Gerald's arrest."

"What happened to Gerald?"

"The police tracked him down to a house in Avon Hills. He was sitting in the living room with an older woman. He was dead. The woman turned out to be Gerald's mother. She sat in her rocking chair singing to him…"

"'You Are My Sunshine.'" Adam spoke as a chill passed through his body. "That was the song she was singing, wasn't it?"

"How in the fuck did you know that? No one knew about that except the three responding officers. It only appears in the report."

"Sean said he heard the man singing it." Adam shook his head. "How did Gerald die?"

"They never determined the cause of death. He had several stab wounds, but none of them were fatal. They suspected that he was poisoned, perhaps by his mother, but they never found any trace of drugs in his system. What they did find during the autopsy were traces of the missing body parts. Apparently he was eating specific part of bodies from the men that he killed." He handed Adam the folder.

"Thanks, Dad, I appreciate this."

"Just be careful."

"I'm sure it's nothing." Adam walked his father back into the living room. "Thanks again." Adam stood facing his father. An uneasy silence fell between them. Adam wondered if he should hug his father—or would a handshake suffice? He couldn't remember ever hugging his father, even at his mother's funeral. He opted for the safe way out. He opened the door and patted his father on the back. Adam locked the door behind his father. He walked over to check on Sean, pulling the blanket up over his shoulders. Adam contemplated another bourbon and Coke. He opted for a pot of coffee to help keep him awake in case Gerald came after Sean again. As the coffee brewed he sat down at the kitchen table and opened Gerald's file.

Everything his father had told him was in the file: the pictures of the various freezers overflowing with body parts, the autopsy with the contents of his stomach, detailed re-creations of Gerald's supposed life. Adam flipped through the pages until he found the police interview with the survivor.

His name was Daniel. He was twenty-four when the attack took place. There were pictures of him in the report. Despite the bruises and swelling to his face, he was a good-looking young man. Adam tried to picture what he might look like at sixty-four. Daniel gave in vivid detail the events of that night.

I met Gerald Brink two nights ago at the Punch Bowl, it's on Essex Street. When he introduced himself to me he was carrying a handful of folded bills. I think he assumed I was selling sex. I thought it was kind of his game—a way to get him off. You know, some weird fantasy sex-for-hire gig. He was well groomed in his light blue three-piece suit. I was drawn to him. So I played along, thinking it was a harmless game. I would have gone home with him even without the money. I like older men. There's something about their maturity, their stability that turns me on. Anyway, I pocketed the two hundred that he gave me and let him take me back to his place.

He was so charming and handsome. He acted as if I was the only one in the world. He made me feel special. By the time we arrived at his place, I actually had myself believing that he loved me. No one has ever made me feel the things he did. So I didn't question anything when things turned a bit unusual in the bedroom. I guess in a way I was already under his spell.

The coffeepot beeped the completion of the brewing cycle. Adam walked into the kitchen, poured the coffee into a large thermos, and grabbed a mug from the cupboard. He sat down and filled his mug. Blowing across the top of the coffee, he took a sip of the rich, black liquid. He continued to read Daniel's statement.

He was incredible in bed. He knew what to say and what to do. The sex went on for hours. At first he was the passive one. I fucked him four times just in the first hour. He couldn't get enough of it. He begged me for more. He said he was a dirty old man who needed to be treated like a dog. He told me to call him my bitch. After I tried to fuck him a fifth time, I told him I needed to rest, to recharge. That's when he turned more aggressive. He started in on me, fucking every hole he could find. He told me that he wanted to tie me up. He said he had never done anything that bad before. He sat another four hundred dollars on the nightstand. The extra money was too much to pass up, so I let him tie me up. He fucked me again. Then he moved to my mouth. He came down my throat. I tried to spit it out, but he just kept fucking me. I didn't have a choice but to swallow it. He even tried to fuck my nose. That's how my nose got so beat up. He fucking busted the cartilage to make more room for his dick. He almost fucked the nose off my face. I started yelling at him. I told him to get off me. That's when things turned bad.

He didn't say anything. He just sat there, staring at me. When he finally climbed off me, he sat next to me with a strange expression on his face, as if he was disgusted with what he had done. I asked him to untie me. He said he couldn't because I needed to be taught a lesson. He called me the Devil's whore—a tempter of men. He got up off the bed and crawled into the corner of his bedroom. He pulled his knees up to his chest. He started crying and rocking himself. He suddenly stopped crying, like a switch had been thrown. He glared at me and began pounding his head against the wall, cursing himself and me for having sex with another man. It wasn't until he started humming that he calmed down. It's one of those children's songs, like a nursery rhyme…Shit…Damn. Oh, "You Are My Sunshine." That's the one. Yeah, he started humming that song. I was so freaked out by this time, I didn't know what was going to happen. I begged to be untied. The more I talked to him, the angrier he became. He started blaming me for his immoral sexual conduct. He came up on the bed, pulled a knife out of the nightstand, and started making these small cuts across my skin. He kept repeating that he needed to make small, slow cuts to drain the evil blood from my body. That it was the only way. I asked him what he meant by that, and he said he needed to spill the blood of sinners in order to be allowed to return. I know this sounds fucked up. I think he knew he was going to die. It was as if he was making plans to…I don't know, come back from the dead.

When he finally put the knife down, he was smiling at me. I thought it was over, that he would untie me. He moved to my feet instead. He licked between my toes, slobbering like a rabid dog. His saliva dripped down my arch and heel. He started sucking on my toes. He bit them. It wasn't a nibble. He was chewing on them, hard. I felt several bones in my toes crack in his mouth as he gnawed on them. He looked up at me. His teeth were red from the blood he'd drawn from my toes. He told me he would be back, that he was getting hungry.

I knew I had to do something before he came back. I knew he wasn't going to let me live. I pulled on the ropes that bound my hands to the headboard. I felt the knot give, then it tightened again. I couldn't slip my wrist out of it. I pulled as hard as I could, twisting my hand. The pressure grew. Tears rolled down my face. I felt a bone snap in my hand. I bit my tongue to hold back the screams so he wouldn't hear me. I ended up biting the tip of my tongue off. I had broken my thumb and wrist. I was able to put my hand through at that point. I reached over to untie my left hand as I heard him coming up the stairs. I laid back down on the bed, hoping he wouldn't notice that my hands were free.

I literally shit myself when I saw him come into the room carrying a large pair of shrub clippers. The hot, wet shit soaked into the sheets. He didn't seem to notice. He crawled up on the foot of the bed, opening the curved metal blades of the clipper. He slipped my little toe between the blades. I wanted to react. I couldn't do anything. I think I was in shock. The handles of the clippers came together. I never felt the blades slicing off my toe. It was the pain after the toe was severed that broke my paralysis. I let go of the wooden slates of the headboard, grabbed the knife, and screamed as I sat up in bed. The handle was slippery from the shit. He turned toward me as I screamed. His face was expressionless. I waved the knife through the air, not caring where it hit him, so long as it did. The blade sliced through his bicep. He dropped the clippers on the floor. He growled at me, then flung himself on top of me. I raised

the knife and shoved it into his back. His heavy weight
fell against me. He was still breathing. I rolled him off the
bed. I yanked the knife from his back and used it to cut the
rope around my ankles. I grabbed my clothes and ran out
of the house. Once out in the street I called the police. By
the time they got there, he was gone.

Adam closed the report. A chill swept across his skin. He
looked over at Sean—he looked peaceful and relaxed. A childlike
smile creased his face. Adam felt a wave of emotions hit him as
he realized that what Sean had been experiencing was real. Gerald
Brink had found a way to come back from the dead. Goose bumps
scattered over Adam's arms. Adam walked over to the couch and sat
down, placing Sean's feet across his lap. Sean stirred. Adam rested
his head against the back of the couch and fell asleep.

Adam awoke to a deep, hollow laugh coming from Sean's
bedroom. Sean's body shook. He kicked his feet hitting Adam in
the gut. Adam's mind flashed to the grave rubbing hanging on the
bedroom wall. He ran to the kitchen pantry to find Sean's toolkit. He
knelt down, dumping the contents out onto the ceramic floor. The
clattering of nails, screwdrivers, and wrenches crashed around his
feet. The hammer wasn't there. He closed his eyes to clear his mind
from the clutter. It was then that he remembered Sean using the
hammer to hang the cloth. He walked into the living room. Adam
looked down at Sean sleeping on the couch. Sean's legs twitched.
His breathing became heavy. The laughter died as Adam reached the
hallway. Adam stayed close to the wall as he made his way toward
the closed door.

Adam pressed the side of his face against the door as he gripped
the doorknob. Through the door, he could hear the muffled sounds of
humming. The humming became intermittent, mixing with words;
then the humming stopped—lyrics took over.

Adam's heart drummed in his ears. His hand trembled, shaking
the door in its frame. He closed his eyes for a brief moment before
turning the knob. He charged into the room. The room was empty.
Everything was in its place. He stood, without moving—waiting.

The silence of the room fell around him as if it were masking Gerald's words.

Through the early morning light, he saw something out of his peripheral vision pass by the glass frame of the rubbing. He focused on the cloth hanging from the wall. He walked up to it. The cloth appeared dirtier, as if it were aging. The wax that highlighted the carvings had become cracked and brittle. Adam bent down, keeping his eyes on the cloth. He stretched his fingers until they touched the metal head of the hammer. He gripped the handle and stood up. He faced the eyes that stared back at him in their dull gray tones. Adrenaline raced through his body. Sweat broke out across his chilled skin. He raised the hammer, aimed, and swung.

The glass shattered. He swung again. The sound of breaking glass gave him a sense of control. A rush of emotions—anger, fear, and hatred—flew out of him with each swing of the hammer. Glass and drywall flew around him as he continued his assault on the wall hanging. The gray wax broke and fell from the cloth. Adam found himself grinning, almost laughing as the hammer tore into the cloth and the framed piece crashed to the floor. Adam fell to the floor, following the rubbing. He gripped the handle of the hammer with both hands and continued his attack.

"Jesus, Adam, what are you doing?" Sean leaned against the door frame.

"I'm sorry, I had to destroy it." Adam looked up at Sean; the tattered rag hung from the head of the hammer. "It's how he did it. It has to be."

"What are you talking about?" Sean knelt down next to Adam.

"Gerald. This is how he came back from the dead. Through the grave rubbing we did." Adam saw the confused expression on Sean's face. The sight of him seemed to calm Adam. "Sean, I'm sorry I didn't believe you. Gerald is real. It wasn't a dream, but you don't have to worry anymore. I stopped him. It's over. I've destroyed his way in."

"Come on. Let's get you out of here." Sean stood up pulling Adam up with him.

The floor creaked in the hallway. Adam and Sean paused, staring off through the bedroom door. Silence. Another creak. Something crashed in the living room. Adam shook with nerves as he heard the familiar song.

"Adam, you need to leave."

"What? No. We're both getting out of here." Adam grabbed Sean's hand and started to walk toward the bedroom door.

"Adam, listen, we don't have time to argue about this." Sean held Adam back.

"What are you talking about? I'm not leaving here without you."

"He wants you to leave. He's not going to let me go. I'm afraid what he'll do to you if I try to leave."

"How do you know this?"

"I can hear his thoughts inside my mind as if they are becoming my own thoughts. I can't explain it. Adam, you have to go."

"Sean, I'm not—"

"Adam, please go. Do whatever you have to do to find a way out of this. You have to…"

"What, what's wrong?"

"He said he'll kill me if you don't leave. Adam, please, you need to go."

"But I don't know how to help you." Tears filled Adam's eyes. He stared at Sean. A tear rolled down Sean's face. "I love you."

"I love you too." Sean pulled Adam into him and wrapped his arms around Adam. "Summerland," he whispered in Adam's ear.

"Summerland? What—" Adam's words were cut off as Sean placed a hand across Adam's mouth. Sean shook his head.

"You need to leave. He's getting angry." Sean squeezed Adam's hand and walked him to the door. "Don't forget."

"Wait." Adam pulled free from Sean. He ran to the dining room table and gathered up the papers from the police report. "I'll find a way, I promise."

"Be careful, Adam."

Adam turned to say good-bye. He stared at the closed door. The deadbolt clicked into place. "I love you," Adam whispered before heading down the stairs. Tears slid down his cheeks, filling the creases between his nose and upper lip. He sat behind the wheel of the car. He glanced up at the window, thinking, hoping it would be Sean. The figure in the window stood taller and more muscular than Sean's frame. It approached the window and pressed its face against the glass. The face staring down at Adam was Gerald's.

Adam turned the ignition over as he stared at Gerald in the window. He put the car in reverse and backed down the driveway. Seeing Gerald's face in the window, knowing that he was in there, alone with Sean, sent Adam into a fit of rage. He was going to beat him. He was going to get Sean back. He took off down the street heading to where it all began, Mount Auburn Cemetery.

The main gate was locked. Adam looked at the clock in the car. The cemetery hadn't opened yet. He wasn't going to wait. He backed out and pulled into the vacant lot across the street. As he stepped out of the car, memories of that night with Sean flashed in his mind. He ran across the road and down the side of the cemetery. He pulled himself through the same opening in the fence. He looked around, questioning which direction they had gone. Everything looked different in the light of day. He turned to the right and headed toward the back of the property.

"What in the hell are you doing in here?" a gruff voice shouted.

"Jesus." Adam turned around. An elderly woman approached him. She walked with a cane, taking tiny steps on the gravel path. Her long, unkempt gray hair blew out behind her in the breeze.

"There ain't no Jesus here, young fella." She paused and looked around. "Nope, Jesus ain't here no more, if he was ever here at all." She walked up to Adam.

"Who are you?"

"Name's Abigail, I watch over the place. Don't you know what closed means? That means we ain't seeing any visitors."

"Look, I don't have time for this. I'm looking for a grave." Adam could smell mothballs coming off the old woman's clothes. It reminded him of his grandmother's scent.

"We got plenty of them. Take your pick. What'd you say your name was?"

"I'm Adam. I'm trying to find a gravesite my friend and I saw the other night. I think it was back over there." Adam pointed off to his left. "Please, I know you're closed, but this is important."

"Nope, sorry I can't do that. You see, there ain't nothing back there. It's not plotted, just empty ground."

"We were there. We saw it."

"Look, young man. I don't let anyone back in that area of the property for nothing. There ain't nothing back there to see. So either you are lying to me, or you and your friend were here when you weren't supposed to..." She paused, shaking her head. "You came here just like you did now, didn't you? Through that hole in the fence?"

"The grave." Adam ignored the old woman's question. "It was for a man by the name of Gerald Brink. I know..." Adam saw a change in her expression. "You know which grave I'm talking about, don't you."

"What in God's name have you boys done?" Abigail moved to go around him.

"Wait." Adam blocked her path. Abigail threw her hand straight out in front of her. The impact hit Adam in the chest, shoving him off the path. Her strength took Adam by surprise. He lost his footing on a small headstone. Adam stumbled to his feet and ran after her. "What do you know about this grave?"

"I know more than I care to. You young people are always getting yourselves into messes that I have to clean up. He's out there for a reason. You boys couldn't figure that one out on your own?"

They stopped at the edge of the small headstone. Adam looked down at the marker, remembering how innocent that evening had felt. "What do you know about this grave or the man buried here? Please, it's important."

"You didn't dig up the body?" Abigail sounded surprised.

"Of course not."

"Thank the Lord for that small blessing." She looked up at Adam. "It's best you leave here and forget you ever saw this grave. Gerald Brink was an evil man. As a child he stayed to himself. He never made any friends. He sat in his room most of his childhood talking to himself. No one ever thought he'd turn into such a vicious killer. He murdered eleven young men just like you over a period of six months. He was gay, just like you…"

"How do you know about me?"

"Don't interrupt an old woman, it ain't polite. He hated himself 'cause of his lust for other men. He felt dirty, ashamed. I kept telling him it wasn't a bad or unholy thing, just different is all. He couldn't see past the rage. It was when he acted on those desires that he changed. He blamed those poor innocent boys. After the first murder, he became a different person. You could see it in his eyes. He craved the kill. It's what kept him going. He lived to torture them, to kill them, and to feed from them."

"Abigail, how do you know so much about him?"

"He was my son."

"Your son? That would make you…"

"One-hundred twenty-six, to be exact." She smiled with a mouth full of crooked yellow teeth. "When you get my age you don't care who knows."

"But how…"

"You don't need to know any more than I've already told you. It's better that way, safer too."

"One last question. Have you ever heard of a place called Summerland?"

"Sweet Jesus!" Abigail crossed herself. "What did you two boys go and do that night?"

"Sean is an artist. Well, he's a photographer. He wanted to do a grave rubbing…"

"Dear Jesus, you didn't." Abigail looked down at the headstone. "You've done gotten yourself into a mess of trouble, young man. I don't like speaking about him so close to his resting place. I sometimes think he listens if you get too close. Suppose we take a walk so you can tell me what you and your friend did here."

"We came in through the opening in the fence back there. We just happened to find his marker."

"There isn't such a thing as just happening when it has to do with my Gerry. He knew you were looking."

"Looking?"

"I'll tell you all you need to know, but first finish your story."

"We finished the rubbing, took it back to Sean's place, framed it, and hung it on his bedroom wall."

"You and your friend are in serious trouble." Abigail stopped. She took Adam's hands in hers. "You brought him back through the cloth, though I reckon you already know that or you wouldn't be here. He's come for your boyfriend, hasn't he?"

"Yes, it's getting bad. You never answered me. What is Summerland and what does it have to do with your son?"

"Let's sit a spell. I'm feeling a bit winded." Abigail led Adam to a small bench. "I knew what Gerald was doing, but I couldn't stop him. He was my baby boy. A mother can't just turn her back on her only child, no matter how bad he is. It wasn't till after he died in my living room and the cops took him away that I found out just how wrong he had become."

"Wrong?"

"After those men rummaged through my house looking for stuff, I found a chest hidden away in the basement. It was full of the black arts: books, trinkets, amulets. He even kept a journal documenting each of the murders. He began eating the body parts of those boys, believing it would allow him access to our world after he died."

"I still don't understand."

"I began studying his books trying to find anything I could use to keep him dead. That's when I first heard of Summerland. The witches of certain traditions believe there is a place where your spirit goes after you die. It's here you are to remain until you have learnt all of life's lessons. Once you have understood everything from your past life, you are reborn. Then the process starts over."

"What does that have to do with Gerald or our grave rubbing?"

"For forty years Gerald laid in that grave over there. I put him there so no one would ever find him. Gerald was too evil a man when he died to ever learn anything from his mistakes, so his soul rotted in Summerland, waiting. Your grave rubbing gave him a way out."

"What does he want with Sean?"

"Knowing my Gerry the way I do, he wants to send Sean's soul back in his place. That way he can live again through Sean's body."

"You have to help us."

"I'm too old to be messing with the kind of magick it would take to stop him. I don't have the strength left in me for that kind of fight." Abigail stood up. "There's only one person I know who has the power it's going to take to stop my son."

"Who?"

"Madam Shata. She lives near Pigeon Cove on the outskirts of Halibut Point. She ain't easy to find, but my guess is she's your only hope. You'll need to follow highway 128 toward Gloucester. From there take 127 through Pigeon Cove until you come to Gott Lane. It's a barren wasteland if you ask me, but that's where you'll find her. Most of the local folks know about her, so if you get lost just ask anybody, they'll direct you. You best be going if you want to help your friend. Time's running out, I'm afraid."

"Wait, you can't just leave." Adam grabbed her arm. "Please, you have to try. He's your son, he'll listen to you."

"My son doesn't exist anymore, hasn't since his first kill. That's when I lost him to the darkness. His soul belongs to Satan now." Abigail shook her head as she looked at Adam. "Oh, no. No, don't you go laying no guilt trip on this old lady. I can see it in your eyes. You had no right coming in here and meddling with things you know nothing about." She bit her lip and placed her hands on her hips. "Damn you boys. Give me the rubbing?"

"I don't have it."

"Sweet Jesus. Please don't tell me it's back there with him? We can't do anything until we have that cloth."

"Please, come with me. It's a short drive."

"I'm going to regret it, but take me to him."

They walked back to the car in silence. Adam struggled with the reality of what was happening and even more with what was to come.

"Remember," Abigail broke the silence as she pulled on her seat belt, "you only have one task, so don't fuck it up. Just get the cloth and make it to Pigeon Cove. That's where you'll find Madam Shata. She'll know what to do."

"I'm going to check on Sean first."

"You will do no such thing, young man. You do this my way, or I won't help you. Is that clear?"

"I'm not going to just leave him there without checking on him first."

"You don't even know if it's still Sean in there."

"What about you?"

"Don't worry about me. Just get yourself out of there and find a way to save your friend.

Abigail patted Adam's knee. "Just remember, no matter what happens, get the cloth and get out."

Adam pulled into the driveway of Sean's home. He looked up at the window expecting to see Sean or, worse, Gerald. The window was empty. Adam and Abigail got out of the car and walked up the steps.

"Sean?" Adam shouted as he unlocked the door. Adam and Abigail walked into the living room. The stale, sour air fell around them. "Stay here," Adam whispered, "I'm going into the bedroom to get the cloth."

"Adam?" Sean's voice drifted through the room. "Adam. Why did you come back? You have to leave."

"Oh my God, Sean, what's happened to you?" Adam ran over to the recliner where Sean sat rocking. His face, covered with several days' growth of whiskers, looked ashen and thin. His lips were cracked. Blood seeped out from the broken skin. His clothes, stained with blood and sweat, hung from his thinning body. Adam pulled Sean into an embrace and began to cry. "Sean…"

"What in the fuck is this?" The deep, rough voice of Gerald

spilled from the hallway. "That bitch has no business here." He walked over to the recliner, picked Adam up, and threw him across the room. "He's mine."

"Sean, please." Adam pulled himself up against the wall. He saw Sean look at him with a blank stare. Sean's lips trembled. A tear fell from his emotionless eye.

"Adam, it's not Sean. You need to leave." Abigail walked toward them.

"Mother, I wish I could say it was good to see you, but I'd be lying."

"Gerald, you don't fool me. I know the transformation is far from over for you. You don't have the strength yet to fight me." Abigail looked over at Adam. "Go!"

"I may be far from perfect at the moment, but you're wrong about one thing, old woman." Gerald charged toward Abigail and grabbed her by the throat. He shoved her up against the wall, which cracked from the impact. "I'm stronger than you."

Adam ran into the bedroom. The shattered remains of the frame lay scattered on the carpeting. The torn cloth was still among the debris. Adam fell to the floor and brushed pieces of the broken glass away. He picked it up and shoved it into his pocket. As Adam stood he noticed Sean standing at the bedroom door. A thin trail of blood ran from the inside corner of each eye. Adam ran to him and brushed the blood away.

"Hurry." Sean looked at him with bloodstained eyes.

"I'll be back as soon as I can." Adam kissed Sean. His lips were cold. He could taste the drying blood through Sean's split lips. "Don't let him do this to you, Sean. You have to fight." Adam hesitated. "I wish I could...the pills." He looked around and saw them sitting on the nightstand next to the bed, along with the glass of water. "Come on." He walked Sean to the bed. "Here, take these. It will knock you out, and hopefully Gerald as well." Adam slipped the pills in Sean's mouth and tipped the water to his lips. Sean managed to swallow them. "Just lay down and let the pills do their thing." He smiled at Sean through tear-filled eyes. He bent down and kissed

Sean's forehead. "I promise, I'll be back before dark." He left the bedroom without looking back. Adam walked into the living room, where Abigail was still struggling with Gerald.

"Why won't you die, bitch?" Gerald growled as he tightened the grip around Abigail's neck.

Adam watched with horror as Abigail's thumbs pressed deeply into Gerald's eye sockets. His mind flashed to Sean with the blood running from his eyes. "Abigail, no!"

She looked at Adam. He was the last thing she saw as Gerald snapped her neck. Her hands fell from his face. Her body went limp. Gerald released her and she slumped to the floor.

Adam took off running before Gerald had time to react. Adam opened the front door and slammed it behind him, hoping Gerald would be too concerned with his own business to follow him. Adam pulled out of the driveway without looking back and headed onto highway 128 toward Gloucester.

An hour later he turned onto Gott Lane. It was nothing more than a narrow one-lane road cut out of the coastal cliffs and ocean vegetation. Adam had been accompanied by the warmth of the morning sun for most of the drive, but as he approached Pigeon Cove the sun was obscured by thick, gray clouds. Adam slowed his speed against the strong winds that pummeled the car.

The narrow path opened up onto a makeshift parking area overlooking the ocean. The car skidded on the damp surface of the granite before coming to a stop. Adam stepped out of the car and walked to the edge of the cliffs. He stared down an eight-hundred-foot drop. Large, angry waves crashed against the jagged rocks below. The wind howled around him. He felt small and insignificant surrounded by such a large expanse of raw nature. To his left he noticed a small path. He followed it with cautious steps as it led him down the side of the steep, rocky cliffs.

The cool, moist air clung to Adam's clothes as he continued down the slope. A faint light appeared through the thick mist. As he approached it, the fog and moisture broke. His vision cleared. A house built into the side of the cliffs opened up to him. A candle sitting in a window had been his guiding light. The small wooden framed house, weathered and gray with age, stood alone against the rocky cliffs. The door opened before he had a chance to knock.

"Adam, I'm so glad you found me." The woman's voice held a power and force under her soft-spoken tones. "Where are my manners? Please, come in out of that dreadful fizz that they call weather in these parts. It does crazy stuff to my hair." She patted down her long, uncombed hair. "I am Madam Shata, the one you seek."

"How did you know I was coming?" Madam Shata was nothing like Adam had expected. She stood less than five feet tall. She had a solid build without being overweight. Her long, dirty blond hair hung below her shoulders, with strands partially covering her eyes. Black roots along her scalp gave away her semi-beauty secrets. She had a round face, yet her features were flat. Adam couldn't help compare her to the angelic face of a shih tzu. He immediately trusted her.

"There will be time later for such trivial questions and answers. We must now put our energies on more urgent matters—the life of your friend Sean." Madam Shata grabbed Adam's hand and pulled him across the tiny room. "Please, warm yourself by the fire while we prepare for what's to come."

"But how...?"

"Shhh." Madam Shata raised a finger to her thin, pursed lips. "Please, we don't have much time. You must put your faith in me, without question, without fail, if we are to be victorious over the dark beast that has invaded your friend." Madam Shata perched on an ottoman in front of Adam.

"Abigail said you would want to see the cloth." Adam pulled the torn cloth from his back pocket.

"Yes, please. I must observe the cloth from which the escaped..." Madam Shata's brown eyes grew in disbelief as she studied the cloth. "Oh dear, this is far worse than I could have guessed. Your friend is in much more danger than I anticipated."

"What, what is it?"

"These eyes." She pointed to the corners of the cloth. "They were on the headstone?"

"Yes."

"I assumed the cloth was the vessel from which his soul was able to escape." Madam Shata shook her head in a slow, rhythmic sway. "I am sorry. That was a deadly assumption on my part."

"What are you talking about?" Adam's voice rose in panic. "Gerald had to have been released into the cloth. It was hanging in Sean's bedroom when all this started."

"Here, there, it doesn't matter where the cloth was located. The cloth was not the portal and the portal was not the cloth. Your friend Sean has been the vessel all along."

"That's not possible."

"All things are possible with a little help from the dark side." Madam Shata slid off the ottoman to kneel in front of Adam. "You see these symbols?" She pointed to each corner with her short, pudgy fingers. "These eyes are part of a curse, if you will. Some folks call it the evil eye. It doesn't matter what you call it, it's not a good sign for your friend. The eyes were on all four corners of the headstone for a reason. They are there to act as a binding spell to keep the evil that rested below the ground from rising. When your friend rubbed the grave, he removed the essence of the spell from the headstone, allowing Gerald to escape. He attached himself to the person who released him—Sean. The cloth was just the medium by which the curse was lifted."

"I'm sorry, I still don't follow you."

"It would be much easier if the cloth was the vessel, for then we could enslave Gerald's soul back into the cloth. We are not so fortunate. Our jobs will be a bit more complicated than that."

"What do we have to do?"

"If the cloth had been the vessel, we could have reversed the spell from the comfort and protection of where we are at this moment. Alas, the Goddess is challenging us today. She is making sure we are worthy of what we are about to ask of her. We must bring both Sean and Gerald to the cemetery. We must reverse the spell that has gripped Sean, while at the same time binding Gerald's soul back to the ground."

"But it's going to work, right?"

"There are many factors that will play a significant role in the coming hours. Our success depends on everything coming together at the right moment. Since we cannot control all the elements in this world, there is no way to be sure of anything. It is time we prepare for our journey." Madam Shata, stood holding her hand out to Adam. "Come."

Adam took Madam Shata's hand and was led into a smaller room. The air, filled with years of varying incense, pricked Adam's nose. He followed her gesture, taking a seat on a large cushion in the center of the floor. He watched her select several candles from the built-in bookcases that lined the short wall. She sat down on the other side of a small wooden table, placed a metal burner in the center, struck a match, and lit the powered contents. The air filled with sage and other heady aromas.

"Hold out your hands with your palms extended upward while leaving some room between the table and the back of your hand."

Adam did as instructed. She repositioned his hands further away from the burner to the edges of the table. He watched as she placed a white candle in each of his palms. Nerves broke through his body. His arms twitched. His hands and fingers trembled as he tried to balance the unlit candles.

"You must remain quiet from this point forward. I need you to clear your mind of everything, including Sean. You must concentrate on my words and nothing else. Can you do that?"

"Yes." Adam closed his eyes. He took a deep breath of the scented air. He focused on the weight of the candles and the smell of the incense drifting around him. Adam heard the strike of a match, then the smell of sulfur. The heat of the flame closed in on his hands. He heard a wispy breath as Madam Shata extinguished the match. Her tiny hands slipped underneath his.

"By dragon wing and dragon claw, may our defense be without flaw. Concealed by the Goddess's light, please remove us from his sight. Go before we prepare to fight, and blind our foe with all your might. Full of rage and terrible ire, burn him with your blinding fires. Dark and terrible by thy wrath, Goddess protect us on our path."

Adam felt her hands slip away. He opened his eyes. The light from the candles danced shadows across Madam Shata's face. She caught him looking. She smiled. She licked her thumb and forefinger before extinguishing one of the candles. She squeezed the black ash of the wick between her fingers and then drew three single lines across Adam's forehead. She put out the second candle, marking her forehead with the same symbols.

"We must gather our supplies and be on our way. Gerald is growing stronger by the minute. Sean, I'm afraid, is weaker. Gerald knows you have found me. The rage in him is powerful. The protection spell should help keep our movements and plan hidden from him, but the spell will not last long. We must get Sean out of the house before it dissipates. Once we're safely out of the house with Sean, Gerald will know where to find us—at his grave."

❖

The drive back to Cambridge seemed twice as long to Adam as the drive out. He had hoped to spend the time asking questions, to better understand what was needed to send Gerald back and how it was going to affect Sean. From the moment they left the cliffs, however, Adam knew his questions would have to wait. Madam Shata closed her eyes the minute she took her seat. She sat in silence. Adam figured she needed to meditate, to draw energy, or just to rest before the final confrontation with Gerald. It wasn't until they had pulled into the driveway of Sean's house that she spoke. Her words cut through Adam like jagged pieces of glass.

"I must warn you that Sean is in terrible shape. The transformation is almost complete. There is very little of him left. He probably won't recognize you."

"We can still do this, right?"

"Yes, I can send Gerald back, but…"

"What? What are you not telling me?"

"I'm not sure how much of Sean can be saved. Much of who Sean is, or was, is now intertwined with Gerald. Sending Gerald back at this late stage may send parts of Sean back with him. There's no guarantee how Sean will end up."

"Let's get up there and get him before we lose any more time."

"Even with the protection spell, Gerald may be able to sense me or my powers. We can't take that chance. You must go alone. The protection spell will keep you safe. I will stay here, ready to leave when you come out."

Adam opened the car door and ran up the steps and in through the front door. The weight of the room stopped him cold. The air was stale, acrid. The silence of the condo was deafening. The early afternoon light cast distorted shadows against the off-white walls as he walked down the narrow hallway. The door to Sean's bedroom stood ajar. Adam pushed it open. It creaked against his weight. His heart sank as he looked toward the bed. Gerald lay next to Sean's emaciated body.

"Sean?" Adam ran to the edge of the bed. He lost control and started to cry. Sean had lost most of his weight. His pale, drawn skin clung to his bones. His eyes moved in their deep, hard sockets, meeting Adam's horrified gaze. His lips quivered as they curled into what Adam thought was a smile. He slipped his hands under Sean's body and lifted him from the bed.

Adam stopped cold as he noticed Gerald stirring. His heart pounded in his chest. He watched as Gerald opened his eyes and looked around the room. Adam stood, paralyzed, waiting for Gerald to notice him. Gerald laid his head back down on the pillow and wrapped his arm around the empty space where Sean had been. Adam, still holding his breath, backed away from the bed. When he reached the hallway, he turned around and took off running. At the bottom of the stairs he saw Madam Shata get out of the car. She opened the back door. Adam slid into the backseat, cradling Sean in his arms. They backed out of the driveway and headed toward the cemetery.

"Come on, sweetie, hold on. We're going to get you out of this." Adam kissed Sean's forehead. His skin felt deathly cold. Tears fell from Adam's cheeks. "Please, babe. You have to hold on. I know you saw me. I saw you smile at me. You just have to hang on a while longer." Adam rocked Sean until they stopped at the entrance of the cemetery. Adam opened the car door and slipped out of the backseat with Sean in his arms. Madam Shata joined him with her large flowered bag slung over her shoulder.

"We must hurry." Madam Shata grabbed Adam's elbow, pulling him along behind her. "The protection spell is fading. I can feel Gerald's emotions. I've never felt such rage coming from one person. He's stronger than I expected, and he's coming for us."

Adam ran behind Madam Shata, trying to keep up. She had veered off the path and now dodged the various tombstones. He had never seen such determination and agility in a person of her size or age. Adam did his best to follow her without tripping over his own feet. He bumped into her when she stopped at the foot of Gerald's grave.

"Sit him down here." She pointed to the ground next to her foot. "He must be kneeling, and in his weakened state that means you're going to have to hold him in position."

Adam lowered himself to the ground. He placed Sean in the position Madam Shata had instructed. Adam watched with growing panic as Madam Shata fell to the ground alongside him and began digging a hole in the center of Gerald's grave. He looked around as a cold wind flew up around them. The leaves on the trees swayed and shook. The branches creaked and groaned against the force. Limbs snapped and flew through the bustling air, their weight shaking the ground as they landed. "Oh my God, listen." Adam felt his heart sink as he heard Gerald's voice, singing "You Are My Sunshine," being carried through the wind.

"You have to hurry!" Adam's voice rose. He tightened his arm around Sean and held him closer, rocking him as he tried to focus on Madam Shata's preparations. She lit a black candle, then tilted it, forcing some of the wax to drip into the bottom of a dark gray bowl. She secured the candle to the hot wax, grabbed a container of water from her large bag, and filled the bowl with it.

"I want him back." Gerald's voice echoed around them. "You took him from me and I want him back."

"We must focus our energy on the flame," Madame Shata said as the wind throttled and beat the flame. It held strong against the wind. "Adam, you must be Sean's vessel. Hold him close. Concentrate on the flame. Send all of your negative energy into the flame. Do not listen to Gerald no matter what happens. Do not break your concentration, or Sean will be lost."

"In the name of the Gods and all ye spirits." Madam Shata's voice rose over the sounds of the wind and Gerald's singing. "In the name of the light and the dark, and the Gods of the Netherworlds, let whosoever has cast this curse upon Sean suffer it for themselves."

"What's happening?" Adam held Sean tighter as Sean's body began to shake and convulse. A brownish gray sludge spewed from Sean's lips. He spat and vomited with each convulsion.

"Concentrate, Adam!" Madam Shata glanced behind them before continuing. "Let this candle be their candle. This burning, their burning. This curse, their curse. Let the pain they have caused fall upon themselves."

Sean's convulsions became stronger. His body fell upon the grave. The foul-smelling liquid sprayed from his mouth and nose, covering his face and the grass he lay in. His eyelids opened and his eyes rolled back in his head. Sockets of pure white stared back at Adam and Madam Shata.

"Fucking bitch!" Gerald's voice blew around them. The sounds of his breathing echoed through the trees, battering their faces and skin.

"Quick, Adam, grab the candle and invert it, sending the curse into the water." Madam Shata's words were cut short.

Adam looked over at her with shock and horror as an invisible force lifted Madam Shata off the ground and threw her through the air. Adam flinched as he heard her body slam into the trunk of an old oak tree.

The fear suddenly subsided in Adam. A calm rushed through him. His mind cleared as if he had been in control the entire time. He knew what had to happen next. He crawled over Sean. His chest and arms fell in the pool of mucus and sludge. He grabbed the candle and tipped it upside down in the bowl of water. "May the curse you have delivered flow back through your veins," Adam shouted. "May—"

"You do it Adam and Sean will die." Gerald's voice echoed through the air. "You don't want to kill Sean, do you?"

"Fuck you, Gerald!" Adam screamed until his lungs felt like they would burst. "May the curse bind you in hell once more!" He poured the water into the hole that Madam Shata had dug, then placed the candle into the water. The ground shook as Adam scooped up the loose earth and filled in the hole.

Adam crawled back to Sean. He covered Sean's frail body with his own, protecting him from the storm that was Gerald's anger. The wind continued to intensify and howl with a deep, guttural sound. Adam could only hope that the vocal sounds he heard was Gerald's agony as his spirit went back to Summerland.

Adam looked across the gravel path at Madam Shata lying on the ground. He wanted to go to her, but Sean had to be his first priority. He knew she would understand. He felt a faint pounding against his arm and realized Sean's pulse had gotten stronger. He sat, bringing Sean up in his arms. Adam kissed Sean's forehead, his cheek, and his cold lips.

"Come on, Sean. It's over. Come back to..." Adam's heart leapt into his throat as a hand fell against his shoulder. He looked up. Madam Shata stood behind him. "Are you okay?"

"It will take more than the likes of Gerald to stop me. I'll be fine, but thank you, Adam, for your concern. It's Sean who needs our attention. Come, let's get him to the car and back home."

❖

Adam and Madam Shata stood over Sean's bed. They had removed his soiled clothes and covered him with layers of blankets to help warm him. Sean drifted in and out of consciousness as his body fought to recover. His moments of lucidity were brief and fuzzy, yet Adam could see recognition in his eyes.

"He'll be okay." Madam Shata broke the silence of the room. "It will take a while for him to heal, but he will."

"Thank you." Adam turned to face Madam Shata. "I don't know how we could ever begin to repay you for what you've done."

"There is no need for repayment. Sean's life is my reward." She placed her hand in Adam's. "You take care of him. He'll need you more than ever." She rose up on her toes and kissed Adam's cheek. "I must go. Take care of yourself, Adam."

"Thank you again." A tear formed in the corner of his eye as he watched Madam Shata walk out of the bedroom. He heard the front door shut as she left the house. Adam crawled under the covers and pulled Sean into him. As he drifted off to sleep, Gerald's song played in his mind.

FOREVER

"Of course I will love you forever," I whispered only yesterday to Tony as my cold lips brushed against his ear. How different "forever" sounded to the two of us. The tone in his voice chilled my thoughts when I realized what he was asking me to do.

I hope he understands my refusal to make him like me. My decision has nothing to do with our love. There is nothing that would make me happier than to spend forever not growing old with him. The joy I will have to imagine. I want to give him what he has asked for, but I cannot do to him what was so violently done to me.

❖

I was born in London. The year was 1719 and I had just finished celebrating my twenty-seventh birthday with some friends. The quantity of spirits we had consumed helped keep us going against the cold November air. I was the bachelor in the group, which was fine with me. I knew I was different. I knew I lusted after men, about which we didn't speak then. I had heard about "Molly houses," where men could go to be with other men. However, I never seemed to have enough courage to walk into such an establishment by myself. At twenty-seven, I was still a virgin.

After my friends dropped me off at my flat, I decided tonight was the night. I felt alive for the first time in my life, and I knew instinctively that this was the night I would experience the pure, raw power of another man's love.

The bells had long ago sounded midnight when I arrived at the ale house in a small, crowded area off Compton Street. I paused just outside the door, took a deep breath, and steadied myself. I opened the door and stepped inside. From within the tiny pub, it seemed as if the world I left outside stopped. Heads turned in my direction, looking at the stranger standing in the doorway. The excitement grew in my breeches, tingling through every hair on my body. I lit up a small pipe, took a long, deep draw, and exhaled before making my way to an empty stool by the bar.

The short, pudgy man behind the bar greeted me immediately—and perhaps impertinently. He looked young, not a wrinkle on his face. He wore a clean white shirt and black breeches. He smiled at me as if he could read my mind.

"Your best gin, my good man," I said even before he asked me. He smiled and poured the drink.

"Haven't spied you here before, m'lord." He set the bottle down next to my glass. "Are you but recently come to the city?"

"Born and raised here, my good man." I finished the small serving off in one gulp and gestured for another. The gin warmed my body and calmed my nerves. I rekindled my pipe as the bartender left. I turned in my seat to take in the sights around me. The lighting was dim, and the billowing smoke made it difficult to see. I hadn't learned any of the signs or signals by which men let other men know of their purpose, so I resolved to face the bar and keep to myself. I was too much a novice to make advances.

I was on my third drink and deep in thoughts of leaving when someone came to sit beside me. I tilted my head to the left and looked at him out of the corner of my eye. He sat calmly swirling his drink. He turned to look at me. His eyes were pitch black, surrounded by the purest white I had ever seen. His face was smooth except for a small scar upon his right cheek. His long, wavy hair hung loosely about his face.

"I do not know you, sir." He spoke quietly, the accent German.

"I am known to my intimates as Stephan." He reached and took my hand in his.

"Are we intimate, then, sir?" His hand was cold. "I am known as Alex."

"So, Alex." He smiled at the indiscretion. "What wind blew you here tonight?" He moved in a little closer to me. "You appear to be lost at sea."

I started to reply. His hand moved upon my leg. I lost my words as I looked down in my lap and watched his fingers trace small circles upon my thigh. The tingling returned to my loins. I could feel myself growing firmer, thicker behind my linens. He noticed the movement and then moved one of his fingers over the bulge in my breeches. A small moan escaped my lips. I reddened with shame.

He laughed. "You have never done this before, have you?" His finger made small circles over my firmness.

"No."

"Surely it is time." He moved his hand from my lap and finished his drink. He stood up. "Will you accompany me, sir?"

I didn't move at first, and then stood to face him. Our eyes met. I could feel his breath on my face. His scent invaded me. It was potent and unfamiliar. Lilac water perhaps, a mixture of beer, a man's odor, and then...something metallic. It called to something in me I did not know existed. There was nothing I wanted more in the world than to surrender my body to this stranger. We left the ale house together.

"My rooms lie near at hand." Stephan broke the silence that had fallen between us. "We can walk there, if you are agreeable."

"Indeed we can." I began to feel a bit uneasy. What would be expected of me upon our arrival? He seemed well versed in the art of hunting men. I hoped my inexperience would not repel him.

Within a few minutes we arrived at a surprisingly elegant building. The servants seemed to have gone to sleep. He opened the door himself and escorted me in.

He shut and locked the door behind us. His rooms were more generous than most in this part of London and well appointed.

Numerous candles lit tapestries, paintings, and a harpsichord lacquered in the deepest red. My attention was diverted from our surroundings when he walked to me and put his arms around my waist.

Stephan was taller than I by as much as a head. His dark, piercing eyes looked at me. No, that's not quite how it was. They looked *into* me. I could feel his desire press against me.

"You tremble," Stephan whispered. "Here, maybe this will help." He leaned down to draw my lips to his. Sudden warmth rushed through me the instant our lips met. My knees felt unstrung as the kiss lingered. He pulled away as gently and as quickly as he had commenced. His finger traced my lips. They quivered.

He removed his waistcoat. I stood transfixed. He removed his shoes and began to loosen his breeches. "Will you not join me?"

He undid the buttons and dropped the garment to the floor. I continued to stare as if frozen by the sight of him undressing before me. Beneath his immaculate shirt, his torso was smooth and hairless. He stepped out of his breeches, leaving his body exposed except for his innermost linen. I could tell his sex was large and heavy by the way it fell against the thin material. He walked to me and pushed my coat off my shoulders, letting it fall to the floor.

"Touch me," he said and brought my hand to his chest. My fingers trembled as they grazed his skin. The softness astonished me. I never knew a man's skin could be so soft. My finger brushed his left nipple. He smiled at my apparent nervousness.

I began to feel like I didn't exist in that time or place, as if I were watching us from above. I wasn't there, yet I could both feel and hear every touch, every word. I closed my eyes and felt his lips against my neck, his tongue licking the salt of my skin. I reached down to feel my swollen nature. I didn't recognize its size.

"Your body delights me," Stephan whispered in my ear as he pulled my shirt open. He kissed my chin and then my throat as he began a descent. I felt his tongue running through the hair on my chest, matting it to my skin with his spit. My breathing turned to gasps as he continued to move downward. I grabbed his head with my hands to steady myself as his tongue reached the end of my shirt and the beginning of my breeches. His hands slid back up my chest and pushed my shirt off my shoulders. He stood upright and kissed me. I wanted more, but didn't know if I could go on. He mesmerized me with his beauty and gentleness.

We stood facing each other in nothing but the flimsiest linen. He picked me up as if I weighed not more than a few pounds and carried me to his bed. He stood and removed the last of his garments, and then he leaned down without a word and removed mine.

He crawled on top of me, our bodies not quite touching. I could feel his sex against my skin as he lowered himself onto me. Our bodies pressed tightly together. He raised my legs and moved them over his shoulders. My heart jumped with his movements as he settled himself between my legs. I could feel his sex pressing against the length of my arse. I meant to enjoy the feeling, then he entered me without warning. He knew what I wanted, perhaps better than I, and how to give it to me.

The pain was sharp and came in waves as each inch of him entered deeper into my body. As the final thrust came, the slow movements we made together began to count a devilish dance.

As Stephan continued to push his way in and out of me, our bodies wet with each other's sweat, he asked me one simple question. "Will you love me forever?"

Without hesitation I replied, "Yes."

The force of his thrusts increased. The room began to spin. I sealed my eyes. My body shook from my very bones. I was covered in sweat. Our bodies seemed to leave the comfort of the bed. Was I floating several feet above it, his arms wrapped around me?

The pain was sharp—not in my arse, in my neck. Panic opened my eyes. I tried to pull myself free. His grip was too tight around my body. The burning in my blood forced tears from my eyes. I felt giddy, light-headed, the room darkening in my vision as I felt myself fall back to the bed.

I don't know how long I slept, if sleep I did, but when I awoke the sun was setting again. I was in my own room. I felt weak, though something else inside me felt strong. I called out to Stephan. There was no answer. Some hunger burned in the pit of my stomach. I tasted blood. Suddenly it came back to me—the night before, what Stephan had done.

Fear and anger raced through me as I absorbed the full impact of my own death.

Questions about my new existence flooded my mind, and I had no answers. I felt completely alone, cut off from everything I had once enjoyed. At that moment, I hated Stephan more than words could speak. I had to find him. He needed to pay for what he had done.

I paced the crowded streets, alone except for my thoughts. No one seemed to heed me. I stood in front of the ale house. Barely a day before, I had stood in the exact same place, nervous and excited about the possibility of finding someone to experience the pleasures of masculine love—someone to give me new life. I stood there less than a day later with my skin cold, my body dead. I stood there not with fear, but with anger and rage.

My senses seemed sharper, more attentive to my surroundings. I found my seat at the bar and ordered a gin. The same bartender served me. I looked around the familiar pub. Stephan was not to be found. As I continued watching the men, the hunger in my stomach grew. I smelled blood, blood that raced through the bodies of these men, these men who were alive. I began to hate *them* as well. Anger ripped through me, taking control of my passions.

Then I noticed someone watching me.

Our gazes locked as he made his way to where I sat. His dirty-blond hair hung about his shoulders. His eyes were a deep blue. As he approached, his scent engulfed me. He stood next to me without saying a word. His warm body brushed against mine. In my mind, I saw Stephan standing next to me. As he spoke, I heard Stephan's voice.

"Looking for a bloke, m'lord?" His voice sounded strong and confident, almost surly. He reached out and touched my chest.

"Yes."

"Looking for a particular lad?" His hand found an opening in my shirt. He slid a couple fingers in and ran them through my chest hair.

"No. You'll do just fine." I looked at him and smiled. I could feel his heart beating faster as I responded to his answer. I moved his hand out of my shirt and escorted him to the door.

I took him to my room. I didn't ask him his name and he didn't ask me mine. No need for niceties; our meeting was merchant's business. I shut and locked the door behind us. His lips were on mine within seconds. I picked him up and took him to my bed and laid him down. The hunger rose as we reached our limits.

I collapsed on top of him, my face resting against his shoulder when Stephan once again appeared in my mind. The anger and need for revenge began to suffocate me. The hunger for blood was more than I could tolerate. I sank my teeth into his neck. I felt his body tremble as my teeth broke through the skin. He tried to fight me, digging his nails into my back. My new strength was too much for him. I drank from him, nourishing my exhausted body, yet the taste of his blood disgusted me. I tore at his skin, ripping the muscles and tendons from his shoulder. I chewed on the tough meat, draining it of blood. I spat it out before tearing another piece from his dead carcass. Before long I was covered in his blood. His skin and bones were scattered across my bed.

❖

Every night thereafter, for more than two and a half centuries, I searched the streets of London hoping to find Stephan, hoping to put an end to my suffering once and for all. Every night I would find someone else to take his place, someone else to nourish my desire for blood and revenge.

Every night until I met Tony.

As the millennium came and went, my suffering remained. If I were ever to escape from the memories of what Stephan had done to me, I knew I had to leave London. I packed my belongings, those with which I could travel easily, and left the rest of my life behind. I headed for America. I stole away on a freightliner, not quite sure where it was headed, and ended up here in Savannah as so many of my countrymen had before.

I was foolish to think moving would change anything. I still needed blood to survive, and each time a young man would approach me, the anger of hundreds of years would surface. The kills were just as violent as they had been in my home country.

Several months later, I once again walked the dark streets and came across a small bar whose entrance was down an alley. I opened up the door and went inside. The place was empty except for a few customers. I walked up to the bar, ordered a gin, and found a small table in the back from which I could watch people.

I was into my third drink and feeling a bit light-headed from the lack of feeding when I noticed someone looking at me. I returned the look and smiled. He seemed embarrassed to be caught in the act. He looked away. I sat there watching him out of the corner of my eye. I saw his head turn in my direction. I raised my glass to him and motioned him over with my finger. He hesitated. A faint smile crossed his thin lips. He stood up and cross the bar.

As he approached, I could smell his scent. It intoxicated me. He stopped at the edge of the table. His hands trembled. I motioned for him to sit down.

"I'm Alex." I spoke with the air of a gentleman, hoping it would set him at ease. He reminded me of my former self, not so much in looks but in manners. His brown hair was cut short—spiked on top. His large brown eyes looked at me with nervous excitement. He wore a tight-fitting T-shirt that showed off his defined chest and stomach. I waited for a response. When none came, I reached out my hand to his. My heart went out to him. It was as if I had known him my entire life. My hand seemed to comfort him.

"I'm Tony." The tone in his voice trembled. "I…" He paused, cleared his voice, and started again. "I like your accent. Where are you from?" He seemed to relax a bit.

"London originally. I've been here in Savannah for a couple of years." I finished off my drink and asked Tony if he wanted another. He said he did. I got up and walked to the bar. I could feel Tony's eyes on my back, watching every move I made. It excited me.

We were silent while we finished our drinks. My head buzzed from the alcohol and hunger. I could smell his blood, feel his heartbeat from across the table. My stomach grumbled letting me know it was angry with me. I feared speaking to him, afraid I would get to know him too well, which would spoil my dinner. I hated feeding on someone I knew.

I knew what he wanted. He was like all the rest of them in that way. He didn't care for me. All he wanted was my body, my sex. I decided it was time to give him what he desired.

"Shall you accompany me back to my place?" I asked as I moved my hands onto his. His pulse was strong. It would be a good feed.

"I…" He stumbled with his words as he pulled his eyes from mine. "I've never done this before." He looked back at me. "I mean, sex with a man."

"Really?" I tried to act surprised.

"I guess I've always wanted to wait, to give my body to someone I loved. Not just for the sake of having sex." His embarrassment over this confession was all too obvious.

"I take it that you decline my invitation."

"No, that's not what I meant. I knew you were the one from the moment I saw you." His voice began to tremble. He continued his confession. "I've never met anyone like you before. There's something special I see in you, something I've never found in anyone else."

I sat there staring at him, shocked at the words I was hearing. *Damn him*, I thought. *He's made this personal. The sooner I get this one over with, the better.*

"You okay?"

"It is sweet of you to worry so. I'm fine. I wasn't prepared to hear such words. We've known each other," I looked at my watch, "for a little less than an hour. It's been a long time, longer than you can even imagine, since I've heard words such as those." He smiled at me, causing my mind to stop. "Shall we go, then?" I added before too much silence passed between us.

We walked along Bull Street, enjoying the warm spring air. We stopped once on our journey to admire the beauty of Monterey Square. The light of the full moon lit our way. Tony seemed to hesitate as we walked up to my home. I took him by the hand and led him inside.

I went to him and ran my finger down his cheek. I traced his lips before leaning down and kissing him. His mouth opened to mine. His taste was sweet upon my tongue. His hands ran down my back and found their way under my shirt. The warmth of his touch aroused me. I stepped back and pulled the shirt over my head. He kissed my neck. Moving downward, his tongue caressed my nipples and they became erect in his mouth. I pulled him off me and pushed him against the wall. He looked startled at my aggressiveness. I studied his body, noticing the stiffness in his pants. In my mind, his body and form seemed to change. In my mind Stephan stood in front of me, glaring at me, mocking me.

I went to him, ripping at his shirt, exposing his smooth, hairless body. The scent of his body, his blood invaded me. I pressed my body against his. I felt his prick expand as my crotch pressed against his.

"Alex," he moaned. "I've never known…"

"Don't speak." I placed a finger to his lips.

I knelt in front of him. I unbuckled his belt and lowered his zipper. He stood motionless as I removed his pants and underwear. His prick fell between his legs. The scent of his overanxious body drew me closer. My tongue lifted his thickness and guided it into my mouth. I could taste his excitement. The salty sweetness was like freshly drawn blood to my hunger. I wanted to love upon him. To give him everything he had waited for, to bring pleasure to him that he would never forget. I released his sex from my mouth and stood up to remove my pants. I picked him up and carried him to the bed. I knew I had to end this. I couldn't let him take control of me like this.

I lay my naked body down on his. His sex pressed up against mine. I raised his legs, preparing myself to enter him. He stopped me.

"Alex. You're too large," he muttered. "I won't be able to take you."

"Don't worry. I know how to do this." I kissed his neck, savoring the anticipation of my next meal. "Just relax, I won't hurt you."

He took a deep breath and relaxed. His virgin ass was small and tight. The thrill of entering him excited me even more. I felt the muscles in his body tighten, working against me. He gasped as my thickness gained access. The warmth of him surrounded me as I moved further inside. The tightness of his muscles squeezed my prick. I moved deeper. His body became wet with sweat, his breath heavy against my face. I slipped further inside him, my stomach churning with desire. I kissed his neck, feeling the blood flowing beneath the surface of his skin—it made my hunger grow. I licked and sucked on his neck, warming the skin for the incision with my teeth. I felt his heart beating faster, the blood rushing through his veins. I licked my lips and exposed my teeth. I raised my head to make the initial plunge.

"I will love you forever!" he whispered into my ear.

My eyes widened; my heart stopped. I froze as my teeth were just scratching the surface of Tony's neck. I jumped up, my sex still inside him. The look on my face must have startled him. He panicked and pulled away from me, pulling me out of him. I looked at him, seeing myself in his eyes. Tears filled my eyes, tears I didn't know I had. Looking at him was looking at myself in a mirror. I couldn't take from him what had been taken from me. I had loved Stephan during that moment, the moment just before he killed me, and I was about to do the same thing to Tony. I turned away from him and sat on the edge of the bed, my hands over my face to hide my teeth.

"You need to leave, Tony." I spoke with a soft tone, trying to hide my hunger for him. I knew he heard my words. "Please, you don't know me. I don't want you to see me as I am." The words he spoke I will never forget—they are engraved in my memory and my lifeless heart for all eternity.

"You don't want me to see?" He moved behind me, his hands rested upon my shoulders. "See what? That you're not like me? I know that. I know what you are."

I turned around, confused at his words, and looked at him. His eyes were warm and caring as they looked at me, at my body. I saw in his eyes that he *did* see the true me. He knew I was not like him.

"Why me? Why would you want to be with someone like me, someone who has to kill to survive?"

"Just look at yourself!" He started to giggle, as if realizing the impossibility of that statement. "Sorry." He pulled me around to face him. "You're incredibly sexy, you're young, and you will always stay that way." He touched my face. "All I want in life is to be able to love someone and have him love me back. I don't want to have to face the day when someone I'm with will die. I don't want to have to face those long, lonely nights afterward, living a life filled with regrets."

"You don't understand my life. It's ugly, cold, and brutal."

"I know you have to kill to survive, and I'm willing to accept that. All I ask is that you let me love you, and that you love me in return. I know this can work, you just have to believe and let me get close to you."

He became quiet in that moment. My mind raced with thoughts and emotions. I didn't know what to say—all I knew was that I loved him. I wiped the tears from my face and kissed him. We fell back to the bed wrapped in each other's arms. I let him enter me, something I had never let anyone do since the night with Stephan. His prick was long and slender, and filled me with immense pleasure. In those moments with him, I felt I was once again alive.

That night was nine months ago. Since that night, Tony and I have become inseparable except for those long, lonely daytime hours when Tony must work and I must sleep. Meeting Tony has changed my life. He has shown me, for the first time, what it is like to be alive. When I'm with him, I feel as if I've been given a second chance. I no longer thirst for revenge against my sire. Instead, my kills are quick and as painless as possible for my victims. I kill to survive, nothing more.

Tony became an integral part of my feeding, and I soon realized that if Tony could accept my feeding—the darkest side to my life—there was nothing that could harm us. How deceitful I had been to myself and to him to think that nothing could separate us.

The deception came to the forefront last evening. Tony asked me to change him, to make him like me so we would never be separated, not even by his death.

I hope he understands what those words did to me. I cannot take his life from him, no matter how tempting the thought of being able to live forever with him. I hope someday he will find these pages and understand why I had to do what I'm about to do.

The sun is almost upon the new day, and it is time I end this journal. To find my way to the ocean's edge and, for the first time in hundreds of years, watch the sun come up over the horizon. The last thing my eyes will see is the glorious colors of a new day. The last thing my mind will see will be the face of my beloved Tony. How strange it seems to know this will be my last entry. I want to leave by saying this.

Tony, I will love you forever.

About the Author

William Holden has published more than forty-five stories of erotica, horror, fictional history, and romance. His short story "Words to Die By" was a finalist in the 2010 Saints and Sinners Short Fiction Contest. His first book, *A Twist of Grimm* (Lethe Press), was a finalist for the 2011 Lambda Literary Award for best gay erotica. William has also written encyclopedia articles on the history of gay and lesbian fiction and has authored five bibliographies for the GLBT Round Table of the American Library Association. He is co-founder and co-editor of *Out in Print: Queer Book Reviews* at www.outinprint.net. A native of Detroit, William now lives in Cambridge, Massachusetts, with his partner, Mark Jordan. He can be reached at www.williamholdenwrites.com.

Books Available From Bold Strokes Books

Night Hunt by L.L. Raand. When dormant powers ignite, the wolf Were pack is thrown into violent upheaval, and Sylvan's pregnant mate is at the center of the turmoil. A Midnight Hunters novel. (978-1-60282-647-2)

Demons are Forever by Kim Baldwin and Xenia Alexiou. Elite Operative Landis "Chase" Coolidge enlists the help of high-class call girl Heather Snyder to track down a kidnapped colleague embroiled in a global black market organ-harvesting ring. (978-1-60282-648-9)

Runaway by Anne Laughlin. When Jan Roberts is hired to find a teenager who has run away to live with a group of antigovernment survivalists, she's forced to return to the life she escaped when she was a teenager herself. (978-1-60282-649-6)

Street Dreams by Tama Wise. Tyson Rua has more than his fair share of problems growing up in New Zealand—he's gay, he's falling in love, and he's run afoul of the local hip-hop crew leader just as he's trying to make it as a graffiti artist. (978-1-60282-650-2)

Women of the Dark Streets: Lesbian Paranormal by Radclyffe and Stacia Seaman, eds. Erotic tales of the supernatural—a world of vampires, werewolves, witches, ghosts, and demons—by the authors of Bold Strokes Books. (978-1-60282-651-9)

Tyger, Tyger, Burning Bright by Justine Saracen. Love does not conquer all, but when all of Europe is on fire, it's better than going to hell alone. (978-1-60282-652-6)

Wholehearted by Ronica Black. When therapist Madison Clark and attorney Grace Hollings are forced together to help Grace's troubled nephew at Madison's healing ranch, worlds and hearts collide. (978-1-60282-594-9)

Haunting Whispers by VK Powell. Detective Rae Butler faces two challenges: a serial attacker who targets attractive women, and Audrey Everhart, a compelling woman who knows too much about the case and offers too little—professionally and personally. (978-1-60282-593-2)

Fugitives of Love by Lisa Girolami. Artist Sinclair Grady has an unspeakable secret, but the only chance she has for love with gallery owner Brenna Wright is to reveal the secret and face the potentially devastating consequences. (978-1-60282-595-6)

Derrick Steele: Private Dick—The Case of the Hollywood Hustlers by Zavo. Derrick Steele, a hard-drinking, lusty private detective, is being framed for the murder of a hustler in downtown Los Angeles. When his brother's friend Daniel McAllister joins the investigation, their growing attraction might prove to be more explosive than the case. (978-1-60282-596-3)

Nice Butt: Gay Anal Eroticism edited by Shane Allison. From toys to teasing, spanking to sporting, some of the best gay erotic scribes celebrate the hottest and most creative in new erotica. (978-1-60282-635-9)

Initiation by Desire by MJ Williamz. Jaded Sue and innocent Tulley find forbidden love and passion within the inhibiting confines of a sorority house filled with nosy sisters. (978-1-60282-590-1)

Toughskins by William Masswa. John and Bret are two twenty-something athletes who find that love can begin in the most unlikely of places, including a "mom-and-pop shop" wrestling league. (978-1-60282-591-8)

me@you.com by KE Payne. Is it possible to fall in love with someone you've never met? Imogen Summers thinks so because it's happened to her. (978-1-60282-592-5)

Bloody Claws by Winter Pennington. In the midst of aiding the police, Preternatural Private Investigator Kassandra Lyall finally finds herself at serious odds with Sheila Morris, the local werewolf pack's Alpha female, when Sheila abuses someone Kassandra has sworn to protect. (978-1-60282-588-8)

Awake Unto Me by Kathleen Knowles. In turn of the century San Francisco, two young women fight for love in a world where women are often invisible and passion is the privilege of the powerful. (978-1-60282-589-5)